"Zoë Marriott has a high level of literary intelligence and is terrific at rebooting fairy tales with wonderful descriptions of the natural world... [She is] a rising star of fantasy fiction." The Times

Zoë Marriott says of *Barefoot on the Wind*: "We all know what the message of 'Beauty and the Beast' is supposed to be: love others for who they are inside. But as I got older, it began to seem more and more strange to me that in the traditional fairy tale, it is innocent Beauty who is forced to learn to love the Beast, while the Beast is rewarded for threatening Beauty's father and taking her prisoner. And so I set out to explore the story from a feminist perspective, asking, 'What if Beauty went after the Beast of her own free will? And how could the Beast redeem himself in order to truly deserve her forgiveness ... and her love?'"

Books by the same author

Daughter of the Flames
FrostFire
Shadows on the Moon
The Swan Kingdom

The Name of the Blade series
The Night Itself
Darkness Hidden
Frail Human Heart

Barefoot on the Wind

ZOË MARRIOTT

WALKER
BOOKS

First published 2016 by Walker Books Ltd
87 Vauxhall Walk, London SE11 5HJ

2 4 6 8 10 9 7 5 3

Text © 2016 Zoë Marriott
Cover illustration © 2016 THERE IS Studio /
illustration and creative lettering by Sean Freeman

The right of Zoë Marriott to be identified as author of this work
has been asserted by her in accordance with the Copyright,
Designs and Patents Act 1988

This book has been typeset in Berkeley

Printed in Great Britain by Clays Ltd, St Ives plc

British Library Cataloguing in Publication Data:
a catalogue record for this book
is available from the British Library

ISBN 978-1-4063-3337-4

www.walker.co.uk

Dedicated to my mother, Elaine Marriott.
With love.

Author's note

While *Barefoot on the Wind*'s setting was inspired by Japan – in much the same way that Tolkien's Middle-earth was inspired by Celtic and Anglo-Saxon Europe – the story takes place in a fantasy realm called Tsuki no Hikari no Kuni, or the "Moonlit Lands". This country is not intended to represent a historically accurate version of any Asian country during any period in history.

Red leaves spiral down
Chase summer's dying warmth. Run
Barefoot on the wind.

One

There is a monster in the forest, whispered the trees.

"I know, Sister." I patted the vast trunk of an ancient cedar with one sun-browned hand as I passed. "I know."

The tree shuddered a little. I turned away to crouch by the body of the serow I had just brought down. Its thrashing and struggling had already stopped. My fingers sank into the soft, greyish fur as I turned it over and looked down into the animal's swiftly clouding eyes. I did not fool myself that its death had been painless – how could death ever be without agony? – but my arrow was embedded deeply in the mountain antelope's heart. It had only suffered for a moment in its passing. That was the best I could do. The animal's death had been necessary, vitally necessary, to our survival. "Thank you," I said quietly.

The serow's meat, hung and cured, would feed us for

many days. Its pelt would make a warm blanket and perhaps mittens for the coming winter. The horns and bones would become a multitude of useful tools. I had seen little game today, and I was already perilously close to the ever-shifting edge of the Dark Wood that encircled the village. The small preserve of trees where it was safe to hunt was anxious, shivering and creaking around me, warning me from wandering deeper.

Digging my knee into the crisp fallen leaves, I pulled the arrow free from the animal's body, examined the horn arrowhead for damage, then wiped it off and, after unstringing my bow, slid both into the quiver strapped to my back. I lifted the serow with a grunt of effort, draping its weight across both my shoulders. A glance down reassured me that the brace of small birds from my snares was still securely attached to the belt of my leather leggings. I turned and made for home. Around me, the trees sighed with relief, leaves shaking gently, as I moved away from the edge of the Dark Wood.

There is a monster in the forest, the trees murmured gently.

"I hear," I told them, weaving swiftly between their trunks. There was no real need for stealth now, but my bare feet, tanned as tough as leather, made little noise. "I hear, Sisters. I'm going."

It was a long walk back to the valley. The other village hunters, working in their pairs, would have sung on their way home, laughed raucously, whooped and cried out, breaking the forest quiet so that no spells could creep over them. But I hunted alone. My hunting-partner was gone, and no one else would take his place; it would be bad luck. The soft pattering of rain in the thick tree canopy and the furtive fluttering and shifting of animals and birds in the branches were my only company.

I paused on the ridge at the edge of the trees to catch my breath, heartened by the glow of fires flickering to life in the deepening darkness below. Evening drew in early at the bottom of the valley.

Rain billowed over the autumn red of the peaks and drifted down onto our steeply stacked rice terraces, mingling with the mist rising up from the river. The small cluster of houses, with their thickly thatched triangular roofs, seemed to huddle together around the swiftly flowing water, as if for companionship. There were less than fifty of them now, though there had been three or four times that number in my grandmother's youth.

A collective shout followed by a burst of laughter drew my eyes downwards, past the animal pens, to where a small group of village children defied the cold. They crouched on the smooth stones of the river shallows, skinny brown legs drawn up like those of the frogs they hunted. One stood on her tiptoes, arms held aloft in triumph, hands cupped around her prize. The ragged hem of her yukata, which had been tucked carelessly into the obi around her waist to keep it dry, was slipping loose, the pale fabric splattered with mud. I felt a sharp pang beneath my breastbone as I remembered the last time I had played at frog hunting.

The empty space at my side – the place where my hunting-partner should have stood – seemed to throb like a new bruise, sending a ripple of sick, cold misery through my soul.

Kyo, Kyo, where are you? Where did you go?

Why didn't you come home, my brother?

Because of you, Hana. All because of you.

I exhaled the familiar pain slowly, and fixed my eyes on the lights of home.

Bracing my knees against the sharp incline of the ridge, I moved downhill, passing the rotting, picked-clean carcasses of two houses that had been abandoned before I was born. No need to wonder why their families had left them. Too close to the forest. Too dangerous. A tangle of pine saplings poked through the green timbers: the wood trying to reclaim the land which we had forsaken.

Two people had already been taken this year, and it wasn't even winter yet.

There is a monster... the young trees warned as I walked by.

"Yes, Sisters," I replied, hefting my burden higher on my shoulders as a shiver snaked down my spine. "Thank you for the warning."

My back and arms ached dully, and now that I was out from under the shelter of the leaves, the rain caught in my hair and drizzled down my face, and wet dirt squelched between my toes. The serow's weight made my steps heavy.

Firelight glowed a soft orange-gold between the gaps in the shutters of my house, welcoming me as I unloaded the antelope, the brace of birds and the rough sack that held my day's foraging onto the porch. With a stretch and a muffled groan of relief, I laid my precious bow and quiver down beside them. I would oil the wood and leather and check my fletchings later.

Our house had once stood neatly at the centre of the village. Now we were its furthest outpost. In the last two years five more families had abandoned their old homes, moving further away from the forest and closer to the perceived safety of the water. And, although no one had ever said it aloud, further away from us.

No one was keen to be close neighbours with such an unlucky family.

Hearing my movements, my mother pushed back the kitchen screen. Her vivid amber gaze checked me over for signs of damage as I washed my feet, using a small stone cup to scoop up icy, clean water from the narrow trough. Dirt and leaf mould coursed away from my skin into the soft moss under the porch.

Wordlessly, Mother handed me a cloth. It was threadbare and rough but so warm that I knew she must have kept it folded on the hearth for me after she had lit the fires. I smiled up at her as I dried my face and ran the cloth over my damp hair, then jerked my head sideways expectantly.

She turned to look, and her eyes widened at the sight of the serow.

"Hana," she said, voice soft with awe as she knelt to run her fingers through the soft fur. "No one has seen one for months!"

"I was lucky," I told her, hitching myself up to sit on the edge of the porch to dry my now clean feet. "There's a pheasant and two pigeons there, as well. And check the sack."

She reluctantly stopped stroking the serow's pelt and opened the rough pouch to reveal a bounty of prized golden mushrooms. She let out a soft breath and lifted her head to look at me, arching a brow.

"It was a good day," I said, twitching one shoulder as I slipped my geta sandals on. The wooden soles were worn in the exact shape of my feet, and the cloth straps were soft, but still they felt heavy and restrictive after a day running barefoot. There was a short silence.

"You went to the edge again, didn't you?"

"Mother—"

"Hana."

"The other village hunters were too greedy this year. They've picked everything near to the valley clean, and the game is wary."

"We can make do. You're on your own out there. What if you ran into a wild boar? What if you walked too far by accident, or the edge of the Dark Wood shifted—"

"There are no boar left," I said wearily, looking at her

over my shoulder. "No one's seen an animal more fear-some than a deer in fifty years. And the friendly trees would warn me before I ever got too close to the edge of the Dark Wood." I did not let my eyes waver from hers even when her expression flickered with uneasiness.

My mother had never heard the trees speak. Nor did she wish to. It was a gift that my grandmother had passed onto my father and me. And I was the only one who still used it.

Useful as such petty gifts were – a certain knack for getting pigs to go where they were wanted, the ability to sense fish hiding under rocks – and common as they had once been in many families, most people in the village preferred to pretend that they did not exist nowadays. I suppose we had learned the hard way that anything un-canny could be dangerous.

My gift meant I could never stumble into the cursed wood that ringed our village, enclosing us within the small pocket of trees where it was still – mostly – safe to walk and hunt. Not by accident. Not even with my eyes closed.

"We needed this," I said firmly. "You know we did."

Mother carefully laid the mushrooms down and shuf-fled towards me on her knees, the much-mended fabric of her old blue kimono catching on the planks of wood. She grazed my cheek gently with the backs of her fingers. "Not as much as we need you."

The cold, ever-present sadness of the empty space be-side me – inside me – eased, warmed by her affection.

I felt grateful tears sting my lashes and ducked my head. When I looked up again, she had already collected the birds and mushrooms and was rising stiffly to her feet to re-enter the kitchen.

"I will deal with these. Go fetch your father and he will clean and skin the serow, and hang it." She paused. "We shan't speak of this."

My tense muscles eased with relief. That meant she wouldn't tell my father where I had caught the antelope and gathered the mushrooms. We both knew that he wouldn't think to ask unless she brought it up. I wasn't entirely sure what he would do if he knew I had walked the edge of the Dark Wood. He might fly into one of his rare, cold furies. He might not blink an eye. I didn't know which would be worse, and I was not eager to learn.

"Tell him not to tarry," she added more briskly, reaching for her treasured cleaver, the one with a metal blade that had been sharpened down to a thin sliver over years of use not just by her, but by her mother, and her mother's mother before that. The steel was the same colour as the lone pale streak in her neatly coiled hair. "Night is almost here, and the Moon is dark tonight."

"Yes, Mother," I replied, letting my tone say, *I love you.*

The crinkle of fine lines around her eyes answered, *I love you too, Daughter.*

The quiet happiness of being understood helped me set my sandalled feet onto the freshly swept stone path that led to my father's workshop. On the way, I unfolded my kimono and plain nagajuban from the obi which had held them up out of the way for my day's hunting. The material, soft with years of washing, fell around my legs with a faint *whoosh*, veiling my leggings from sight. I ran my fingers lightly over my tightly plaited hair, brushing back the few stray strands from my face, and took a deep breath as I reached the closed door of the workshop. My posture altered, stiffening into the correct, straight stance of a dutiful daughter. I tapped on the door.

"Father?"

A long pause, punctuated with small noises: a rattle as some tool was laid down in a ceramic dish, a hollow sliding as something wooden shifted. Overhead, a robin let out a sweet, mournful trill.

"Enter."

I pushed open the door slowly, carefully. "Mother sent me to fetch you."

My father sat at his bench with his back to me, although his work – a wooden shutter from one of the elder's houses by the look of it – had been carefully moved aside. One of our precious pig-fat candles guttered by his wrist. The flame limned his shadowy profile in gold as he turned his head, and cast direct light on the long, slender lines of his fingers. Kyo's hands had been like that.

Father was our village's master carpenter. We had plenty of people who could hammer a board over a broken window, or patch a hole in a roof, but my father's skill at making and mending was unparalleled. He could save items that anyone else would have given up for scrap wood, make a cartwheel that would last a lifetime, balance and hang a door so that it would never slam, and carve or inlay ordinary items so cunningly and subtly that even after years of living with them, you would sometimes stop in awe at their loveliness. People whispered – sometimes with gossipy friendliness, at other times more uneasily – that his talent was almost like magic.

"It is still light," he said, just flatly enough to be a reprimand. His hair, worn long and pulled back into a ruthlessly neat topknot, was almost all silvery-white now, though he was still young. For a moment he looked heart-breakingly like my grandmother.

My throat tightened, and when I spoke, my voice was rough. "I … I caught a serow today. Mother would like it cleaned and hung. And … and tonight is—"

"I know what night it is."

My hands clenched into knots as he reached out to pick up a wooden brush, the gesture a clear dismissal.

"I will come when I am finished. Go back to the house now, Hana."

"Yes, Father." I bowed, though he couldn't see me, and turned away without shutting the door. If he intended to keep Mother waiting, he would at least have to get up and shut it to avoid the damp draught blowing on his neck.

I gulped in a rasping breath as I walked back down the path, my eyes dry but burning. The sense of empti-ness, of absence, flowed around me again. Like an arrow piercing my heart, the memory came of another autumn day like this one, when Kyo and I had returned, noisy and triumphant and covered in dirt, to show Father the white hare we had caught. How pride had lit Father's face, how he had gently touched Kyo's wild, tangled hair and laid his hand firmly on my back.

There is a monster in the forest, whispered one of the apple trees as I passed.

A growl vibrated in my chest. "I know!"

I leapt onto the porch, kicked off my sandals with a heavy *thump-thump*, and darted into the steamy warmth of the kitchen without stopping to look at the serow again. It wasn't enough. Nothing was ever enough.

And nothing ever would be.

"There is a creature in the Dark Wood that surrounds the village," loving mothers tell their children as they tuck them into bed at night. "A terrible beast that no man has ever seen and lived to tell of. At the dark of the Moon, when Her light cannot protect us, the monster grows hungry, and calls to the people of the village, and beguiles them from their safe warm beds out into the forest."

"What then?" the half-frightened, half-thrilled children will gasp.

"It eats them," the mothers reply, softly, sadly.

"But … why don't people sleep in shifts? Bar the doors? Tie their feet together?" the children begin to ask as they age, as the story stops being a story and becomes reality:

harsh and close enough to touch. To hurt.

"It doesn't work, my dear ones," the mothers say, still soft but resigned now, firm. "People have tried. Of course they have. For a little while it works. For a little while we think we might be safe. But then the monster grows hungry, too hungry to be denied. The watchers fall asleep. The doors open themselves. The sleepers squirm out of their bonds. They go. And they don't come back. No one ever comes back from the Dark Wood. You must never stray too far into the trees, my dear ones. Never go out at the dark of the Moon. There is a monster in the forest, and it craves human flesh."

We cannot leave this mountain. We cannot even stray far from our valley. The Dark Wood imprisons the village – unbroken as an iron fence, though it shifts and changes like a shadow in the wind – and no one who tries to pass through it ever returns. So we are trapped here, a dwindling, frightened handful, scraping the best living we might from what little land we dare to farm and hunt.

We do not know why.

Why this curse fell upon our mountain, or how the forest, which once was as much a home to my people as their own hearths, became haunted. We do not know where the monster came from or what its true form is. All we know is when it began. One hundred years ago. One hundred years ago the first villager was taken. One hundred years ago, everything changed.

The curse came with the frost. It was the middle of a bitter winter, and everything that could freeze on the mountain was already frozen. But inside, the screens were drawn, fires were stoked, and people huddled close, warm and safe. Yet that night the cold crept in. When the villagers awoke, their fires had gone out, their clothes and skin were rimed with ice, and icicles hung from the rafters above their beds.

They ventured out of their homes to discover that the familiar forest tracks, the travellers' marks carved into the broad trunks of the trees and the rutted mud road down to Tsuki no Machi – the great City of the Moon – had all disappeared. The wood had changed. Wandering further from the valley, the villagers found new trees. Where there had been bare branches, patches of wintry sunlight and the sight of clear sky, now towering dark evergreens formed a great ring around the village, their dense boughs packed almost solid, like the planks in a fence. Bushes with thorns as long as a man's finger and as black as a tanuki's claw sprouted between the trees and climbed high above their heads. It was a new wood. The Dark Wood.

Something had come into the forest, and made the forest its own.

Most of the village hunters turned back in fear, but one man – braver, bolder than the others, or perhaps simply more foolish – refused to walk away from the dark tangles of trees that had sprung up overnight. That man was my great-grandfather. It was he, with his family gift of tree-speech, who heard the first warnings of the monster that lurked within the Dark Wood. He passed that warning onto his fellow hunters. He was the greatest tracker and woodsman the village had. He refused to be barred from the place he thought of as his own home – and so, alone, he walked into those trees. Into the deep, Dark Wood. He was never seen again.

The first of our family to be taken, but not the last.

My grandmother was not yet born when it happened. Her mother told her – as all mothers tell their children here – what happened, and she told me and my brother.

Then, when I was ten, the monster took her too.

After that, my brother and I told each other the stories, so that we would not forget. Kyo was two years older than me, and in the dark, lying in our futons next to each other, he whispered the words as our grandmother had, pausing when she had, emphasizing the same parts as she had. It was a way to keep her alive, I think. A way to show that, although she might be gone, disappeared from her futon one morning with nothing to show that she had ever existed but the faint tracks of her feet disappearing into the trees, she had been ours, for a little while.

We thought losing Grandmother was the worst thing that could ever happen to us. But when I was twelve, the monster took Kyo.

Every day, the trees warned, *There is a monster in the forest.*

Every day, I wished – oh, how I wished – that the monster had taken me instead.

Two

What happened to Kyo was not my fault.

My mother told me, over and over again: "There was nothing you could have done, Hana. You are not to blame."

For months afterwards, grave-faced ladies and smiling old men up and down the valley would stop me as I passed, ask how I was, press a new basket, or a carefully wrapped packet of dried fish, or a ribbon, faded and frayed but soft, into my hands. *You're a good girl. You must not blame yourself. No one could have known. How you must be feeling, you poor thing...*

Even the other children, who would have died before saying such disgusting things aloud, showed me their own variety of sympathy, patting me roughly on the head and back during our games, offering to share some coveted treat made by their mothers, and taking care never, ever to mention Kyo's name in my hearing.

If I had been a prouder person, a stronger person, perhaps I would have hated this attention, the smiles and gentleness that did not quite hide the pity. Instead I clutched at the kindness as a baby grasps its mother's hand. I armoured myself with the assurances I was offered. No one – *none of them* – thought I was to blame. I knew this in my head, the same way I knew that water flows downhill, or that the sky is blue. I had to know that, or I could never have gone on.

But in my heart I was aware of a deeper truth. For water stops flowing when it freezes, and sometimes the sky is not blue but black.

One person held me responsible for Kyo's fate. As long as he could not forgive me, it would be impossible for me to forgive myself.

It was such a silly mistake. A childish, foolish thing that in any other place would have ended with no more than scoldings – perhaps even laughter. But not on the mountain. Not for us.

We were down at the river. I crouched in the shallows, feet numb with cold, eyes wide with anticipation. Catching frogs. It was a child's game, but a useful one. A half-dozen fat frogs would make a tasty meal for our small family. Kyo stood on the bank, holding the covered basket in which my prey, if I were fast enough, would be placed for safe keeping. He had declined to shed his sandals and wade into the autumn chill of the water, thinking himself, at fourteen, too old for such sport.

Or so he said. I thought it had more to do with the presence of the weaver's pretty sixteen-year-old daughter, washing out reams of newly dyed cloth downstream, and always ready to giggle and blush at any boy who came within ten feet of her.

Father had told Kyo to keep an eye on me, but I remember thinking peevishly that he hadn't glanced at me once since he had caught sight of Misaki bending over the water in her thin, kilted-up yukata. Kyo and I were hunting-partners, used to spending hours at a time in each other's company in the hush of the friendly trees, and then laughing and singing our way home to display our catch in victory. We shared our triumphs and our disgraces. We shared our fears and hopes. It made us far closer than any normal pair of siblings – best friends, really, despite the difference in age and gender – and I wasn't used to being ignored. Especially for a girl who screamed when she walked into a cobweb, I thought rather scornfully, pretending to myself that I hadn't done the same thing just that morning.

After a couple of attempts to reclaim his attention, and a couple more to get the pair of them to hush and stop frightening the frogs away, I gave up in exasperation and waded upstream away from them, finding a new hunting ground where the river curved sharply.

I only glanced back once. He was standing against the

blaze of autumn leaves, awkwardly rubbing the back of his neck with a hand that was just beginning to broaden out into the likeness of our father's. His too-long, shaggy hair was tangled, and there was an embarrassed laugh tugging at the corners of his mouth. I was too far away to hear it. That last glimpse of him is how I will always remember my big brother.

It didn't occur to me, as I waited patiently for the frogs to come, that night was drawing in.

It didn't occur to me that the Moon would be dark that night.

It didn't occur to me that Kyo, looking up to find, from his point of view, that his little sister had vanished from the river without a trace, would panic.

Of what happened next, I know only what I worked out for myself, and what others could be coaxed, in reluctant dribs and drabs, to tell me. While I crouched under an overhang of rock, silent and still as a hunting heron, Kyo searched the river for me, racing up and down the banks, calling my name. I didn't hear him. I tell myself I didn't. That the water must have drowned out his voice. That I would not have been so petty as to ignore him if I had heard. But memory is a mutable thing, and ... I cannot be sure.

All I know for certain is that I did not answer.

Everything would have been different, if only I had answered.

Kyo rushed home. Our mother was out visiting a friend,

so Kyo went to Father's workshop. What our father said to him then, no one can tell me. No one knows except Kyo and Father himself, and Father has never spoken of it. All I can gather is that he sent Kyo out to search for me up along the valley wall, above the rice terraces, where I sometimes liked to play hide-and-seek among the abandoned houses. Father himself hurried in the other direction, rousing his neighbours as he went, calling for them to light lanterns and join the hunt for his daughter.

I heard the villagers shouting as I was climbing out of the river onto the bank. I was chilled and tired and furious with Kyo for running off and leaving me without a word. I was even more irritated that he had taken the basket with him, so I had to release two frogs back into the water instead of bringing them home for dinner, because I could not hold onto them. When my father caught sight of me, he gave a great shout of joy and relief, and for a little while it was like the ending of a fairy tale, where everyone laughs and weeps with happiness. In that happy chaos, lit with the lanterns from the search, true darkness fell over the mountain without anyone noticing it.

Even then, it took far, far too long for me to ask: "Where is Kyo?"

My father's arm was still wrapped gently around my shoulder. His fingers flinched against my upper arm and then dug in, clenching, clenching, so tight that tears sprang to my eyes. I let out a choked cry of pain, and he released me as if I had burned him. As my mother caught me in her arms, I turned to see that my father wasn't even looking at me. In the bright yellow light of the lanterns, he stared up at the impenetrable darkness of the mountainside, where the forest blended into the Moonless sky.

He whispered, "But … but I…"

And then his face – changed. When he looked at me again, I could see his thoughts as if they had unrolled before me on a paper scroll.

What had happened to Kyo was not my fault. But I will take to the grave the memory of my father's eyes telling me:

He is gone because of you.

I wish it had been you instead.

Nothing was the same after that. My mother continued to love me, and my village showed me kindness, but from that day I was no longer truly welcome in my home. In an instant I had become a stranger to my father. Sometimes it was as though we spoke two different languages composed of the same words, and only my mother was able to translate between us.

I felt my brother's absence like a void in the fabric of my life, in my heart, in the place at my side that had always been his. It was more than grief, or even guilt. Where Kyo had once been was only emptiness, a wound that never seemed to fade, or heal with time, as other people assumed it must. It left me hollow. And worst of all, I knew my father could see it. He preferred that empty space to me, to the living child that reminded him of what he had lost.

I grew from a skinny village waif to a sturdy hunter, with strong legs and steady hands. I learned how to braid my own hair, tight, tight, so that not a single long strand straggled free, how to run barefoot on the wind, fleet and soundless as the clouds overhead, and how to catch game where no other hunter could see it. I worked as hard as two hunters to provide for my family, and the kindness of our neighbours gradually became respect.

When I turned fifteen – marriageable age – our family's ill fortune kept most of the village boys away. But while I was not pretty, or delicate or fine, and I no longer laughed as freely as I used to, I was a hard worker, and I was healthy. These things were valuable in their way, and one or two young men began to show an interest in me.

Shouta was the nicest and most persistent of the boys who tried to court me. His family hadn't lost anyone to the monster since his great-aunt, before he was born, and perhaps this made him less fearful of my family's reputation, because he never treated me any differently than any of the other village girls – except in a certain warmth in his eyes when they rested on me. In any case I … liked him. He too had endured the death of an older brother – although his had died of a fever. But I did not know what to say to him, how to deal with his attention. I did not know what I wanted.

One day he caught me as I drew water from our

family's well and said plainly: "Hana-san, forgive me – I must ask. Do you intend to marry?"

I hesitated, pretending to concentrate on balancing the full, heavy wooden bucket against the stone rim of the well without tipping it. In the tiny pause, Shouta stepped close – too close – and took the bucket from me. His arms did not tremble at all as he lifted my burden smoothly, and then placed it at my feet. The movement barely disturbed the surface of the water. It was an impressive display of strength.

Reflections shimmered and wavered in the bucket. Leaves stirred gently over our heads, clouds passed above them, and between, was the nearly soundless thrum of a flock of birds taking flight. Nothing that I could see stayed still for an instant. Nothing except the featureless shadow of my face leaning over the water: a black, unmoving void against the pale sky.

I knew that if I said I did hope to marry, Shouta would ask me to be his wife. Probably straightaway, right here by the well. I allowed myself to think about it. To marry would be to leave my father's house. To have a place of my own. Maybe even to find some peace.

And yet wherever I went, whatever I did, I would carry the sick, hollow ache of my brother's absence with me.

"Shouta-kun," I began tentatively, almost in a whisper. I stopped, annoyed at myself, cleared my throat and began again. "Shouta-kun, after Nori-san passed into the Moon's arms, did you feel ... do you still feel his loss every day?

As much as when he was first gone? Do you think of him, every day, all the time, even now, until sometimes it overwhelms you?" I took another bracing breath. "Sometimes, do you wish … wish it had been you instead?"

I finished with a faint gasp, almost of relief. It was the first time I had dared to speak these thoughts aloud. But in the next second I realized how clumsy my hurried speech had been, and how it must have sounded. The dawning look of dismay that filled Shouta's eyes made it obvious. I shifted away. The urge to leave the bucket where it sat and flee towards the shelter of the trees was almost irresistible.

"We all have sad days," he told me with ponderous gentleness. "And of course I miss my brother when I think of him. But you can't give into those feelings, you know. In my family we always say that you can choose to be happy. I believe that, Hana-san. It's up to you. You can't sit and dwell upon your unhappiness until … well, until you start thinking … silly things." He seemed to balk a little then, as if unsure whether he should go on. Finally he finished, "You must pull yourself together. Focus on what is good, and get on with your work and soon that sadness will pass, you'll see."

Something – something wild – something dangerous – was rising in my throat. I felt torn between bitter laughter and furious tears, and looked down sharply, pressing my lips together to keep hot words from spitting out to scald him. After all, what had I expected? It was the sort of well-meaning speech that I might have been offered by half the village if I had been so foolish as to share my real thoughts with them.

It was just that … no one who had ever felt the way I did could possibly say what Shouta had. No one who had been so lost in despair that they had forgotten how happiness even felt could believe that being happy was a choice. It was like telling someone with the lung sickness that there was plenty of air, if only they pulled themselves together and chose to breathe it. Feelings – my feelings – didn't work that way.

I had hoped…

No. It was no use wishing. He didn't understand.

"Your advice is good, of course," I told him, when at last I raised my head. My voice sounded gruff and rusty, as if the force of the words I'd kept inside had burned me. "Thank you, Shouta-kun. Now that you have answered my questions I may answer yours. I do not intend to marry."

And as I explained that I couldn't leave my father's household when my parents had no son any more who would bring a wife into the family to care for them as they grew older, and how it was my duty to stay with them and make sure they were well looked after, I felt no disappointment. No relief, either. Only a kind of numb acceptance. I should have known.

If Shouta himself was disappointed, he hid it well, expressing only admiration and approval. Later on I realized, from the renewed looks of pity everywhere I went, that Shouta had taken it upon himself to pass word of my decision onto the entire village. But at least boys stopped following me around and trying to give me wildflowers or rice balls and flirt with me.

And it wasn't as if I had lied.

Though I had lived there all my life, no one in our village truly understood me. They did not know me, and after Shouta's reaction, I was sure they never would. How could I expect anyone to perceive or accept my hollowness? My strange, dark thoughts and the wild silly impulses that drove me? Or to understand and love the friendly trees as I did, and run through them barefoot as I did, without fear of the edge of the Dark Wood, even after all the terror that place had brought us? No. It was better to keep on as I was. Alone.

And so I filled my days with work, the hunt, and prayer – but it was never enough. Nothing ever changed. My father still had not forgiven me. The terrible debt of my brother's life was still unpaid. So, yes, I often wished the monster had taken me instead. I would have offered myself up to it gladly, to bring Kyo back. Often I looked up at the bright face of the Moon and begged: *Anything, I'll do anything. Help me, please.*

My grandmother was a wise lady. When, as children, she heard Kyo and I offering up frivolous prayers for a new toy or a favoured treat, she would warn: *Be wary if you ask favours of the Moon. She does not grant our wishes. She answers our prayers.*

It was only when my chance at redemption finally arrived that I began to understand what those words truly meant – for it came with a scream, in the darkness of the night.

Three

"Hana! Hana, wake up!" my mother cried, her voice high and thin, and made jagged by fear. It cut me free of my murky nightmares with a jolt. I sat upright in my futon, gasping.

"What is it? What's the matter?"

She huddled on her knees by my bed, just barely visible in the faint silvery light that edged the closed shutters. Her breath rasped and then drew in sharply, and in the silence that followed I felt my spine go cold with terror – because there was a sound I should have heard, a sound that should have broken that terrible quiet. My father's voice.

My mother was crying, and my father was not there.

My father was not there.

It was the dark of the Moon, and my father was not in the house.

"No. No, Mother, no—" My words rose tremulously, a thin wail-like wind ghosting through the broken shutters of a long ruined home. I scrabbled out from beneath my blankets, cursing them when they tangled and tripped me. I kicked free savagely as if I was in a fight for my life. In the other room, the twin piles of bedding where my parents had slept side by side all my life lay empty. My mother's was a mess, like mine, the result of a panicked exit. My father's covers lay neatly folded back, as if he had taken care not to disturb them when he rose.

In another moment I was pushing back the screens, almost slipping on the frost-rimed porch. When I leapt down, my bare soles crunched on the icy grass, and my breath clouded in a long plume before my face. The sun was just lifting beyond the highest peak of the mountain, setting fire to the ragged clouds. Even in that dim light my eyes – hunter's eyes – could see the trail of footprints marked in the soft dark mud, before it had frozen. The tread was heavy and dragging, as if the walker had been immensely weary. But the trail did not waver, or turn back. It led, straight as one of my father's door lintels, towards the ridge. Towards the trees.

Into the forest.

My mother's thin and shaking hands were on my shoulders, scraping at me like the brush of dry dead twigs. She turned me away from the forest and took me into her arms. She was talking. Crying. But I couldn't hear anything through the awful echoes of silence in my ears, through the overwhelming, aching cold of all around me. Inside me.

My father had gone.

The monster had taken him.

There is a monster in the forest... whispered the trees.

"*No one ever comes back from the Dark Wood,*" my grandmother murmured in my memory.

But I had traced its edge. I had stalked in the shade of the dark trees and even, once, laid my hand on their gnarled bark and walked away again. And I was fast. Faster than anyone in the village.

Faster than my father on his very best day.

I tore free of my mother's hold and ran. She cried out in protest behind me, but I did not stop. My feet caught flame in the cold of the hoar frost, frozen puddles cracking beneath my weight and showering my light sleeping robe and bare legs with icy water that burned and then numbed. I bolted up the steeply cut terraces, heaved myself onto the ridge and crashed through the tangled brush on the treeline. My hair snagged on stray branches and ripped free painfully as I plunged forwards, lungs already working like the blacksmith's bellows. But I would run until my heart and my lungs and my legs gave out. I would run until—

My foot caught on a tree root.

I landed on one knee, my hands slamming down on the earth for balance.

Except my hands did not touch icy dirt, or leaves.

Instead, they found skin, and cloth.

It was not a root that had tripped me.

My mother's cries – and perhaps my own – had awakened our nearest neighbours. A dozen or so men and a handful of women, tousle-headed and hastily dressed, were just beginning to mount the lowest terraces as I began my descent of the highest in the brightening light of dawn.

There is a monster in the forest, the trees twittered unhappily. For once, I did not answer.

There was a collective shocked exclamation as the villagers caught sight of me. Further away, in the village, I heard screens and shutters squeal open and bang shut as more families, disturbed by the outcry, left their houses to see what new outrage had befallen us in the night. But silence fell as they gathered there at the bottom of the slope, faces upturned, watching my laborious progress with wide eyes and open mouths.

The first of our neighbours had gathered expecting to follow my trail into the forest, and drag back a weeping, irrational girl – if they were lucky enough to catch me before I passed the edge of the Dark Wood, and the point of no return. The second wave of villagers expected to hear that another of us had been taken, and were already praying that it was not a close relative or friend.

What none of them, not even my mother, had expected to see was me emerging from the trees of my own volition, with my father flung across my shoulders like the bloodied carcass of a wild creature.

I had hoisted his limp body up just as I had carried the serow the day before, wrapping my left arm around the backs of his knees and my right hand around one of his trailing arms to hold him in place. His deadweight was a great deal more than the mountain antelope's had been, and I was wheezing with effort, breath coming in short huffs that tasted of blood. My back creaked with each heavy footstep. I kept walking. There was nothing else I could do.

No one ever comes back from the Dark Wood.

My mother's voice cried out suddenly, faint but clear. "Help her! Someone help my daughter!"

As if a spell had been broken, the people stirred and surged forwards. Shouta was the first to reach me, then Goro, the big burly weaver, with my father's particular friend, Hideki, close behind. Shouta's face blanched at the sight of my father's back. Hideki hastily turned his eyes away.

"Let us take him. Let him go now, Hana-san," Shouta said. His words blended into Goro's gruffer ones: "It's all right now, girl. We've got him."

I resisted for a count of two painful breaths, but my strength seemed to have fled. I could tell by their voices, their eyes, that they thought he was dead. They thought I was carrying my father's corpse. I had been sure he was alive but ... that was impossible, wasn't it? Kyo never came back, did he? No one came back from the Dark Wood. No one…

I couldn't hold on any more. What was the point in holding on? My fingers lost their grip, and my father's weight was gently lifted from me. I staggered, dizzy, and someone – Hideki – rushed to steady me, a too-firm hand under my elbow and one on my back, bruising and uncomfortable.

"Kaede-sensei," I panted, naming the village's healing woman. "She—"

My words were drowned out by a shout.

"He's alive!" Goro yelled, voice cracking in his throat as if even he didn't believe what he was saying. His head jerked up and his gaze found mine. "Hana-san, he's breathing – he's alive."

My whole body tingled with a rush of pure, undiluted relief. I felt the sunlight touching my hair, and the rough earth beneath my feet. The light-headedness, the nightmarish sense of unreality, faded.

"Praise the Moon," whispered Hideki.

"Take him to Kaede-sensei," I said. "Quickly. She'll know what to do."

Before I had finished speaking, Goro and Shouta were rushing away down the terraces, my father cradled between them. He lolled back limply in the chair made of their arms. I trotted after them, and Hideki scurried worriedly behind me. At the bottom, my mother, who had stepped aside to let the two men pass, reached out to grasp my sleeve. Her eyes remained riveted on my father as she tugged me onto the pebble path that wound through the centre of the village. I was grateful for the way Shouta and Goro had turned my father when they took him from me, so that she couldn't see … the blood.

"Where – how did you find him? You were so fast…" she questioned. She was trembling all over, fingers clutching desperately at my kimono. "Hana, how?"

"He was on the ridge. Right there, on the ridge. He was already almost home." Distantly, I noticed the reaction to my words ripple through those who were silently following us. I ignored the quiet murmurs and shocked looks, and the way my mother's last question hung unanswered in the air. I wrapped one arm around her, pulling her into the shelter of my sturdier frame to share my warmth, and to hold her steady.

"Ichiro…" She covered her face as she whispered my father's name.

Someone had run ahead of us to wake Kaede's household. By the time we arrived, the two large wooden screens that opened onto her great room had been pushed back, and sticks of precious incense lit inside. They filled the air with the distinctive spiralling blue smoke that meant illness and death to us. We had smelled it when Shiro's ox gored him and he lost his hand. We had smelled it when Atsuko died bringing her little daughter into the world, and for three days after while Kaede fought to keep the baby alive.

The sensei did not waste her precious incense. She only burned it when there was still a chance. We never smelled that sickly sweet perfume on the wind when the monster took one of its victims, for then there was nothing Kaede could do.

Breathing it in now fanned the tiny spark of hope inside me into an ember that smouldered under my breastbone, painful in its intensity. My whole body wanted to curl up around it – but whether to smother it, or shelter it, even I could not judge.

"Bring him in, and then get out," the healer snapped as she smoothed a threadbare but shiningly white sheet into place over a thick futon. The worn tatami mats were covered in squares of clean cloth. Some held rolls of soft bandages, some earthenware pots and chipped ceramic jars, and one had strange metal tools that glittered menacingly beneath my worried gaze.

Shouta and Goro shuffled past all this and gingerly laid my father down, rolling him at the last moment, so that his uninjured front pressed into the futon. There was a collective murmur of horror as the villagers crowding behind me saw the terrible wounds for the first time.

The back of his worn cotton yukata was soaked through with blood. Half-dried, almost black and sticky like the sap of the dark pines, it marked three long gashes, inches apart, that stretched from the top of his left shoulder all the way down to his right hip. Claw marks. Claw marks from a paw wider than a man's back.

Father's face was turned towards us, and it was grey: the colour of fine ash when the wood has all been consumed and there is nothing left for the fire to eat. The long silvery hair straggled, knotted and wild, around his head. He would have shaved himself bald before he willingly allowed himself to be seen undone this way. He was so still. So quiet. All the lines of his face had smoothed away into blankness. I barely recognized him.

I felt rather than heard Mother's gasp. Her jaw tightened and she blinked frantically.

"Did you all go deaf overnight?" the healer demanded, staring at the people filling her porch. "Get out, I said! How can I work with you people taking up all my patient's air?"

As people began sheepishly shuffling away, the sensei's gaze, dark and shining with fierce intelligence in her wizened face, ran over my mother and me. Her eyes lingered on me the longest, and her expression softened a little. "You must go too. This is no place for you now. I will do everything I can."

One hand, the fingers gnarled with age, came to rest almost tenderly on my father's head. I used my hold on my mother's arm to urge her back a step, over the threshold of the room. Kaede-sensei nodded sharply, and then turned away, calling for her apprentice, who scurried out to pull the screens back into place, blocking my father from our sight.

Mother shuddered. "Hana – oh, Hana..."

"None of that! It will be well, you'll see," cried Hideki's wife, appearing beside us with a look of desperate cheerfulness. "Just you leave the sensei to her work. Come on, come away, that's right…"

Mother's friends surrounded us, leading us inexorably from the healer's house like a flock of small birds that chirped and squawked and fluttered softly, but could not be escaped. We were escorted home and pressed firmly to sit in the kitchen. The fires were lit, our stores rifled, cups of tea forced on us, the shutters thrown open and the futons tidied away. Goro had gone back to his own home, but Hideki and Shouta came with us. They drank tea too.

No one ever comes back from the Dark Wood.

The hot tea grew cold in my grasp, and was replaced. People moved and talked around me. Shouta and Hideki eventually had to leave to go about their day's business. In the doorway Shouta spoke my name seriously. When I glanced up, he gave me a look, long and complicated, that I was too slow to interpret. I stared at him blankly. He bowed his head before turning away.

Some of the women left too. Others soon came to take their place. The sun moved behind the shutters, and patterns of light shifted across the mats to gleam upon the polished wood of our family's Moon shrine.

The sense of helplessness, the suffocating kindness of the villagers that made me want to scream with frustration and cry with gratitude in the same instant – it was all too horribly familiar. I felt as if I had lost my mooring on reality – was slipping from my place in time. I closed my eyes for a second, and I was twelve years old again, weeping under my mother's arm, staring at my father's back and willing him to turn and look at me.

My mother's hand found mine, shaking fingers closing tightly around my palm. She was chilled. I clasped her hand in both of my own, trying to warm the icy skin by rubbing gently. Her eyes were like scorch marks in the paleness of her face.

"He – he came back," I whispered, not sure what she needed me to say. "He almost made it on his own."

The words were hushed, but I felt the sudden stillness in the room, a sense of breath being held. When I looked up, my mother's friends rushed back into motion, back into speech. They seemed almost as frightened as we were.

There is a monster in the forest.

Never go out at the dark of the Moon.

No one ever comes back from the Dark Wood.

How could the rules of our reality, shaped by the last hundred years, be rewritten so utterly, without reason or warning? What did it mean?

Oh, Moon, merciful mother of our lands, would my father survive it?

Four

A cloudy purple-grey dusk had fallen before Kaede's apprentice came to fetch us. Mako was a slight, unassuming woman, a little younger than my mother, and her voice never rose above a soft, hoarse whisper – but she nonetheless extracted us effortlessly from the gaggle of Mother's friends and our well-meaning neighbours and made it very clear that we were to come with her unescorted.

Though it was not yet full-dark, no children ran shouting down the pebbled path, no old ladies sang as they sewed on their porches, no young men laughed and gossiped outside our village meeting house. All I could hear was the rough, quick rasp of my mother's breath and the snared-rabbit thrum of my own heartbeat as we walked together, our shoulders brushing, through the quiet houses to Kaede-sensei's place. Shutters and screens slid open as we passed, and I felt the eyes upon us. Fear lay like thunderclouds on the village's rooftops, waiting to burst through the narrow streets in a crackling flood.

The healer's house was lit up as if for a festival night, with lanterns shining brightly through her screens. As we politely shed our shoes outside the door, the sensei herself came to greet us. Her face seemed more lined than it had this morning, the harsh light making black shadows crawl into the deep wrinkles around her eyes. With her shoulders slumped in weariness, she only came to my chin. She clasped each of our hands silently. My mother's wide, anxious eyes kept my mouth closed as we followed her inside.

In the great room my father lay on his back, clad in a plain white robe, with thick blankets and a mottled, slightly moth-eaten red fur pulled up under his waxen face. His hair was neatly combed and all traces of blood and dirt were gone. He looked clean and peaceful.

He looked like a corpse.

As I hesitated on the threshold, stricken, my mother moved forwards. She sank to her knees beside him and laid one hand on his forehead.

"Is he...?" My mother's voice trailed off as a movement at the other end of the room made us both start.

To my surprise and resentment I realized that the village elders, two men and a woman were gathered opposite us. The arrangement was familiar from judgement days, when the elders sat in exactly such a neatly spaced line in the meeting house and heard disagreements and grievances, and made decisions on the matters involved. Normally Kaede was with them, but she had knelt by my father to adjust his covers instead.

"Why are they here?" I asked. My voice came out louder and more demanding than I had intended, and my mother gave me a repressive look.

"Hana, we are honoured if the elders choose to interest themselves in your father," she said. But the words were not precisely a chastisement, which spoke volumes about how she felt to see these people gathered in her husband's sickroom, apparently allowed to see him before we had been.

One of the elders, Hayate, met my eyes. "You are fretted and worn with sorrow," he said, not unkindly. "And wish only to learn that your father will be well. But what has happened to him concerns all of us here in this village. Remember that, please."

I ducked my head. "Of course. I ... I am sorry."

The other two elders nodded gravely. Kaede made a flapping gesture at me with one hand. "Sit. You'll give me a crick in my neck, towering over us all like that."

Reluctantly I eased down at my father's feet, feeling somehow as if I had ceded precious ground.

"Kaede-sensei, please," my mother said.

The healer squared her shoulders. "Physically, things are not as bad as I initially feared. His back was ... cleaved open, almost as if by knives, and he must have lost a great deal of blood. But the wounds were – well, they were *clean*. I have washed and stitched and bound them, and I believe they will heal well, if we can keep infection out, which I plan to do."

"Then he is well?" Mother asked, unable to conceal the hope in her voice.

"As for that…" The usually unflappable healer seemed to run out of words. She licked her bottom lip uneasily, and my mother's brow creased.

Hesitantly, I asked, "Were there other wounds we cannot see? Something—" I swallowed. "Something worse?"

"It isn't that. At least, I don't think so," the sensei said. "You see, he won't wake up. We have tried everything we know, but nothing works. He doesn't flinch or stir when we prick him with needles, and his pupils do not react to light. I've seen people sleep like this before in one or two cases, but there was no blow to his head, as far as I can see – and apart from the claw marks in his back and a few minor scrapes and bruises, he seems unharmed. There is no reason why he should lie like this, unmoving. It is … an *unnatural* sleep."

"Will he recover?" my mother asked.

At the same moment, I demanded, "Unnatural how?"

"I fear – I greatly fear – that whatever called him out into the woods still has him in its thrall." Kaede glanced up at the elders and let out a long sigh.

"The monster?" My mother choked on the words. "The … the monster has a hold upon him, still?"

"That's the only explanation I have. I've always thought that people must sleepwalk into the Dark Wood. Well, he's still caught in that sleep. And he won't eat, and we can barely coax a little water into him. When a person doesn't move, can't eat or drink much, their body starts to fail very quickly. Like this ... we might be able to keep him alive until the Moon is next dark. Perhaps."

The words hung in the air like the sickly stale scent of dried blood.

"Isn't there anything...?" Mother's voice wavered, her hands curling into fists on her knees.

"I'm not a magician, or a witch, or a seer. I can't undo what's been done to him."

Mother drew in a sharp breath at the seeming cruelty of the blunt words – but I sensed something hiding beneath Kaede's apparently fatalistic attitude. A faint edge of ... excitement? I laid my hand comfortingly on my mother's shoulder, staring at the healer. "But?"

"I'm not a magician, or a witch, or a seer," Kaede repeated with more emphasis. "But it stands to reason, doesn't it, that if magic is keeping him like this – some spell or curse, whatever you would name it – then the only way to help him is to break it?"

There was a long pause, in which the silence hummed like the plucked string of a shamisen.

"This is why the sensei spoke to us first, and asked us to be here," Hayate said finally. "We must decide what action to take."

"I don't..." My mother's eyes darted to the elders. Her hand rose to clasp mine on her shoulder.

"Break the curse," I said slowly, hardly believing such insane words were leaving my mouth. "Break the monster's magic. You're saying – you're saying – the monster must be ... destroyed. For my father to live, it must die."

My mother's head turned between me and the sensei, her eyes running over both of us incredulously. "How?"

Kaede again glanced at the elders. "I don't know. I don't know how or if such a thing could be done. I only know that for the first time in one hundred years, a man has walked into the Dark Wood at the dark of the Moon and survived it. Maybe the curse on the mountain is weakening. Maybe at last something has changed—"

"Or maybe it was just chance," the most ancient of the elders – Hirohito – interrupted. "We cannot know."

"Then what is to be done?" I asked them. My thoughts churned slowly, turning over and over until nothing seemed to make sense any more.

The female elder, Yuu, cleared her throat. "Honoured Kaede-sensei has suggested that now might be the time to – to mount some kind of – of exploration. An expedition. In daylight, of course, and heavily armed. If they could penetrate the Dark Wood, seek out the beast while it slept, perhaps—"

"But who is to say that it is *possible*?" Hirohito interrupted. "Who is to say that because one man walked into the Dark Wood and returned, others can too? We have lived under this … this foul enchantment for a century. No one has ever been able to break it!"

Without thinking, I snapped, "No one has ever tried."

Hirohito opened his mouth again, met my eyes – and looked away suddenly, blinking.

"It would be a very great risk," Hayate said. "Very great. We have already lost so many. To send more into that cursed forest, to face that darkness, by *choice*…"

"We could ask them?" my mother suggested softly. "Lay the facts we have before the village, and ask if anyone would go? Give them a chance to decide for themselves if they feel the possibility of freedom is worth the risk."

"They would," I whispered fiercely. "I know they would."

Yuu sighed wearily. "Everyone must know about this – that is not in question. Everyone saw Ichiro-san return. Everyone knows something has changed. They are frightened, and the longer they have to wait to hear what is going on, the more frightened they will become."

Reluctantly, the other two nodded. Kaede made a small noise of satisfaction.

"Very well then," Hayate said. "We will tell them about Kaede-sensei's idea, and let them make up their own minds. Tomorrow." The elder climbed creakily to his feet. The discussion was at an end.

I dreamed that night, for the first time in many years.

Sometimes, when my mood was at its lowest, and I

felt sorrow and grief weigh as stones upon my breast, I wondered if the emptiness my brother had left behind wrapped itself around me in the darkness and drank down my dreams, denying me even that refuge. At other times, I told myself it was just the honest exhaustion of hard work that kept both dreams and nightmares at bay, and I should be grateful for it.

But that night, I dreamed.

I walked into the wood again, and saw again my father just as I had found him that morning. He lay sprawled on his front, one arm outstretched as if he had been reaching for home even as he fell. His pale grey yukata – almost identical to mine – had turned black with blood.

I could not tell if he was breathing.

The light of the rising sun slowly pierced the bronze leaves above, dappling the wood with spots of gold. The trees shivered but did not speak. Nothing stirred – no birds sang, no animals called. I knelt over him, unable to speak, unable to touch. Paralysed, not by fear, but by disbelief. Nothing seemed real. Nothing made sense.

No one ever comes back from the Dark Wood.

And then something happened which did not come from my memory. My father's ashen face twitched, and his bruised eyelids lifted. Yet instead of the familiar dark brown gaze, I found myself looking into pleading eyes the same sharp, vivid green as sunlight shining through a new spring leaf.

"Hana," he whispered, and his voice was not my

father's, but another voice that was ageless and tormented and terrible. "Help me."

"How?" I asked, my hands reaching without thought to clasp his. "Tell me what to do."

His cold waxy fingers closed around mine, tight, tight. Distant dream-pain panged through me. A lone droplet of blood, intensely red, trickled through our joined fingers and splashed onto the pale gold of a fallen leaf. With a gasp, I tore away – and saw three deep claw marks raked across the skin of my palm.

"What—?"

"Hana." Those impossible, unnatural eyes bored into mine. "Kill me."

Five

The morning was crisp and still. Amber sunlight spilled through the open screens of the meeting house and through the gaps in the ceiling and walls, painting gilded patterns among the blue-edged shapes of the other village folk. Everyone had come, except for a few older ladies who had volunteered to watch the littlest children and keep them quiet. I had never seen the small building so full.

I wanted to look properly at the sea of familiar faces. From my privileged position at the foot of the raised dais where the elders sat, it would only have taken a quick glance over my shoulder to examine everyone's expressions and try to determine their reaction to the elders' words. But my mother's shoulder pressed heavily into mine, forcing me to support almost half her weight, and a sudden turn sideways on my part would cause her to stumble. I could almost hear her willing me to behave: *Be still, Hana. Be patient. It does no good to fidget.*

Hayate cleared his throat, and in my peripheral vision several people flinched.

"We have told you all we know," he said. "At this juncture, our plan is the only hope for Ichiro-san, and perhaps – perhaps for all of us. Every resource we have will be at the disposal of the volunteers. We will fully arm and provision them from the village stores, so there is no need to worry about stealing precious supplies from your families. In the event that something goes wrong … of course those who are left behind by the volunteers would be cared for by us all, and not allowed to suffer for their loss."

"Although we would encourage any man with a young family to think very carefully before volunteering," Hirohito put in quickly. "And ask those without siblings and with parents still living not to consider it at all."

It was a struggle to keep a grimace from my face. No need to ask for whom that comment was intended.

There was another uneasy pause. At last Kaede spoke up. "You will wish to speak with your families and consider everything we have discussed before you make any decisions. The volunteers should return here to the meeting house at – let us say … sunset."

I heard the people behind me shifting, stirring and stretching, like ones awakening from a strange dream. But they were so quiet – almost completely silent. There were no muffled exclamations, no frightened or excited whispers. It was eerie. My mother must have felt me tense. She leaned against me harder than ever, her hand fastening around my upper arm, like a vice, to keep me in place. The other villagers filed out of the meeting house in that unnatural hush, leaving just me and Mother alone with the elders.

"It is done, for good or ill," Kaede muttered. "Now all we can do is wait."

Mother finally let loose my arm, and bowed respectfully. A moment later I followed her example, rather less gracefully.

"I should like to sit with my husband while we wait," my mother said. "Is that acceptable?"

"Of course." The healer heaved herself nimbly to her feet as the other elders slowly began to rise. "We can walk together. You too, Hana-san?"

I didn't want to. I didn't want to see him like that again, still as death and emptied of all the frozen rage, dry disapproval and occasional flashing humour that made him – made him *himself*. I didn't want to imagine him as another aching void in my life. Or look at him and remember my dream. But still less did I want to let my mother down.

Schooling my expression into composure, I bowed. "Thank you, Sensei."

The healer's house was stiflingly hot, and the great room where my father lay was filled with thick billows of blue incense that made my throat close up. I had not expected to see any change in him – the sensei would have told us if there had been – and I tried to believe that it was a good thing. Change was unlikely to be beneficial now. At least he wasn't beginning to wither yet.

My mother settled at my father's side and took one of his limp hands in hers. I took up a place a little behind her where she could not easily see my face, hoping my presence was some kind of comfort, at least. To my frustration, much as I wracked my brains, I found I had nothing else to offer. So I watched her as she watched him, quietly awed by her unwearied patience. Sometimes she gazed down at him with intent, searching eyes. Sometimes her gaze went distant and I knew she was remembering. At other times her lids fell shut and her lips moved silently as she prayed.

It wasn't as if I was unused to waiting. To stillness, and silence. Half my life had been bound up in those things. When I hunted, there were quite as many hours spent crouched motionless waiting for prey to show itself, as there were hours stalking, running and climbing. Yet in a nest of leaves, surrounded by soft forest sounds and with the potential to burst into motion at any moment, I never had trouble finding the stillness within myself that made waiting bearable. Today, trapped by obligation as much as by these walls, there was no peace in my heart. Every nerve and muscle seemed to twitch beneath my skin, fired with the urge to do something – anything. But there was nothing at all that could be done.

After about an hour, my mother's free hand came to rest on my knee, startling me so badly that I sucked in a too-large mouthful of the incense smoke and suffered a coughing fit.

"Poor Hana," she said softly as I wiped my watering eyes. "I had hoped the quiet would help you to calm yourself, but it isn't working, is it? Your father will sense you have been to visit him, and be comforted, I am sure of it. There is no need to force yourself to sit for … for the whole day."

Until sunset, she meant. Until we knew who would go into the Dark Wood for us, and when they would go, and how they planned to hunt the beast down…

"I can't leave you alone," I protested.

"I am not alone. Kaede-sensei and Mako-san are on the other side of the door – and your father is right here. Go, Hana. Just…" She stopped, and took a short shuddering breath. "Just stay away from the trees."

"Yes, Mother." I bowed my head and squeezed her hand before rising to my feet. I despised myself for the relief I felt at leaving the room – and both my parents – behind.

"Is something wrong?" Mako asked in surprise as I emerged into the small vestibule and drew the door closed behind me. She set down the basket of herbs she held and made as if to hurry into the great room again.

I stopped her with a hasty gesture. "No – no! I only… My mother has sent me out to … to undertake some chores at home."

Mako frowned a little. "I am sure the sensei could ask

one of the men to look in at your house and take care of any urgent tasks. You need not leave."

"Let the girl go, Mako-san," the healer interrupted, appearing from a room deeper in the house. "There is nothing for her to do here. No doubt she has been fidgeting her poor mother to flinders." Despite the blunt words her eyes, resting upon me, were kind. "Go stalk another serow if it will ease your heart, child. Just make sure you return by sunset. She will truly need you then."

I gave her a deep bow of wordless gratitude, and fled, barely taking the time to slip my socked feet into my sandals as I went.

Outside I stopped to savour the sweet clean air on my flushed cheeks, and then forced myself to walk away calmly, taking the well-worn village paths with slow, graceful steps. Hidden inside the voluminous sleeves of my soft yellow and green kimono, my hands curled and uncurled, curled and uncurled, trembling with strain. I couldn't seem to make myself stop, and could only hope it would go unnoticed. I may have been unable to control my fear, worry and self-consciousness – unable even to offer my mother the support she needed and deserved – but I refused to let my feelings show for everyone to pick apart and comment on. I had endured enough of that in my life already.

There was no need to have worried. Polite nods, jerky bows, and swiftly turned backs were all I was called upon to deal with. The scent of pity in the air was thicker than the pungent clouds of incense in the healer's house. *Bad fortune in that house. Bad luck. Such a sad, unlucky family...*

Although I had intended to honour my words to Mako and retreat home, when I reached the fork in the path, I yielded to some faint, internal prompting and veered left. My soft-soled sandals squeaked over the smooth, wet stones as I picked my way carefully down to the edge of the river.

The river was the greatest friend of our settlement – but she was an inconstant companion, changing her moods as often as a fine lady changes the combs in her hair. Today, when I would have welcomed the sight of raging white water, she was calm and smooth, greyish blue and almost clear under the glare of the low autumn sun, and her song was gentle in my ears.

No children played here this morning to pierce me with bittersweet memories, and so I was left alone, save for a small group of older men wading a little further up, where the water deepened, looking for fish or crabs with their nets at the ready. It seemed an ordinary day for them. Just a normal day in the valley, like any other. And yet it was a day that could – that must – change everything.

We were asking so much of our people, my mother, the elders and me. But what other choice did we have?

What other chance would we get?

It was already too late for so many...

The aching hollow that Kyo had left behind seemed to unfold itself then, devouring everything else inside me until all that was left within my body were grief and guilt, longing and despair. I imagined I could see it, see the emptiness, like dark wings curving above my head, streaming and flowing at the edges of my perception. A single harsh sob ripped loose before I clamped my jaws together.

Kyo, Kyo, why did you leave us – why didn't you turn back, why didn't you come home…?

Because you didn't call me back, sister. You didn't answer me. It's because of you.

I put both hands over my face, wheezing through my teeth.

Breathe. Just breathe. This will pass, it will pass. For now you must breathe. Just breathe…

There under the open sky, alone, I found my stillness at last.

When I came to myself again, the sun had slunk a little way across the sky to hang above me. My joints ached with the chill mist that had crept up from the river, and fine shivers prickled my skin with gooseflesh.

I knelt to drink, gathering my trailing sleeves up in one hand as I cupped the other in the icy water. My parched throat begged for more and I drank again, and then again, before I was satisfied and able to turn towards home. I was numb, all through, and grateful for the numbness.

When at last I entered the safe solitude of my family's house, I busied myself with familiar, useful tasks. Changing from my furisode kimono – which had been passed down from my grandmother's mother, and was the finest thing I owned despite the patches and worn spots – into a ragged old yukata and leather leggings took the blink of an eye. Freeing my hair from the heavy, uncomfortable knot at the base of my skull and rearranging it into its accustomed tight plait was only a little more time-consuming. Then I looked around eagerly for other chores to occupy my hands.

I lit the fires and banked them. Then I drew water from the well in case my mother wanted tea or to wash when she returned. In the rapidly warming kitchen, I cleaned and polished my bow, stringing and drawing it carefully to maintain its flexibility. I checked my arrows, washing off streaks of dried blood, mending some fletching, and replacing a chipped horn arrowhead with a new flint one that I had made the week before. There was a small split in the bottom of the quiver to be sewed shut, and the ancient, cracked leather deserved a careful oiling. Finally, I plucked the birds which I had brought home the day before, and which my mother had hung in the pantry, finishing by collecting all the precious feathers and down, and storing them carefully away.

By then I was warmed through and longing to be outside again. Taking the small, quartz-bladed hatchet from the hook by the kitchen door, I went to chop wood and bring it into the house to dry out.

It was there, at the woodpile by Father's workshop, that Shouta found me.

I heard the footsteps crunching through the fallen leaves when he was a few yards away and turned to watch him approach.

"Good afternoon," I greeted a little uncomfortably.

"It is evening now," he corrected.

When I squinted upwards, I realized he was right. The sun had passed out of sight beyond the roof of our house, and the sky to the east was growing dim. It must be almost sunset. Hurriedly, I gathered up a last armful of wood and headed back towards the house. I brushed carefully past Shouta where he stood like a tree stump, apparently unwilling to move. As our arms touched, he seemed to jolt, and then clumsily reached out to take some of the split logs from my arms. He followed me to the porch.

"Thank you for coming to fetch me," I said, piling the wood untidily outside the kitchen door. "I lost track of time."

I hung the hatchet back in its place and wiped wood dust and splinters from my hands, wincing as a sliver of wood drove into my palm. I pulled it out with the ease of long practice and pressed my thumb over the tiny wound.

"You needn't have done this," he said, dropping the few pieces of wood he carried on top of mine. He took my hand to examine it, ignoring my instinctive move to withdraw, and grunted with satisfaction when he saw that the bleeding had already stopped. "I would have been happy to chop the wood for you. Anyone would have."

"It's all right." I pulled at my hand again, more strongly, and this time he let go. "I don't mind splitting a few logs – I'm used to it."

"It is not all right, Hana-san," he said slowly. "Chopping wood, hunting and trapping, spending half your time in the trees by yourself – you shouldn't be used to that kind of work. Those are jobs for a son, not a daughter."

Taken aback, I tried to make out his expression beneath the shadow of the porch roof in the deepening dusk. He had never spoken to me like this before. I always thought the reason he liked me was because I was sturdy and strong, and willing to lend a hand to any task.

I am a better hunter than any son in this village, a small part of me thought rebelliously.

My movements brisk, I began to untuck my yukata from its obi. "Shouta-kun, I'm sorry, but I don't have time to talk to you about this. I must go to Mother. The elders will be at the meeting house with the volunteers—"

"There are no volunteers."

The words were stolid and matter-of-fact. I froze in place, unable at first to make sense of them. "What did you say?"

"There are no volunteers, Hana-san. The plan the elders suggested is crazy. It is like asking us to slit our own throats and lay down for the crows to feast upon our bodies. You must have realized that. You must have realized that no one would be willing to go."

"That ... that isn't true." Shaken, I gaped at him.

"It isn't crazy. Something has changed – it must have changed. This is our first chance, our only chance to – to *change* things. To break the monster's hold on us. *Someone* must be willing to go."

"It is a chance to die, and nothing more," Shouta said flatly. "No one comes back from the Dark Wood."

"My father did." It was fact, inarguable fact.

"There are some who say he shouldn't have. No one blames you. We – well, most of us – think what you did was brave. You always have been brave. You've stood unbending under your father's cruelty for years, done whatever he asked, tried to be as good as a son to him without ever asking for pity—"

I thought I might be sick. "Don't say that about him!"

He went on as if I hadn't spoken. "You did a good thing. You brought him back so that your mother could say goodbye, and he could be buried here. But that's enough now, Hana-san. It's enough."

My mind whirled with confusion, and disbelief – I was too shocked yet for anger – but one thing above all others stood out. "You're speaking as if he was already dead. Does everyone think that way? Is this what they're all saying?"

His expression held the sort of patient kindness I would have expected from someone forced to deal with a small, recalcitrant child. "This is reality, Hana-san. Your father was dead the moment the monster called to him, the moment he set foot in the forest at the dark of the

Moon. If your mother had any sense she wouldn't have let you—" He cut himself off swiftly. "No, I don't mean that. But there's nothing else to be done for him. She must accept it. You both must."

Dazed, I did not resist as he reached out to me. His broad, capable hands made contact with my bare forearms tentatively, thick fingers encircling my wrists with more confidence when I did not struggle. "You are free of him now. Do you understand? You and your mother are free. Your father's house was cursed with ill-luck and everyone knew it. Your ancestor was the very first to be taken, then your grandmother, then Kyo, and now him. One from every generation. No other family has ever lost so many. But he is the last male of his name. The bad fortune will die with him. You won't have to live this way any more. You can make a new life." He swallowed audibly – the first sign of uncertainty he had shown. "With me. If you want."

I ripped my arms free with a violent, angry jerk and took two unsteady steps back. "My father lies dying. How can you speak to me like this now? What is wrong with you?"

"I am sorry—"

"You're not sorry! You're glad! You think, all of you think, the village will be better off without him. That we will be better off – that I will. Dear Moon, will no one help us?"

"I will always do anything I can to help you," he said with his usual firmness, as if his speaking the words made them fact. "But I am not willing to die for him. None of us are."

I spun away, clasping my hands around my head. "Mother. Have they told her?"

"The elders are with her at the healer's house," Shouta said, sounding just a little discomfited. "She is … upset. She asked for you. She said you must come to her right away. I shouldn't have – forget what I have said, Hana-san. Forget it for now. Come, I will walk with you to Kaede-sensei's place."

"No. No. Leave me. Go away."

"Your mother—"

"I said leave me!" I cried. I sucked in sharp, shuddering breaths. "I – cannot go to Mother – like this. I must calm myself first. Tell – tell her – tell them that I shall come in a moment. I just need to…"

He shifted from foot to foot. "I don't think I should leave you alone."

"Shouta-kun, if you do *not* leave me alone, I will scream. I swear by the *Moon*. You said you wished to help me, so go to my mother and tell her that I will come very soon. Go."

Disappointment tugged down the corners of his lips, but he nodded, and after a small pause turned away, stepping off the porch and disappearing down the path into the village.

I put my hands over my face and let out a hoarse shriek, and it was an effort to stop. For a moment it was all I could do not to lose control completely – not to keep on yelling until my breath was gone. *Cowards*.

They were all *cowards*.

Hiding their cowardice with the pretence of ... of common sense. Disguising their fear under a thin, oily patina of justifying words. They thought I should have left him there in the trees to die alone. They – they *welcomed* the opportunity to rid their village of him! How could I bear to live amongst them knowing that they would look upon the miracle of my father's return as some kind of ... ill-chance?

But I would *have* to live with them. There would never be any way out of this place if no one was willing even to try to break the curse. I dug my fingers into my hair, welcoming the faint sting as my nails scratched my scalp.

If it had been anyone else, any other father or son or sister or cousin in this village who had been dying in Kaede's house, I knew I would have wanted to help. I had believed these people, people I grew up with, spoke to or saw every day of my life must feel the same.

Perhaps that was the rub. If it had been anyone else in the village – anyone but my father – their decision might have been different. He was not an easy man. Not a likeable one. Not since Kyo. His skills made him valuable, and he had friends who had known him from a child, who had stayed loyal even as his tongue turned bitter and his temper uncertain. Apparently that old friendship only stretched so far.

We are not willing to die for him.

But then who would? Who would, if not his friends, his neighbours, his family in all but blood? Who else would risk their lives for him if not them?

The answer swum up from deep inside, as if it had been waiting there all along:

You, Hana.

You.

I had not thought of it – not let myself think of it – not even before Hirohito's pointed words this morning. My mother relied on me. Not just for practical things, but as any mother will rely upon her sole surviving child, especially when her husband has gone far away inside himself. What was more, she loved me. If she were here, she would forbid me from going without a second's hesitation.

But she was not here.

I took a deep, slow breath, dropping my hands from my face as I stared unseeingly through the open door into the house. Gradually my gaze fixed itself upon my bow, lying on the kitchen table where I had left it, the curving red-brown wood washed with shifting patterns of firelight. I stepped inside and picked up the weapon. A shiver moved through my body.

You are free, Shouta had said. Was that what they all thought? They had it wrong, so wrong.

If my father died now, without forgiving me, then I would never, ever be free.

If I let this glimpse of hope slip through my fingers without even trying to catch hold of it, none of us would ever be free.

Shouta may have scorned me for behaving more like a son than a daughter, but I was still the best hunter in the village. I knew the woods as no one had in a hundred years. I heard the whispers of the trees. I had carried my father back out of the forest when anyone else would have given him up for lost.

If anyone alive had a chance of tracking the beast and slaying it, surely it was me.

But I had to go now. Now, before anyone else came to seek me out. Now, before I had to face my mother, and she read what I was thinking in my eyes. Now. Before my courage failed.

In a single swift movement, I slung my quiver over my shoulder, stowing the unstrung bow inside with the arrows. I left the warmth of the kitchen, took the hatchet from the wall where I had hung it moments before, and drew the door carefully closed behind me. Then I turned my back on home and village, faced the gathering shadows of the night, and began the climb towards the forest.

I did not look back.

Six

There is a monster in the forest! the trees protested as I entered their shelter.

Full dark had not yet spread its mantle across the mountain – but the trees still had almost all their leaves, so the shadows were deep beneath the dense canopy of branches. I stopped a few feet into the wood and closed my eyes, allowing my sight and my other senses to acclimatize. All the normal woodland noises were still there, if a little muted. Somewhere in the undergrowth a determined quail was letting out its soft *kukroo krrr, kuckroo krrr.* The wind sent waves whispering through the forest, and the trees creaked and groaned, uneasy with my presence. Eyes still closed, I lifted one hand and found the whiskery trunk of the venerable old kusunoki beside me, breathing in the bitter, herby scent of its foliage.

"Hush," I whispered. "Hush, all will be well."

The creaking noises around me died down a little. When at last I opened my eyes, I could see the pale brown blur of my hand against the dark grey of the tree bark.

"Grandmother, you and your sisters have kept me safe all these years. I know I can trust you. Help me, as my own people will not." The trunk seemed to shudder under my touch. The forest stirred and then stilled: listening. "I cannot do it by myself. I need you to guide me. Show me the way to the Dark Wood."

A long, gusty sigh moved through the trees. Leaves rustled, and boughs swayed and trembled overhead. Then:

Help.

Hana.

Walk. Walk. Walk.

The voices were faint, beckoning me away from the treeline, deeper into the forest.

"Thank you."

I patted the kusunoki and started off, following the soft murmurs through the towering hollows, mossy clearings and overgrown deer trails of the wood. At first I travelled ways that I knew well, taking comfort from the distinctive shape of a large rock that glowed with yellow-gold lichen even in the deepening darkness, or the position of a fallen tree over the clear trickle of a stream. The forest floor was dry, soft and almost warm beneath my rough soles. The wind kept pace with me faithfully.

Exertion made sweat spring up on my skin, but my friend the wind swept the moisture away and left a chill in its place. I shivered as I forced a path through the prickly, trailing tendrils of a hop vine, wishing I had stayed at the house a moment longer to don my much-mended, down-stuffed jacket. But it was useless to think like that. If I had stayed but one or two moments longer to put on a warm coat, then certainly I should have tarried for three or four more and packed a bag with what food could be spared from our pantry. I hadn't eaten since breaking my fast that morning, and my stomach was now reminding me, pointedly, that it was empty. And if I had delayed for that long, then why not roll up a blanket to strap to my quiver, for extra warmth? Take flints to light a fire? Except then I would have run out of moments altogether, and found myself listening to the arguments of whomever my mother sent to fetch me next – or worse, looking into the knowing eyes of Mother herself, and not able to leave at all.

To plan, or prepare, or even to think, was the end of hope. It was already a narrow enough, fragile enough hope. The only way to do something impossible was to do it. It was too easy for fear to creep in, else.

I believed I could find the monster. It had been found by countless others before me, after all, who never even meant to seek it. And I was sure I had as good a chance as anyone to deal it a death blow; it would not be used to prey which fought back, and there had never been any animal on this mountain that could escape me once I laid eyes upon it. These things I knew without question.

But if I stopped to think, then I would have to confront the knowledge that killing the beast and surviving it were not at all the same thing. This hunt was very different to the one the elders had proposed. I was alone. I was armed only with a quartz and wooden hatchet and my bow and arrows. And it was the dark of the Moon. The Dark Wood's evil magics would be at their peak.

There was a soft, trembling place huddled deep inside me that flinched from the truth of what this meant, a tiny frail voice that whispered: *I am not ready to die.*

So I could not think of it, any more than I could think of my warm coat. I had a debt to repay. There was only that. Only the hunt. That was how it must be, if I was to succeed.

Deeper into the wood and the shadows I went, with the trees closing in around me and their branches interlocking over my head until even my night vision almost failed, and I walked face-first into low boughs, and thin twigs lashed my skin. The mountainside began to feel like a great, alien intelligence, unloving and unknowable, that sought to slow me or even turn me back. Yet through it all the soft whispering voices of my friends the trees called me on:

Turn now. Turn.
This way.
Walk. Walk…

My steps came slower and heavier, tiredness causing

me to trip and falter. I had no idea where I was on the mountain any more, or of the way back, if there was one. I knew I must have been walking a long time, hours and hours, though there was no burning candle nor sight of the circling stars to tell me how long. If I had entered the forest on a normal morning and simply walked straight, I was sure I would have encountered the wall of strange dark pines by now. A dreadful suspicion that the trees – whether well-meaning or malicious – were sending me deliberately in circles caused my stomach to turn over.

"Is this the right way?" The words were panted more than spoken as I stopped to lean wearily against a young larch, wiping my forearm across my face. I licked my lips and found them dry and beginning to crack. I tasted my own sweat on them, and the metallic tang of blood too.

Look up, the trees replied.

Look ahead. Look behind.

Look.

I lifted my gaze from my feet and glanced over my shoulder. Very little of whatever weak starlight gleamed above penetrated these shadows. I had to squint to make out my surroundings. Following blindly where the trees called me I had been aware that I was climbing for a while without really thinking about it. Now I stood at the top of a ridge, and I realized – with a shock that brought me fully awake – that I could see the distinct, foreboding line of closely growing evergreens at the bottom of that slope … several hundred yards behind me.

I had passed into the Dark Wood without even knowing it.

Slowly I turned to look at the forest ahead. Was it my imagination that the twisted trunks and low-hanging boughs seemed more shadowy still than the ones I had left behind? I could not see what lay beyond them. In truth I could barely see a thing.

A great, rolling rush of wind moved through the wood, and the trees – the trees of the Dark Wood! – spoke to me again: *There is a monster in the forest.*

I did not answer this time, but the warning was well heeded. I pulled my bow from its place on my back and strung it, working by feel and memory alone and allowing the methodical movements to steady me. Taking an arrow, I held it at the ready between two of the fingers that grasped the stock of the bow. With my other hand, I loosened the cord that held the hatchet at my waist so that it could easily be pulled free. Then I began to walk once more.

The trees stirred unhappily as the wind gusted between them, sending dry leaves spiralling around me as I moved forwards. *There is a monster in the forest,* the forest groaned. *There is a monster!*

Fear squirmed down my spine. I nocked the arrow and drew it, my eyes straining at the dark as I entered a hollow in the mountainside where there was a small clearing amongst the trees. The ground dipped steeply under my feet, and I could see glints of deep midnight blue – the night sky – among the wildly tossing leaves of the overhanging branches.

A monster!

The wind rose higher and higher, buffeting and shoving me back. My arm muscles quivered as my grip tightened on my bow and its string. Eyes watering, I pressed on until I reached what I sensed rather than saw was the lowest point of the hollow and the centre of the clearing.

Monster!

I hesitated. The ground climbed sharply ahead of me, rising up to a dark crest many feet above my head. There was no way I could make it up that slope without both hands. But I very much did not want to move any deeper into this enchanted place without my bow at the ready.

Monster!

The trees were almost writhing now, their branches bending, trunks creaking, as if they sought to rip their own roots from the ground.

MONSTER!

I flinched – but all at once, as if that last tearing wail had exhausted their strength, the trees fell silent. The wind died and the leaves stilled. Silence rang like the chime of a bell.

High on the crest above me … something stirred.

It shone in the blackness, so radiant with its own light that my night-blinded eyes could hardly bear to rest upon it. A sinuous shape, glowing like new-fallen snow under a full moon.

The creature emerged almost lazily, its steps decep-
tively swift, and boneless and alien in their grace. In a
liquid, effortless motion, it coiled and sprang. The leap
carried it halfway down the slope in just one bound –
and it was that which helped me believe what I saw, for
only one animal could move that way, on four legs, with a
spine so flexible it could almost bend in two.

This shining thing was a cat. A great, white cat, bigger
than an ox. Bigger than any animal I had ever seen.

Sleek muscles rippled beneath a silver-white pelt
marked with jagged dark streaks – stripes. It stood still
where it had landed, a long, black-tipped tail flicking in-
dolently in the air behind it. A luxuriant silver mane grew
around its great triangular face. As it tilted its head, I saw
its eyes for the first time. Each one was bigger than the
width of a man's palm. And green. An impossible green,
glassy and glowing. Those eyes were too vivid, too bright
to belong to any earthly creature.

It stared at me. I stared back. A bare twenty feet apart,
the beast and I regarded one another, motionless. Around
us the forest seemed to hold its breath. My arrow was at
the ready, my bowstring taut with tension, arms trembling with readiness. But I could not move. I couldn't
even breathe. I was mesmerized with terror and awe. It
was beautiful. This shining silver monster was the most
beautiful thing I had seen in my entire life.

I hesitated too long. My fingers had grown numb. My
hand twitched, and my grasp on the bowstring slipped.

With a low twang, the arrow loosed, piercing the air in a perfect arch. For an instant it seemed to hang there – as if I could catch it, snatch it back. I cried out involuntarily: "No!"

My arrow sank deep into the great cat's chest.

The beast's immense jaws unhinged. It roared. The sound clapped at the air like thunder, shaking the ground beneath my feet. Behind ivory teeth longer than my fingers, the great cat's mouth glowed crimson, as if some impossible fire raged within its belly. A white-hot cloud of steam rolled out between its fangs.

As I watched, immobile with disbelief, the arrow that had been embedded in the cat's flesh quivered and then – somehow – ejected itself from the animal's chest. The beast stepped upon the arrow, crushing it to dust with one massive paw, and then blasted the night with another roar. Its eyes bored into mine with a terrifying, feral intelligence.

No droplet of dark blood marred the monster's white hide. It was unmarked. Unwounded. My weapons could not touch it. And now the beast knew that.

I thought I had felt fear before, but it had been nothing, *nothing*, compared to the all-consuming blaze of my terror now. Any hope I'd cherished of fighting the beast was gone.

I was going to die.

The monster leapt forwards.

I turned and ran, throwing myself at the soft, crumbling earth of the slope. My hands scrabbled and my feet dug in desperately, and my precious bow caught on a spiny branch. It flew out of my grasp. I could not even spare a glance to watch it fall. There was a flash of white in my peripheral vision – instinctively I dropped. A heartbeat later a paw twice the size of my head carved a yawning scar in the earth where I had been.

Arrows scattered out of my quiver around me with a sound like dry bones as I rolled and launched myself away. Some remote instinct scolded me for not stabbing the creature in the gut with an arrow while I passed, and I nearly laughed at the absurdity of it. I could not kill what did not bleed. No one could.

I should have listened to Shouta.

I never should have come here.

Kyo's voice, low and sneering and contemptuous as it never had been when he was alive, echoed in my mind: *Oh, but you were always coming here, weren't you?*

The blast of the beast's breath rolled around me as I zigzagged and jumped, ducking and dodging the lash of its giant paws over the uneven ground. The space of the hollow was narrow and the monster was so massive that it could barely turn around without crashing into the trees and bushes that edged the clearing, offering me feeble cover. But it was fast. Impossibly fast.

I can't keep this up.

I was already so tired. I had to get out. Up. Away. Yet the monster was somehow always there, batting me down again before I could even think of trying to escape. I took a glancing blow in the stomach from one of its paws and went flying. I slapped my hands against my throbbing abdomen as I landed, expecting to feel my entrails sliding out between them.

There was no blood.

It had swiped me with its claws sheathed...?

That look of alien intelligence in its eyes – I had a flash of memory – barn cats toying with a mouse before they ate it—

I am the prey.

Up. Up. Get up – get away.

No. Not yet.

The ground trembled. I lay still, waiting, waiting. Playing dead. The beast was nearly upon me. I could feel those unnatural eyes burning into me.

Now!

Its jaws snapped inches above my shoulder as I darted away, sweeping under its lashing tail. The head whipped around as I passed – *too close, too close* – and I surged to my feet and jumped, flinging myself recklessly upwards towards the low-hanging branch I had seen as I fell. If I didn't make it, I would drop right down into its jaws—

My hands snagged the bough, and I swung my legs up with everything I had, muscles burning, choking on my gasp of relief as I thudded into the trunk. Spitting out a leaf, I began to climb.

Go, go, high as you can, away—

The cat circled the tree as I scrabbled through the

branches. Its low, savage snarls rose up through the leaves and scraped down my spine. The tree was young, its branches slender and flexible. Barely enough to support my weight. The beast could not climb it.

Please don't climb it…

I hissed as something banged against my bruised hip. The hatchet. I had forgotten about it. My shaking fingers reached down to touch the handle. It was all I had left.

The air exploded with the unbearable thunder of the beast's roar. Below me the glowing white shape lunged forwards, and the tree shook. Branches tossed around me, scoring thin lines on my skin. I grabbed at the trunk with one hand. The other clenched fast over the quartz hatchet.

The beast roared again, and flung itself once more against the base of the tree. With an agonized shriek of tearing timber, the roots ripped free of the earth and the tree began to fall. I screamed as the clearing rose up to meet me.

My head rebounded from something hard – a rock, a knoll of wood. Vision fanned out into a blur of wavering images as I struggled to move, dragging myself out from under torn tree limbs. But I couldn't stand. My legs wouldn't obey.

The monster seemed almost to flow into existence before me, its edges scintillating, stretching and reforming against the darkness.

Red mouth opened.

Green eyes sparked.

I flung the hatchet with a yell of defiance. The quartz blade bounced uselessly away from the cat's breast. The monster roared in my face. Then its claws struck home, raking down the side of my body and through my right arm in a single furious swipe.

The power of the blow flung me away. Boneless as a rag doll, I tumbled, slid sideways, and then slipped ... down. Down. Down.

Deep, moist darkness embraced me as I slithered into the earth itself, like being born in reverse. Distantly I realized that the monster had knocked me into the crevice left by the tree roots when it had wrenched them out of the ground. My own deadweight had dragged my body to the very bottom of the hole.

Giant white paws scrabbled at the edges of the crack in the earth, sending cascades of dirt and pebbles flying. A green eye stared in. Infuriated, the monster bellowed and snarled, and the ground trembled again. It stalked past, and then returned, then thundered away once more. It couldn't reach me.

Too late. Too late now.

Agony washed over me in sickening waves. The stench of my own blood, thick and coppery, made me want to retch. I could feel the liquid gushing out in warm rivulets down my side. I thought I must have lost my arm – there was no feeling there but the pain. I didn't dare look, and I couldn't find the strength to move, even if I had wanted to.

Wretched whimpers spilled from my lips. I didn't try to hold them back. It didn't matter any more. Nothing mattered because ... because this was it. This soft earth ... would be my grave. I was going to die here, in the Dark Wood ... like my great-grandfather ... like Grandmother.

Like Kyo.

Amidst the dirt and blood and pain, the thought brought a strange sense of peace. Yes. It was right... I had tried my hardest, tried so hard for so long ... but it had never been enough. I had never been enough for Father... Now I had failed him again. For the final time.

I had always been coming here, hadn't I?

Coming here, to the Dark Wood.

To be with them.

Soon I would see them again... My grandmother and my brother... Soon it would all be finished.

I would finally be free...

The pain was ... not so bad any more. I was starting to feel sleepy.

The narrow sliver of light that fell into my grave was changing. Gradually warming with the golden flush of dawn. That was ... nice. I was glad to feel the sun on my face...

My grasp on consciousness slowly slipped away, but my eyes clung to the light until I could hold them open no more.

Seven

Consciousness came back in a starburst of agony.
Fire seemed to flow through my flesh, eating away
at me in long glowing runnels, like rivers of molten
metal burning my shoulder, my hip, and deep, deep
into my side. I tried to cry out. All that emerged was
a high, thin wheeze that whistled between my teeth.
The effort made the hurt surge up over the rest of my
body like a red tide, and if I had possessed the breath
in that moment to do it, I would have begged the Moon
for death.

What happened where am I what's wrong no no I can't
make it stop please make it go away—

"Be still, be still, you're safe. You're safe now. Don't
move."

I heard the voice only distantly: my own pained,

panicked breaths drowning everything out. A large, shadowy shape moved across the orange screen of my closed eyelids – I couldn't seem to open them – before a strong hand cupped the back of my head and tilted my neck up. Something touched my lip. The rim of a cup, rough and unglazed.

"Hurts," I whimpered.

"I know," the voice rumbled softly, soothingly. "Drink this. It will help."

The cup tipped. I tried to swallow, but the bitter liquid made me choke and cough. The pain flared, and I let out a weak, stuttering sob. I felt fingers knead the tight muscles of my neck, like an apology. "Keep trying."

The liquid was lukewarm, and it tasted awful. I choked again – just a little – but I did keep trying, and finally the cup was taken away.

"Who – why…?"

"Just rest. Sleep and get better."

He laid me carefully back down, my head nestling into some soft, spongy pillow – but the movement jarred my shoulder, which made me flinch, which made my side and hip scream. I bit my lip but couldn't hold in another sob.

"Breathe out," the voice – whose voice? – rumbled. A damp, cool cloth passed over my forehead and cheeks, wiping away sweat and tears. "Breathe in. Slowly now. Breathe out. It will pass. Pain always passes. Breathe in. What we know will pass, we can endure."

I followed the rhythm he set, breathing slowly and quietly until both the clawing fire in my side and the panic had eased enough to be bearable. I sensed more than heard him shift away and stiffened.

"Don't leave me. Don't go." I didn't recognize his voice yet, but I … I didn't want to be alone.

"I'm not going anywhere. Be still now." He began to sing. *"Copper fish, dance, dance… Leaves falling on silver pool… Autumn rain, fall, fall…"*

My mind slowly clouded over as the stuff he had made me drink took effect. I fell asleep to the gentle, rumbling growl of the sweet lullaby that no one had sung to me since I was ten years old…

I woke again with a start and let out a wordless cry. Instinctively I twisted, trying to get away from the pain, but it burned brighter in response, until I thought my whole right side must be consumed down to the black-ened bones.

Hands – big enough to cover almost the whole length of each of my forearms – held me still with a steady, careful weight. I blinked my eyes open, trying to make out who was there, but my vision swam with tears. It was too bright. Everything was too bright. I only saw a shadow against the shifting firelight. I didn't recognize anything.

"You must be still. Be still, be still, please, please…" the deep voice murmured, a soft repetitive litany that calmed me almost against my will.

"Who are you?" I begged. *It hurts it hurts why does it hurt so much?* "You're not my – where is my mother – who are you? What is your name?"

"Listen to me," he said urgently. "Your wounds have only just stopped bleeding. If you thrash about, you will open them again. Please be still. You've already lost a lot of blood, and I don't want you to die."

I croaked, "What happened to me?"

But before he could answer, an agonizing twinge scalded me anew, and I fell away from him, back into darkness.

"Who … who are you?" I asked again when I woke the next time. "Where is this?"

"I am nobody," he answered, already lifting me – one-handed, I realized, and with seemingly no effort at all – for the cup. "And where you are is safe. That's all you must know."

I stared up at him with wide, blurry eyes. I thought I could make out … something, some kind of hood or fabric that shadowed his face. For the first time I realized – or fully accepted – that I did not know this person. He was not of the village. I had never met anyone not of the village. I had never met a stranger. How was this possible? How could it be real?

"I don't know you," I fretted. "I don't understand."

"That's all right. You don't have to understand

anything now," he said, pressing the clay rim of the cup a little more insistently to my mouth. "You only need to rest and heal."

So I drank, and slept again.

A beast – glowing, lightning and shadows – eyes like green fire – its roar shakes the earth and its gaping maw burns red, red breath, white heat like the centre of a forge—

No!

The scream resounded in my chest, but I trapped the sound behind my teeth before it could escape. It was a dream. Only a dream, some nonsensical nightmare, not real. I didn't want to wake my parents. I didn't want to wake Kyo.

No, that's not right. That's not… Kyo is gone.

He's gone and it was my fault… Where did he go? Why didn't I stop him?

Why can't I remember?

Eyes squeezed tightly shut, I tried to make sense of what I knew – but instead of flowing together smoothly from the past into the present and away towards the future, my memories were … shattered. Opaque fragments on the surface of a dark, cold river. I struggled to capture the fragments as they bobbed by in my mind, and to make sense of them, but they … they made no sense. Kyo standing on the edge of the river, laughing. Mother crying. Long spirals of choking, dusty blue smoke – no, incense. Trees looming against the night sky, leaves tossing, and a burning white thing that ate up the shadows: a fallen star consuming all it touched with fire...

Terrible green eyes. Glowing. Glowing in the dark.

Terror arced through my body, locking me into stillness like a small wild creature facing a predator that it cannot hide from or outrun. *Only a nightmare,* the voice of common sense insisted. *No such thing exists. It was only a dream. An awful dream, and no more.*

Bone-deep discomfort, clawing through my right side, slowly drew me back to reality. I was hurt. My body's warning throb made it clear that I should be very careful about trying to move my arm or shoulder. Pain radiated through my abdomen, through my hip and the top of my thigh. I struggled to coax my gluey eyelids to lift, wincing them shut again as the light blinded me and flooded my vision with tears.

Forcing my left arm – heavy and limp – to lift and reach across my torso took an alarming amount of effort. I persevered, panting. My slowly questing fingers encountered thick wrappings on the injured shoulder. Not the soft, slightly frayed bandages I had been expecting, though. Something ... waxy, with dry, curling edges, but faintly damp. Oily damp.

My shoulder was wrapped in leaves. Layers and layers of leaves, soaked in a salve or ointment.

What in the Moon's name had I done to myself that Sensei had needed to cover me with *leaves*?

I let my fingers follow the strange dressings downwards as far as I could, and discovered that they covered most of my torso. A heavy robe, made of thick, stiff fabric, had been wrapped around my other side and over my left arm. A thin blanket pulled up over that covered me from armpits to toes. I let my arm relax back to my side and, groping beneath me, found that I was resting on what felt like some kind of strange, thick, springy mattress covered in a soft fur.

It is very quiet, I thought suddenly. There was birdsong, high and sweet and golden … and completely unfamiliar. What kind of bird sang like that? I had known the call of every bird in the woods by the time I was seven – my grandmother had made sure of it. But somehow this song I did not know.

Somewhere close by, water gurgled. It was the sound of a small, swift-moving rill, nothing like my family's deep silent well. And I could hear the whispers of a light breeze through leaves, but the sound was too far away to be our apple trees, and at the same time much too close to be the trees up on the ridge above the village. I couldn't hear anyone breathing, either. No one was sitting with me.

Without knowing how, suddenly I was sure that I had been ill for a long time.

When a person doesn't move, can't eat or drink much, their body starts to fail very quickly…

I frowned crossly. Strange… I was sure it was Kaede's voice I was remembering. But when had the healer told me that? Could it be something I had overheard while I lay here, barely conscious?

Blinking rapidly, I let the tears from my watering eyes soak into my cheeks and hair as my sight slowly adjusted. I was sheltered by a dim, curving roof, high, high above me. I thought it was made of stone but of a kind I had never seen before, sandy yellow-ish in colour. There were vines, miles of them, leafy green and criss-crossing the circular roof space. Narrow, arching windows ringed the walls, too high for any human to be able to gaze out of them. The openings let in shafts of greenish light, and more clustering vines.

My eyes tracked downwards. Curving stone walls, with strange round pillars carved into them, also cloaked in thick tendrils of green. The space was large but seemed mostly empty. The entire floor was covered in green and yellow moss. I thought my head must be pillowed on the stuff.

From the corner of my left eye, I could see a dug-out hearth, circular like this room, cut into the mossy floor and ringed with stones. The fire there had died down to pale ashy embers. A stand of blackened branches held a clay pot suspended over the heat. Other signs of human habitation – a squat iron teapot, a cup, small bowls, a chipped spoon and a rough pestle and mortar made of two rounded stones – were carefully and precisely arranged on the floor around it.

The sight of the pestle and mortar brought a sudden

flash of memory: bitter, vile-tasting liquid that shrivelled my tongue but eased away pain and let me sleep. It felt like ... like a very familiar memory. Something that had happened not once but over and over, until the shape of the memory was rubbed smooth in my mind. A large, warm hand cradling my head, and a cup pressed to my lips, and a quiet voice that hovered near by, always. Of course. The voice – the stranger. The man not of my village.

Where had he come from? And where was he now?

Where ... where was I?

Weathering the unpleasant twinges that the motion sent down into my shoulder, I rolled my head on the mossy pillow to look to my right. That was where most of the light spilled into the room. A wide, arched doorway with no door led out into – I squinted, eyes watering again – some green space. Very green. Grass? And the line of a tall hedge, perhaps?

I did not recognize any of it. This was nowhere I had ever been, nowhere I had ever seen before in my life. How could that be? And then, like an icy cold hand laid upon my breast, the thought: Had the stranger been the one to bring me here? Away from my village and everything I knew? Where was my family? Why had they let him take me?

Or had they?

My hands curled into fists – or tried to. My right hand only twitched, and the movement sent a terrible burning twinge up along my arm that only added to the sense of panic. I was helpless. Weak. Utterly dependent on a man whose name I did not know and whose face I had never seen. Who was he? Why wasn't my mother here – or my father? Had something happened to them?

What happened to me?

Against my will the air began to huff between my lips with a hard, desperate panting noise. It was the sound a deer made when my arrow had pierced its body but not struck its heart, bringing it crashing down without ending its life outright.

A confused whirl of images from my nightmare assaulted me. Running in the dark. Falling.

Something terrible had happened. Something terrible had happened to me.

I am the prey. I am the prey. Run!

No, I told myself fiercely. *I am a hunter. And I am not afraid. I will not be afraid.* I squeezed my eyes shut, searching for stillness inside.

I had to get up and find out where I was. I had to try to get home.

If I could move at all, I must move now.

Holding my breath, I shifted cautiously from side to side, testing, then made myself roll towards the hearth, onto my left shoulder. My right side seemed to catch fire at the pull on my injuries – a swoop of sickness turned my stomach and sweat sprang up over my whole body. I braced myself and rolled again, onto my front this time, getting my good arm under me with a muffled grunt.

Pain washed through me in hot, queasy waves as I pushed myself upright into a kneeling position. I set my jaw. With a painful heave, I managed to gain my feet – but the effort sent black and silver phantoms darting across my vision. Blindly I flailed for balance. My hand hit something. Something solid. A wall. I leaned into it gratefully. My skin was icy with cold sweat.

But I was up on my own two feet, and the doorway was before me.

Pulling the stiff fabric of the robe up over my bandaged arm and clutching it close around my torso with my good hand, I shuffled forwards. The sun's light fell directly into my face as I stepped outside, and I was so grateful for the warmth that I allowed myself to still for a precious heartbeat to bask in it. Then I blinked the water from my eyes a second time and looked around.

And gasped. It was a garden. But *such* a garden.

No workaday, muddy plot of earth for vegetables and fruit trees and pigs and chickens, this. It was … it was like one of the fancy noblemen's gardens, or the Moon Prince's public parks, which had so impressed Grandmother's grandfather, when he visited the City of the Moon over a hundred years ago.

The garden was deserted, silent under the still soft light of early morning, curls of mist rising up from the tall, dark hedge that seemed to enclose it. Beneath my feet, velvety turf, glittering with dew, had been cut into

long bands that curled and flowed in repeating, sym-
metrical patterns. In between them, raked smooth, was
shining white sand. Whenever several bands of grass met,
they formed intricate knots, and in the centre of each
knot was some small miracle of a gardener's art: an explosion of vivid, unfamiliar flowers trained to cascade over
an iron frame in the shape of a sunburst; a perfect miniature landscape formed of tiny rocks and trees and shrubs
trimmed into pleasing shapes; a softly muttering fountain
in a jewel-like tumble of smooth quartz stones.

At the very centre of the knotting patterns of grass
lay the place from which I had just emerged. It was a
tall, round building, slender and golden, rising five or six
storey's high. Nothing like the squat wooden buildings I
was used to. It must have been impressive once. Now it
was clearly ruined; no shutters or paper in the thin windows, no door in the arched doorway. Perhaps there was
no roof. But enclosing the entire stone building, so that
only random sections of its walls could be seen, was an
immense tree. I had never seen or imagined such a tree
before. The greyish-purple trunk soared into the sky like
a mountain, its lush green canopy spreading so high that
clouds drifted in ragged wisps amongst its branches. It
looked like something from a fairy tale.

I turned back again, to look at the rest of the garden. The hedge that surrounded this place was taller than
my head, and dark. Beyond that, the sun cast its light on
more trees, more leafy giants, in the distance. Everything

was in bloom. As if it were midsummer. It was impossible. Everything I could see was all impossible. This was more than fantastic. More than beautiful.

   Magic.

Eight

Somewhere not far off there was a liquid, mournful cry: a bird or some other creature. I started, and shook myself out of my daydream state.

Time enough to work out if this place was a trick or a hallucination or a … a spell, later. When I had figured out where on earth it was. When I knew I could find my way home.

My unsteady feet trod slowly over the patterns of turf and sand, reluctant to ruin their beauty. The tall, dark hedge, I saw as I came closer, was in truth little more than a dense tangle of thorns. Each of the thorns was as long as my finger, and wickedly barbed. Not a good match for the beauty of the rest of the garden.

To attempt to push through the hedge would be not only painful but pointless; I didn't have the strength.

I needed to find a real opening. A gate. A gap. Anything. Following the curving line of the hedge, I began to circle the garden. I heard again that sad, lilting cry. A moment later an outlandish animal – a bird, it had to be a bird, but how on earth could such a bird ever fly? – walked past with stately indifference. Its body was the size of a toddler, its long, slender neck extended gracefully, a sweeping tail of feathers dragging behind it. The small head was adorned with a sort of crown of stiff black feathers, but the rest of it was snowy white, save for the dark, jagged, diamond pattern that marked the fan-like shape of its tail. Its beady eyes passed over me with no hint of fear as it continued its stately progress and disappeared into a stand of those blue-flowered trees.

I stared after it, trying to make sense of a bird of that size and that colour which had no wariness of hunters. It took me longer than it should have to realize what I'd just seen.

The bird must have come *through* the thorns.

I took two cautious steps forwards. There, sure enough, was a neat opening in the hedge.

A way out.

But when I stepped eagerly through the gap, my heart sank. Another hedge faced me – identical to the first, and running parallel with it. The two hedges formed a sort of corridor that ran as far as my eye could follow in either direction. It wasn't a way out – only a way into a different part of the garden.

But a garden, no matter how strange, could not go on forever.

The sun was just visible beyond the towering distant trees. If I headed east, maybe I would eventually encounter some sign of the river that flowed along the east side of the mountain, and through our village's valley.

That day I learned the relentless misery of walking when you are wounded, and in pain, and nothing but liquid has passed your lips for days. Each footstep feels like the last you can possibly manage. Yet as that foot falls you must find it within yourself to lift the other and go on again. The fire in my right side ebbed and flared with each heavy step. I was weak, and hunger made me weaker, and soon thirst added to that. At first I cursed myself for not stopping to drink from one of the fountains around the giant tree, but then I realized I could not have been sure that even the plain water would be safe in such an alien place.

The sun rose ahead of me. The sky deepened into a clear, lovely blue. A warm breeze stirred the leaves of the distant trees and made the thorns rustle together dryly. And I walked. When the next break in the wall of thorns came, I was so focused on keeping myself upright that I almost walked right past it.

Relief breathed new strength into me. But it drained away when I stepped through the gap. This was no way out either. The opening led to another enclosed garden, circular like the first but smaller.

Here the pale trunks of dead trees, still rooted in the mossy earth, had been carved into flowing, elongated shapes. The bare branches spiralled up and out, stretching gracefully towards the sky. Between the statues, long ropes of tiny glass bells were strung, glinting in the light. The place had an air of tempting tranquility.

Yet ... on a second glance, something triggered a strange uneasiness within me. The more I looked, the more their graceful forms seemed ... tortured. Human?

The wind brushed through the branches, making a soft, silvery kind of music among the bells, quieter than I would have expected. The gentle tinkling sound set my teeth on edge. I felt uneasily that there were voices in it. Voices that wept.

Something was very wrong with this place.

I dragged myself away as fast as I could.

There must be a way out. There must be a way home. There must.

The path marked by the thorns stretched on and on. The sun was overhead now, and my shadow was a dark puddle around my feet. The misery of my injured side and my unquenched thirst were such that at first I hardly noticed the chill that had me clutching the heavy robe tighter for warmth. But I could not ignore the rising cold for long; soon my breath began to cloud in the air before my eyes. Underfoot, the grass had gone from warm to icy. Frost glimmered palely among the thorns and flowers of the hedge. All the while the sun shone down, undimmed.

Something itched on my face. When I tried to release my grip on the robe to reach up and scratch it, I found that I couldn't. My fingers seemed frozen in place. The skin looked ... odd. Almost blue.

My thinking was fuzzy and slow. Frighteningly slow. I shook my head to try and clear it, and tiny ice crystals rained down around me. From me. Ice ... was forming all over me. I had been shivering before, but suddenly I realized that the shivering had stopped. It was too cold here. Too cold. I had to turn back...

I moved too hastily. Deadened feet slipped on the slick grass. I crashed down onto my good side, my pained cry escaping as a cloud of white vapour. There was a sharp prickling sensation under my cheek. Delicate spears of ice were forming around me, criss-crossing and over-lapping, latching onto the fabric of the robe, onto the cracked layers of frost on my skin. Trapping me.

No, no, I must move, I must get up...

I heard, as if from a very long way off, an explosive, growling roar. The bestial sound shook the ground, and even in my half-dead state, I quivered with a spasm of instinctive fear.

A shadow fell over me and I was scooped up in a quick, violent movement. Thin pieces of ice cracked and tore away from my skin, and the wounds in my side flared anew with pain.

"You're alive," rumbled the deep, soft voice I had grown to know in that strange little tower in the tree.

"Thank the Moon. You're still alive."

It was the stranger. I still couldn't see his face – frost coated my lashes and clogged my eyes almost shut. I gasped for breath but couldn't force out the words: *Who are you? Where are we? What is happening to me?*

"It's all right – I've got you," he said. "I must get you out of this place."

Then we were flying. The world whirled away into a blur around us – gales tore at my hair and whipped his cloak wildly around me. He was running faster than the wind itself.

Sunlight suddenly disappeared, and the wind died down as he slowed to a walk. I cracked open my eyes to see that he had retraced my steps through the thorns already. In only moments, we had returned to the first garden, the garden of knots. My teeth grated together as a convulsive shiver worked through my body.

He carried me through the shadow of the giant tree, and ducked to fit through the doorway of the little stone room from which I had fled hours before. I could never have imagined I would feel such overwhelming gratitude to see it again. We went straight over to the hearth, where he folded down into a cross-legged position and propped me up against his shoulder. Holding my shivering body steady with one arm, he drew open the heavy folds of his cloak with the other and wrapped the fabric around me with swift but painstaking care. The sudden warmth was intense – almost painful – but at that moment I would have dived headlong into an open fire if it meant an end to the cold. I burrowed into the cloth, inadvertently nudging up against him. I was only barely aware of his small, shocked breath and jerk of surprise as my hands glanced against the rough fabric at his side. I didn't care. I did not know this person, but I must get warm, or I would die.

"Your hands are like ice," he said quietly. His voice was the same calm, deep rumble as always. "I'll light the fire."

He kept me close with one hand, using the other, by the sound of it, to arrange a wood chimney in the hearth. I heard the unmistakable scrape of flints and felt the lapping warmth of the fire against my side as the little blaze grew. He shuffled us both closer to it, tucking the cloak around my legs more tightly.

There were more sounds at the hearth – clinking, pouring water, dry rustlings. After another few moments had passed, he shrugged the shoulder where I leaned to get me to straighten up. I forced my eyes open to see a very recognizable rough ceramic cup being held before me.

The sleeping draught.

"Drink this."

"No," I croaked, and turned my face away. My skin was still crawling with shivers and if he tried to push me away from the fire, I would resist with every bit of strength I had – which wasn't much – but I wouldn't drink that stuff any more.

There was a short, puzzled pause, then a small sound, as if of realization. "It is only tea. Or the closest thing to tea I have."

Tea? I felt a surge of longing for the familiar drink. But … it was clear now that he had been keeping me drugged, maybe for days. I shook my head again, tensing in anticipation of a display of displeasure, even anger, at my defiance.

"I don't blame you for being wary," he assured me evenly. "But won't you at least try the tea? It won't make you sleep, I promise. You're shaking. Just try it and you'll see."

I reached out a trembling hand for the cup. I hissed and jumped a little when the heat of it seemed almost to scald my chilled palm, and sipped cautiously. The brew did not taste like tea. Not any tea I'd ever had, at least. It was also nothing like that bitter, herby liquid he had dosed me with before. This was slightly sweet, and had a sort of warm, gingery aftertaste, and I sipped again, with more enthusiasm this time, savouring the slight burn as the tea slid down to my stomach.

I did not feel sleepy. He had been telling the truth.

"I'm sorry that you didn't like the pain draught," he said – a little hesitantly, I thought. "You needn't drink any more, if you don't want to."

That sounded … reasonable. Kind, even. He had been kind to me, so far, hadn't he? Perhaps he really was what he seemed to be now, a well-meaning, gentle … stranger.

But I still didn't know who he was.

I took a large gulp of the delicious warm drink, coughed a little, and – gathering my courage – choked out, "I am Hana. What is your name?"

There was no response. The barrel-like chest against which I rested seemed to go still, as if he had stopped breathing.

"I don't know. Don't remember," he corrected himself stiffly. "It's been … so long since I heard it. I am alone here." A long pause. "I have been alone for a very long time."

My lips parted in surprise, even as a memory seared through my brain, a memory of asking who he was once before, and his reply: *Nobody*.

What a terrible, lonely way to live.

Unhappy silence fell then, filled only with the low snapping and whispering of the fire. Just as I was beginning to think that I could trust him, I had managed to say the exact wrong thing. His silence and stillness felt like a chasm yawning between us now. And I found that I was sorry – and I wanted somehow to bridge the silence. Not to ask all the questions that burned inside me, to discover just what he meant – how could anyone forget their own name? – or where this strange home of his was, or what had happened to bring me here. Not even to attempt to placate him for my own safety. I had hurt him and I wanted to soothe the wound.

"Itsuki," I said experimentally, testing the sound of it.

"What?" The word was distant, as if he had forgotten, or wished to forget, that I was there.

"It means—"

"Tree. I know."

"You are as strong as a tree. Almost as big. And nearly as quiet. I must call you something, so if you do not mind, I will call you that. Itsuki-san."

"Itsuki-san," he repeated, but his voice wavered as if he was winded, and I felt him take a deep, deep breath. "Very well." And then after another slightly too long pause: "Thank you. Are – are you feeling much pain now?"

Instinct immediately urged me to deny my true vulnerability. "Just ... just a little."

"Only a little?"

I did not answer.

He sighed. "I would like to examine your injuries. I am worried that what happened today may have caused the bleeding to start again."

"I don't think it has. I would feel it, wouldn't I?"

"Perhaps. Still. There's a salve I can apply which will numb you a little, and your bandages should be changed now anyway. They've dried out."

What he said was sensible enough. I could not argue with it. But I wanted to.

Swallowing hard, I tilted my head back to look up at him. Though the fire burned brightly with golden light behind me, I could not make out his face. The heavy hood of his cloak hung low over his head, and he had turned a little away from me, so that the shadows hid him completely. I couldn't even see the tiny glints of the firelight in his eyes. He had seen my wounds – seen me at my most broken and vulnerable – many times, and yet he would not let me see even his face. He was hiding from me on purpose.

He twitched – an almost imperceptible movement – under my steady gaze. As though I had held his eyes for too long and discomforted him, even though I had no idea where, in that too deep shadow under his hood, his eyes might be. His head turned away even more, ducking almost shyly.

"Itsuki-san—" I began quietly.

Wordlessly, he shook his head. The great shoulders hunched, and still he did not speak.

"Let me see you. I must see who you are."

I didn't allow any hint of pleading to creep into the words, but he seemed to feel it anyway. He made a tiny hissing sound, as if through his teeth. "You won't like it. You – you'll be afraid."

"I am already afraid. Don't you understand? I cannot let you do this unless… I have to see your face. You have to let me see who you are. Please."

He let out his breath – a shaky, almost pained exhale. Then he carefully took my empty cup from my good hand, placed it down on the hearthstone behind me and unravelled me from his cloak. Leaving me on the tattered, colourful rug, he straightened up and took two long paces back.

Chilled by the silent withdrawal, I thought he would turn and walk out of the little room. Instead he lifted his hands to the hood of his cloak. The long, slender fingers seemed very pale against the dark material as they clenched down on it. His knuckles stood out, yellow and red with strain, trembling visibly.

Then he pushed the hood back – and in the same movement he pulled away more layers of dark fabric that had lain beneath it, swathed around his face like bandages – allowing his hair to spill out. He lifted his head to look at me. To let me see him.

My suddenly nerveless fingers slipped, and the fur fell away from my shoulders as I stared.

His hair was a thick, luxuriant curtain, raggedly chopped off at chin-length. It was pure white. White as the Moon, white as bone, white as death. His skin was almost as pale, smooth and poreless, without blemish or line or scar. His features were exquisitely carved, with high, round cheekbones, a perfectly proportioned nose, full lips and a firm yet faintly delicate, pointed chin. And his eyes. Such eyes. Large and deep-set, ringed with soft, silvery lashes ... and *green*. The colour of Michi's prized glass bottle – and glowing the way the glass did when the sun fell upon it and lit it up from within. No one had such colouring. No one. No one had such features. Every detail of Itsuki's face was perfect.

He was the most beautiful thing I had ever laid eyes on – and the most terrible.

His beauty was *alien*. Repellent. Like the vivid jewel-like colours of the most vicious, venomous snake, like the eerie garden of tormented dead trees and the music of its glass bells. It frightened me. No human face should be so perfect. No human face could be so perfect. He looked like something … inhuman. My mind rejected it, crying *wrong wrong wrong*.

He had been right to warn me. I wished I had never seen him. And yet I could not tear my gaze away.

At last, with a ragged sob, I managed to squeeze my eyes shut.

"I'm sorry," he said, blankly. There was a soft rustle of fabric. "Sorry."

Pressing my fist against my lips, I tried to compose myself. "No, I – I'm sorry. I can't – it's not – not your fault," I mumbled from behind my hand.

There was more movement, and my eyes flew open as I realized that now he was walking away, heading for the doorway. His back was bent, and his shoulders slumped. The hood was back up.

"Itsuki-san," I said, remorseful. I was driving him from his own home. "Don't go."

"You are frightened." The gentle voice was dull.

"I'm not. Not any more. I don't want you to leave." I forced the words out, but as I said them, they became true. With more conviction, I continued, "I don't want you to go away. I promise, Itsuki-san."

His head lifted up a little, and he turned around.

Slowly, as if each step were a struggle, he came back to the fire. I pointed at the threadbare rug where I sat, and more slowly still he sank down and seated himself beside me, though not very close.

"I'm sorry," I repeated. "You warned me. I should have been able to … control myself better."

"The first time I saw myself…" he whispered, so softly that I thought he half-wished I wouldn't hear at all. "Saw my face reflected in a pool of water, I was sick."

Dear Moon, grant me your strength. Grant me your wisdom. Let me think of the right thing to do. Cautiously, I reached out to him and laid my hand – my large, square, strong hand that still seemed tiny and fragile compared to his – over his long fingers, where they twitched restlessly on his knee.

His head jerked up. I saw the shape of his chin and his lips outlined in gold from the fire – he hadn't had time yet to rewrap the cloth around his face. As unobtrusively as I could, I averted my eyes, trying not to shudder. "Do you still want to examine my wounds today?"

The twitching fingers quieted. After a moment, he said, "Let me fetch my supplies."

Nine

Based on past experience, I expected the peeling of the makeshift leaf bandages from my injuries to be excruciating, and braced myself to be as stoic about it as possible. But after the first layer of flaky, brittle leaves was lifted away, the ones beneath seemed still to be damp, and flexible, and rather than cracking scabs or ripping away painfully dry skin, they slid loose with barely a careful tug on the stranger's – Itsuki's – part.

"I soak them in oil made from the bark of this tree." He waved a hand to indicate the walls around us. "It helps wounds to heal, and stops the leaves from adhering to the skin. The leaves come from it too. They have a quality which helps to prevent infection."

I nodded, fixing my eyes firmly on the orange and gold ripples of the fire. Not just because I wanted to avoid another horrifying glimpse at his face but also because letting anyone, let alone someone I barely knew, so close to me when I was weak and vulnerable was uncomfortable, like fine cuts dealt by paper, stinging all over my body. It took a great deal of effort to stay still.

Clearing my throat, I said rather unevenly, "My village healer would happily murder you for the secret of such a thing."

He made an absent-minded humming noise that could have been agreement or negation. "You were right, there's no sign of blood here. I'll put the salve on. It may sting, or be a little uncomfortable when I press. Tell me if it hurts too much."

I nodded again, breathing in deeply through my nose, feeling my nostrils flare like a nervous horse's.

"Hana-san. I mean it. I don't want to hurt you."

Despite my unease and embarrassment, I felt a crooked smile pull at one corner of my lips. "You are a strange healer. Normally they tell you to shut up and take your medicine and not whine about it if you know what's good for you."

He let out a little puff of breath. "So far, whining is not a problem I have encountered very much. My … patients aren't ones for chatter."

I only just stopped my eyes from flying to his face in surprise. I had assumed that he was here alone. "Your patients?"

"Animals large and small. Birds. And myself, of course.

A quiet group, generally. You will tell me if it's too much?"

"I will," I said, not sure if I was telling the truth or not.

"Very well then."

There was a little squeaky noise as he unscrewed a jar and then a sharp smell like crushed pine needles, perhaps, or camphor, or both and yet … different. It was so strong that it made my eyes water. The salve felt cool as Itsuki tracked it over the most tender, aching, burning hurts on my side, my arm, my hip. He touched me so lightly that it tickled, and I bit down on my lip to stop a faint snort-laugh slipping out. He paused.

"It's … it's all right," I said. "It doesn't hurt at all."

The coolness had become a tingling sensation, like pins and needles, but growing stronger by the moment. Entirely against my will my eyes flicked away from the fire to look down at the wounds for the first time. A choke of shock escaped me.

I had been carved almost in two.

Ugly red wounds slashed deep, gouging my flesh into puffy pink runnels. No wonder I couldn't move my arm. I might never move my arm again. At best I would be scarred for the rest of my life.

What had *happened* to me?

Screaming as the ground rose up to meet me.

What had happened to me?

Pain in my head. Vision wobbling and blurring, fighting desperately to move, to free myself, to stand.

What happened to me?

Starlight white sizzling in the black. Hot red jaws, gaping, eyes burning green. A colossal sound like thunder breaking around my head. Pale talons striking home—

What had happened?

"Hana-san, listen to me, listen to my voice. *Hana!*"

I coughed, whimpered, sucked in a whistling breath through a throat that seemed to have shrunk to a raw, dry channel three sizes too small, and opened eyes I didn't even realize I had closed. Itsuki was leaning over me. His hands were firmly planted on my forearms, holding me still. The glimpse I got of his expression before I ripped my gaze away was stricken.

"Listen to me. You're safe, Hana-san. You're safe here. Just listen to my voice. Breathe out. Breathe for me. Come on. Breathe."

I choked again and felt the panicked gasps turn into wet, undignified sobs as I finally caught my breath. "What happened to me?" I gasped roughly. "How did I get such wounds?"

He turned his head so that all I could see was the drooping folds of his hood, and removed his hands from my arms. "I don't know," he said. "I don't... Don't *you* know?"

"I can't remember. There's nothing but nightmares. Nothing real. Will I – will I be able to... My arm. How bad is it?"

He turned back quickly, and I saw the light reflecting from his wide, bright eyes. "Your arm will heal fully. You will use it again just as you did before. Even the scars will fade too in time. I give you my word."

I let out a slow, shuddering exhale of relief. "Thank the Moon. You're sure? My hand—"

"I give you my word," he repeated, and his emphasis made it clear that he considered it an oath, a vow.

I nodded, letting my head roll sideways on its mossy pillow. I realized Itsuki's salve had worked – the stabs of hot pain in my side had simmered down to a dull ache again, and without the constant pain, my body was slowly going limp, heavy with exhaustion. "Thank you. I'm … I'm so sorry. For all this trouble."

"There is nothing to thank me for, and nothing to forgive."

What a strange creature, I mused sleepily, *to distain both apologies and thanks, no matter how richly deserved.* "Don't I need more … leaves?" I asked. "Bandages, I mean?"

"Yes, but not just now. You've been through a lot today. You can sleep."

I hummed gratefully, letting my eyes drift shut, then frowned. The wounds… They were red and vicious looking … but they were almost completely closed, as Itsuki had said. I was no healer, but surely…?

"Itsuki-san," I murmured muzzily. "How long have I been here, with you?"

There was a barely noticeable hesitation. "Time may not pass here as it does beyond the thorns – in the outside world that you know. All I can tell you is that the sun has set on the maze ten times since I found you."

At the very back of my mind, an alarm sounded, ringing like the village warning bell, and bringing faint ripples of remembered panic and fear. Ten times? Ten *days*? Could that really be true? Itsuki had no reason to lie, surely, but … I had been here for almost a fortnight already? Ten days was too long. Far too long. I was running out of time. *But … time for what?*

My stomach churned with the feeling that I had forgotten something – something very important indeed. But as I reached out to try and grasp these thoughts, they turned to mist and dissolved, leaving nothing but a faint sense of anxiety behind.

Why can't I remember? What can't I remember?
What happened to me…?

By the time my exhausted slumber broke, it was dark. I was sure I had never been so ill before, so seriously injured, but I wondered if all invalids experienced this side effect of time swooping away in great expanses whenever they paused to rest or closed their eyes. And if so, did they find it as disconcerting, frightening, as I did? Days were slipping through my hands like grains of sand. Time was running out.

My brows knitted together as I tried to work out what it was, this thing that I had forgotten to do. Why so urgent? The memories that could have lent my feelings a solid foundation, or even just context, remained elusive.

When I turned my head towards the light of the fire, the stranger – no, Itsuki, I must remember that – was there, stirring a battered old iron pot hung over the hearth. When he saw me looking at him, he replaced the lid on the pot, stood, and moved around the fire towards me. Something in the set of his shoulders and hooded head conveyed concern.

"I'm all right," I assured him, voice croaking. "It's dark – did I sleep for hours?"

"Not for many hours. It is only evening. The shadow of the tree swallows up the sunlight early." He was kneeling beside me as he spoke, and drawing the basket filled with the oily leaves towards him. "Do you ... feel strong enough to sit up?" His hands curled and uncurled around the handle of the basket as the words trailed off.

I thought about all the times he must have bandaged and unbandaged me when I was bleeding and unconscious, or perhaps raving and fighting him, when he had not known yet if I would live or die. Not pleasant remembrances for him.

"I can sit," I said, extending my hand to him.

Itsuki shook his head. "You'll strain something that way. Here."

He bent over me and lifted my body up into a sitting position without so much as a grunt of effort.

"Show off," I accused, half-serious. I wasn't sure I liked anyone feeling free to heave me around just as they pleased. Even this man. Especially this man.

Again that soft huffing noise. "Says she who went running around the maze alone the moment she could stand from her sickbed. You were lucky you didn't kill yourself. You must have the constitution of an ox."

I didn't have an answer to that – or none which it seemed wise to utter. "You called it that before," I said, a few moments later, when Itsuki was fully engrossed in rebandaging my shoulder. "A maze. Is that what this place is?"

"Yes, a maze of thorn hedges, as you saw."

"But then who made it?" And once one question had slipped out, I couldn't stop the rest. "Am I still on Otsukimi no Yama? Where do all the strange animals and plants come from? I didn't recognize a single one, and I *know* plants and animals. How could it get so dangerously cold so fast? I was walking in broad sunlight!"

His hands didn't slow as he replied. I wondered if he had had been preparing himself for this blizzard of questions while I slept. "The maze was created by some kind of great magic, or curse, which I do not pretend to understand. My home, this garden, lies within it, but is only a tiny part of the whole. As far as I know, the maze is hidden within the deepest forests of Mount Moonview. The animals and plants ... they are foreign to me, too. Or they were, when first I came here. I do not know if they hale from other lands, or if perhaps the enchantment created them. But they are real now, and they live and die as other plants and creatures do, though some of them have qualities or ... abilities that I have never known before."

Like you, I thought, but did not say. "And what of the cold?" I asked, more cautious now, since his avoidance of that question had been obvious.

He sighed but did not falter or look at me. "The maze is filled with wonders – but also with danger. There are other gardens than this one, some of which seek to beguile or even entrap. There are … beasts that roam the thorns. At the very centre of the maze dwells its creator. I call her Yuki-Onna. She is a creature of ice. Ice and magic. If you stray too close to the centre of the maze, to her home, the ice will find you."

I stared at the side of his head until he moved around me so that he could apply leaves to the back of my arm. The Yuki-Onna – snow maiden – was a beautiful female spirit who approached travellers lost in the snow and either stole their lives by tricking and freezing them to death, or, very occasionally, saved them from the storm by guiding them to safety. I supposed it might not be beyond the power of such a creature to create a magical maze and populate it with traps for the unwary visitor.

Yet I could not help but notice that, although Itsuki spoke of this woman – or creature – and her home as dangerous, there was a sort of warmth, a softness in his voice when he said "her". And Itsuki was not precisely a normal human man himself, was he? Could it be…?

"Is the Yuki-Onna your – friend?" I asked delicately. "Is that why you chose to live here?"

He leaned away from me to select more leaves from

his basket. The silence lengthened. At last he said, "She is not a friend to anyone. Certainly not to me. I do not choose to live here, Hana-san. This is a prison, and I am its prisoner. I cannot leave."

A prison? I stiffened in alarm, and winced as my wounds protested. "How did I come to be here, then? And how will I get out?"

"Be calm," he ordered me, laying a hand so softly on the blade of my shoulder that it felt like the flutter of a bird's wing on my bare skin. "The forest beyond the maze is part of the Yuki-Onna's demesne and it is ... not quite a normal forest. It is alive. Sometimes, and I know not how, it brings me things. Birds. Deer. Foxes. Creatures which are injured and will die without my help."

"The Dark Wood," I murmured. I knew the place he spoke of and yet ... I knew I was forgetting something important about it.

"If you like. The forest brought you here and laid you at my door. But this place was not built to hold you. You are not its prisoner. The Yuki-Onna has no reason to wish to keep you against your will, for you have done nothing wrong. She is ... not ... unreasonable. Most of the time. If you wish to leave, you will have to face her, eventually. But you must get better first, so that you can endure the long walk through the maze, and the cold. And so that if – if I am wrong – you are strong enough to run from her."

That is ... not entirely reassuring.

I turned what he had said over in my mind, once

again feeling that rising sense of urgency that I did not understand. "How long will it be before I am well enough, do you think?"

"You are strong and healthy, and your wounds are healing well. It will not be very soon. But it will not be very long, either," he said. Maybe it was my imagination, but I thought he sounded a little sad.

I chewed on my next question for some time before I eventually spat it out. "Itsuki-san, why did the Yuki-Onna build a prison just for you? What is she punishing you for?"

"I do not wish to speak of it," he said immediately — without anger, but without any hint of hesitation or soft-ness. "It is between the snow maiden and me. I promise that no harm will come to you at my hands, and I will do all I can to protect you while you are in this place. I would ask you not to bring it up again."

I stammered, "I— A–as you wish. Of course."

So my saviour was a captive. A prisoner in a cursed jail, held here against his will by a powerful, magical crea-ture. It seemed … an unlikely story. Not that I questioned the truth of what Itsuki had told me, not really. He had no real reason to lie. But without knowing more — the whys that Itsuki did not wish to discuss and the hows he ap-parently did not understand – it all seemed too fantastical and outlandish to be real.

There was also the puzzle of Itsuki himself. What manner of person was he? Where did he come from? Had he been born with that face? What chain of events had led him to this pass? He was not an angry, defiant prisoner, railing against the bars that held him, that much was clear. He did not seem hopeless or despairing, either – but I thought his serenity, or seeming serenity, was hard won.

Yet … there was more to it than that. He spoke of the maze and its creatures almost with affection. And perhaps his captor, too. He had some feeling for her. Could a prisoner whose freedom was unjustly taken really come to love his prison – or pity his jailer? I didn't think so.

That would mean Itsuki's imprisonment was a just one.

What did he do?

I swallowed. He was trapped here in his strange prison – and for now I was trapped with him. Perhaps … I didn't want to know what he had done to deserve the sentence.

Perhaps it was simply best to hope I never found out.

After I was firmly and completely wrapped up once more, Itsuki removed the heavy lid from the pot over the hearth and dished out a generous helping of savoury hotpot. There were chewy pale noodles in it, far thicker and more substantial than the ones I was used to, and several kinds of nutty mushrooms, and unfamiliar root vegetables, and a purple thing that Itsuki told me he thought was a kind of onion, which was sweet and still a little crunchy. He seasoned the dish with a sprinkle of dried moss. None of it tasted like anything I had ever eaten before, but it was good. After two slow and careful spoonfuls, my stomach woke up and began growling viciously, keeping up its protests until Itsuki – huffing with quiet laughter – had served me a second bowlful and some crispy, flat, golden cake-things that, again, he had made himself.

"I'm only surprised it took this long for your stomach to start complaining," he said, as I sheepishly patted my faintly swollen belly.

"Me too," I said, risking a tentative smile, "if all I've had for ten whole days is that pain draught."

"The pain medicine is a powder. I put it in a soup of stewed herbs for you to drink. I know it is bitter and unpleasant, but it's very nourishing. I'm not sure if anyone could survive on plain water for almost two weeks after having lost as much blood as you did. You would have become very weak. Maybe too weak to wake up."

When a person doesn't move, can't eat or drink much, their body starts to fail very quickly...

I frowned as the words drifted through my head, then said, "It's a shame we have nothing like these herbs in my village. Something like that would have helped us through our hard winters, when the stocks get low and we're almost willing to peel the paper out of the screens and eat it."

"There is no winter here, save for at the centre of the maze," Itsuki said. "But without these herbs I would have starved myself, my first few years in this place, before I had learned its ways. When – when you leave, you could take seeds. Cuttings. Plant them in your home and see if they will grow there. Something to remember me by."

I opened my mouth – but before I could reply, his sudden, obvious tension silenced me. Very, very carefully he put down the flat stone on which a few of the golden cakes remained. Then, as though that small gesture had used up all his restraint, he doubled over.

One hand slammed against the packed dirt floor hard enough to dent it, and he fell forwards onto his front. A long, agonizing ripple seemed to move down the line of his back. The knotting and clenching of his muscles was visible even through the folds of his cloak. He let out a muffled, broken sound, all the more pathetic for being nearly soundless.

There was a sharp, sickening crack, and his leg, clad in rough dark leggings, which had been exposed when he sprawled forwards … twisted. The foot turned inwards at an angle that ought to have snapped his shin bone in two, and might well have done, given that noise. At the same time his knee bent back obscenely. There was another crack, and he shuddered. The broad straight line of his right shoulder seemed to buckle inwards. Yet he still did not cry out. He expected no help. He expected no one to care. No one to comfort him, as he had comforted me.

"*Itsuki-san* – Dear Moon – what is it?" I cried, shaking off the horror that had paralysed me and beginning to crawl towards him. "What's wrong with you?"

"Stay back," he grunted. In disbelief I saw him snatch at the corner of his cloak, jerking his bent leg in as he did so to hide it from sight. "Please."

"Let me help," I demanded. "There must be something—"

He shook his head. The next words emerged as a groan. "It. Will. Pass."

I drew in a deep breath, understanding at last. No matter how sudden and horrifying this seemed to me, it was no unknown thing to Itsuki. The terrible twisting and cracking in his body was something he had suffered through before. Perhaps – many times. What had he said when I cried out with the anguish of my wounds? *Pain always passes. What we know will pass, we can endure…*

Still, I could not bear to simply sit here and watch him writhe. There was something I could do to soothe him, one thing that he had done for me before. I would try it. Licking my lips to moisten them, I softly began:

"Sakura, sakura, covering the sky,
Drifting like mist, and clouds…
Sakura, sakura, covering the sky,
Come, come with me now and see them…"

I had no great singing voice, and the song came out low, and mournful, because that was how I felt – but I could carry a tune at least. It seemed to be enough. The faint sounds of shallow, pained panting from beneath the cloak eased slowly into a deeper, healthier rhythm, and though the dreadful spasms still travelled through his frame they seemed to torment him a little less. That last could have been my wishful thinking. In any case, my singing was the best I could do. All I could do.

When at last the attack – or whatever it had been – passed away, Itsuki lay curled into a tight ball on the floor, every bit of him drawn into himself and hidden under the dark cloak. My voice faded away, leaving the room echoing with quiet. The fire had died down again and night had fallen in earnest. Outside, somewhere in the distance, came the peculiar, liquid cry of the white bird that I had seen earlier. Itsuki shivered.

Was this an … an illness? Old injuries suddenly paining him? *No, of course not,* I scolded myself. It was too sudden and too extreme for that. This suffering was nothing natural – and that meant it must be magic. A further punishment from his jailer – that cold and vengeful ice spirit? I had to know. I had to ask. My mouth opened again – and Itsuki finally spoke, his voice hoarse and quiet, barely a whisper.

"Thank you," he murmured, voice breaking on the words. "I'm … sorry."

I heard more in the words than simple gratitude. They were almost a plea.

Do not ask. Do not pry. I do not wish to speak of it.

I sighed. Of all the mysteries in this place, this stranger was the biggest of all. Yet he did not want to be solved, and I must respect that. It seemed little enough to ask, given all the trouble I had put him to. I repeated his own words back at him: "There is nothing to thank me for. And nothing to forgive."

But we both knew that I was giving in. No more questions.

He shuddered once more, then seemed to relax. Neither of us spoke again that night.

Ten

A sound like thunder splits the air, trembles the ground. Behind jagged ivory fangs, the mouth glows, dark red, fire raging inside; steam rolls out as the jaws open wider, wider—

"… We might be able to keep him alive until the Moon is next dark…"

"No one comes back from the Dark Wood."

Kyo, why didn't you come home? Kyo, where are you?

I sat upright with a gasp that turned into a tooth-gritted groan of pain as my wounds caught fire at the movement. I wheezed, the room swooping and trembling around me, until the agony began to fade.

"Are you all right?" Itsuki asked, a little tentatively, from his place by the fire. Over the past few days he had learned I did not always appreciate that question.

As the physical pain subsided, the deep, empty

ache of loss took its place. My brother was dead, and I would never see him again, and it was all my fault, and *I couldn't remember why* and somehow that made it all so much worse. It took an effort to make myself nod, even if brusquely, and to keep my voice polite. "Yes. It was only a dream."

My head might have been jumbled and confused, but of some things I was certain. I had to get better quickly. I had to get better so I could face down Itsuki's Yuki-Onna, escape this maze, and go back to my village. They needed me. *Time is running out! Hurry! Hurry!*

But frustratingly, I could not force it to happen. My injuries would heal in their own time, and I had enough common sense to realize that bullying my body would most likely only set my recovery back. That didn't make the waiting any easier.

In this, Itsuki was both ally and hindrance – for he was the most truly patient person I had ever known. Whether he had been born that way, or learned it through experience, it seemed as natural as breathing to him now. There were times when I wanted to scream at him, prod at him, throw things at his head – anything to disturb his endless, stolid serenity. But of course, I did not. He was still, ultimately, a stranger to me. One whose reactions I could not really predict, and whose tolerance I did not seek to test.

So instead I tried to learn from him. Tried to grasp his unhurried gentleness, his kindness, the soft rumble of his voice, and draw them into myself, to smooth down the jagged edges of my need to be up, moving, doing. At times it seemed to work, and those times were enough to make my enforced inactivity more bearable. But not always.

At first I needed an exasperating amount of sleep, and rest. The most ordinary activities exhausted me, and sometimes, I dozed off mid-sentence, a habit that amused Itsuki immensely, even if he never said it flat out. He did make the mistake of telling me, once, that I snored. It was a very *nice* snore, he assured me. Lady-like, even. He didn't quite manage to hide his soft huff of laughter.

I resisted heaving my cup of tea in his face, but only just.

As I began to get a little stronger, though, the days fell into a bizarre semblance of routine. When we woke – or rather, when I woke, for Itsuki had usually been up for hours by that time – we ate together, and he enquired if I had slept well, if I felt any pain, or if my bandages were flaking. Assuming the answer to these questions were yes, no, and not yet, he would bring me a pan of water and a soft cloth and make himself scarce for a short while so that I could wash my hands and face, and the rest of myself as best I could with only one working hand.

Finished with the task, or having just given up, I would pour the pan of dirty water away into the little hole bored into a corner of the stone room, and answer nature's call there, too. After I had eased a robe closed over myself, I would call my quiet friend back, and he would help me to tie the sash tightly at the waist, since my bad hand still did not have the strength to hold or pull the cloth. And then we would go out.

In the beginning Itsuki had tried – most emphatically tried – to persuade me to stay in his little room and doze the days away. Whether he wanted to keep some distance between us, or was worried about the danger to me in the enchanted prison-maze, his determination to keep me idle caused something dangerously close to our first real argument.

I wanted to be good. To be patient, and rest, as he had urged me. I knew that his advice made sense. But common sense meant little to me when each day I felt more like a prisoner. And Itsuki, no matter his kindness, more and more like my jailer.

"What is the matter with me?" I muttered into the silence of the little stone room after Itsuki had left it, my good hand pleating restlessly at the skirt of my robe. "Why can't I be still? What is wrong with me?"

There was no answer. But that was only the first day.

By the second day I swore I could see the damp walls pressing in and down upon me with each unmarked hour, and I felt the tide of hopelessness – *I would never get better, I would never get out, no one was looking for me, I was nothing but a burden, I might as well die* – rising up to meet that oppressive ceiling until I thought that it would drown me.

I twitched and fidgeted, coming perilously close to hurting myself in my desperation to move. Despite the strict orders of my healer, I eventually gave in, heaved myself to my feet and paced, slow and heavy, leaning against those hateful walls for balance.

It didn't help.

You are hollow, a new voice – a sneering, hateful voice – whispered in my mind. *You are a useless, broken thing...*

Useless.

Useless.

The voice sounded like Kyo.

"What did I do? What did I do wrong?" I begged of the endless, circling recriminations in my mind.

It was your fault. All your fault, sister, was the only answer. And I felt the rightness, the terrible echo of it, aching dully in the marrow of my bones. *That's why no one wants you.*

The ache made me want to cry. To scream. To run from the room as I had done before. But I did not have the strength for any of it. I found myself eyeing the pot where Itsuki kept his powdered sleeping draught with longing. Perhaps, if I could just sleep as he asked me to... Perhaps ... perhaps if I took a lot of the stuff, I would sleep for a long time and wake up all better...

In the back of my mind Kyo murmured: *Perhaps it would be best if you never woke at all.*

"I cannot get better like this," I told Itsuki that evening, over the cooking fire. It was an effort to keep the words from trembling. "You must let me go out."

"You think you know your body better than I do," he

said wearily, "but I understand more about how close you were to death. You must rest. You cannot not push yourself before you are ready."

"Who is to say I am ready if not me? It is my body, Itsuki-san. It is my own well-being, and I *do* know more about that than you can."

"Why won't you listen to me?" he questioned, standing and pacing to the wall and then back to the fire. "What is this ... this wandering spirit in you that cannot be content to be still even for a few days?"

"I don't have a wandering spirit. I have ... I have..." I stopped, swallowed, as a memory of a tall, broad-shouldered young man with a square face, and a pitying expression swam though my mind. *Shouta.* The conversation suddenly felt miserably familiar.

"Idleness is a poison to me," I began, fumbling to find words.

Itsuki broke in with the closest thing to impatience I'd yet heard from him. "That is admirable, I suppose, but—"

"Let me speak!" I said abruptly, my voice sharp with trepidation. "Let me finish. I have ... a hollowness inside me. I do not know what it is, but if I cannot move ... it threatens to swallow me whole. I *need* occupation – or my emotions ... fall into a kind of – of misery. Cruel thoughts torment me. I do not expect understanding, but at least believe me when I say that it is no kindness to force me to be idle. *I must have work.* Please."

I held my breath for his reaction, trembling a little with

the force of the words which had torn out of me. There was a faint, soft noise, as if of a sigh let out very slowly. At last he spoke, low and serious, and almost – ashamed.

"My apologies. I was wrong. I do … believe you. I do understand."

And it seemed – miraculously – that he did. For though he fashioned me a sling for my injured arm, and made me promise to tell him if ever I was in pain, he did not try any longer to stop me from doing things, even though I tired much more easily than I could have guessed, and needed the support of his arm often.

I must have slowed him down terribly on those careful excursions. His long legs would have outpaced me easily even when I was at my fittest, and although I was determined to help him with his work wherever I could, I was wretchedly clumsy with my left hand, and unable to use the other at all as yet. However, he never implied he found my efforts tiresome, and gave every evidence – as much as a quiet man with a carefully concealed face could – of enjoying my company. In fact, he welcomed me into his daily life, and led me unerringly through the safe parts of the maze, always able to find his way, even though each curving thorn corridor looked exactly the same as any other to me.

Every day, as I strove to get better faster, was different. One task took us to a garden of beautiful flowers – Itsuki called them roses – with an addictively sweet fragrance, and small, needle-sharp red thorns on their graceful stems. Itsuki harvested their petals and the orange-coloured berries left on the flower heads, from which he made a sweet paste to spread on his golden cakes. The next morning saw us picking flexible reeds from a garden that was mostly water, to weave into baskets. In another garden there was a rockery of glittering silver-black stones, nearly as tall as Itsuki's ruined tower, covered in delicate ferns and mosses, many of which went into Itsuki's healing remedies.

A family of goats lived among those rocks. The animals were far prettier than the ones we kept in the valley. They had long, soft coats of dappled grey and orange and cream, and impressive curling horns, and seemed to consider Itsuki as a part of their extended family. The nannies came forwards instantly when he entered their domain, and ate rose petals from his cupped palms before letting themselves be milked into Itsuki's battered black pot.

My favourite outings were those where we visited animals. I had always liked them, but it was impossible ever to get attached: our life in the valley was too harsh for that. But Itsuki didn't eat meat. He said he didn't need to, that the maze gave him all the food he required without going to the trouble of having to catch or kill anything. I remembered what he had said about living on bitter herbs to stave off starvation in the beginning, and concluded that either he had never learned how to hunt, or – as seemed more likely the more I got to know him – that he was simply too soft-hearted to harm the creatures of the maze, which looked at him with no fear, and came to him like old friends.

When I was with him, the animals treated me the same way. Birds would sit on the fingers of my outstretched hand and eat seeds from my palm. Goats and antelopes and deer shyly rubbed their faces against my knees and nibbled tufts of grass if I offered them. Golden tanuki and tiny red squirrels chattered eagerly and tugged at my robe with tiny paws until I fed them some of Itsuki's store of dried nuts.

One afternoon, over a week after I woke up, Itsuki was checking on a litter of "kits", the babies of orange-coated, weasel-like creatures. I sat on a rounded stone, playing with the parents. They chased each other around and around on my lap, my laughter apparently only encouraging them to greater speed. Every now and again one or both of them would stop for me to scratch the snowy-white of their chins, or so that they could swarm up my arm to sit on my shoulder and check what Itsuki was doing to their babies.

Itsuki looked up from gently tapping a powder for mites into a young weasel's ear, and I could feel his gaze, even though I could not see his eyes. "Does that hurt?"

At first I had no notion of what he meant. I looked down at my lap, where I was stroking the silky backs of my little friends with my injured hand.

"Oh…" I breathed.

I flexed my fingers with a sense of growing excitement. There was still a deep, itchy sort of throb at the movement, but it wasn't a bad pain: more like the feeling you get when you stretch out a cramping muscle to its fullest extent. I hadn't registered it at all. I hadn't even noticed when I slipped my arm from its confinement in the sling. I was getting better. At last.

Hurry! No time!

"No," I told him, as calmly as I could. "No pain at all. It feels fine."

He seemed to hesitate, then said, "In that case, how would you care for a proper bath?"

"I might *give* my right arm for a proper bath," I said, watching him as he stroked his last patient goodbye with the tip of his finger. "But how?"

"Hot springs," he said, a smile in his voice, as he reached to help me to my feet.

"You – you have hot springs?" I demanded, torn between happiness and indignation. "And you kept them a secret from me? Why?"

"It seemed kinder not to mention them until you were strong enough to go in on your own."

Something came together in my head. "That's where you disappear to every morning before I'm awake, isn't it? No wonder you always smell good."

He cleared his throat. "Mmm."

"And I stink like a pigpen in midsummer," I said bitterly.

"It's not that bad." He paused. "Yet."

I shot him a poisonous glare and he rewarded me with

a nearly soundless huff of laughter. One corner of my own lips tugged reluctantly up.

It was easier than usual to match my pace to his when we went back out into the confusing warren of thorn hedges. Itsuki was walking with a decided limp in his step that day, as if his hips or lower back were paining him. Since I had woken up last night to sing for him as his whole body twisted into knots, I didn't have to wonder why.

I would have liked to be allowed to ask him if he was sure he was well enough to be going about all his usual tasks, but I didn't. In exactly the same way the question "Are you all right?" often made me snappish and short-tempered, nothing made him clam up so quickly, or turned his mood as dark, as my enquiring after his well-being. For someone so solicitous of my health, he seemed to hate nothing more than being reminded of his own.

We turned a corner and Itsuki stopped dead.

My gaze shot up to his hooded face, fearing that he was about to have another of his terrifying attacks. But no. His shoulders and back were straight, and he made no sound of pain. I quickly looked around and saw nothing out of the ordinary except ... one of those tall white-and-black birds, with the fan-like tails.

The creature was slowly stalking into view ahead of us, its tail of feathers not dragging on the grass behind it today, but held stiffly spread-out behind its body, making the jagged patterns – like eyes – on the feathers even more striking. It seemed to see Itsuki. One of those strange, mournful cries rang out.

Before I knew what was happening, Itsuki had shoved me almost violently behind him, hiding my smaller form from the beady black eyes of the bird with the bulk of his body. I could feel the tension vibrating through him as I leaned a little dizzily against his back, and could only guess that for some reason he was ... staring the bird down? Warning it off?

With another, longer call, the bird swept away, moving out of the corridor of thorns into a garden that lay near by. Itsuki let out a long sigh. His shoulders unhunched and most of the quivering rigidity ran out of him.

"Why did you do that?" I asked warily.

"Those birds – the white peacocks – are the Yuki-Onna's eyes and ears in the maze. If she were to catch a glimpse of you here, with me ... she might come to investigate."

I gnawed at my lip. "I saw one of those birds when I first woke up. And it saw me. I had no idea it was different to any other animal in this place. Is it very bad?"

Taking my arm again, Itsuki quickly got us moving away from the garden where the white peacock had disappeared. "Maybe not."

He didn't sound sure.

"But that was days and days ago. Perhaps she wasn't paying attention." I tried not to let venom leak into my tone when I uttered the "she". I had a grudge against her that I tried not to admit to myself was not entirely on my own behalf.

"It could be. Or perhaps she has decided she has no particular interest in you, and is content to wait for you to seek her out. Or…"

"Or?"

His other hand came up to cover mine on his arm – an unconsciously protective gesture which warmed me against my will. "Or she is paying attention, and she is interested … and she wants to see what will happen if she leaves you here with me."

I blinked at that. "Other than the riveting spectacle of us eating, sleeping, and looking after the animals?"

"Yes," he said softly. "Other than that."

There was that odd inflection in his voice again, the one he only had when he was thinking about her. While I was still making my mind up on whether to break my vow not to pry at his mysteries, or to let it pass once again, Itsuki steered me through the hedge into a new garden.

Tall, slender trees, with papery white trunks and vivid yellow-gold foliage, stood sentry around a raised mossy mound. There was a path of small white pebbles leading through the trees on its flank, and before we had reached its end, I could smell sulphur and wet rock, and see the thick clouds of steam rising up.

A pool of opaque, storm-cloud-coloured water took up almost the entire top of the hill. It was clearly very deep, and was roughly oval in shape. The spring that fed it gushed down over red-streaked stones. A tiny frog with jewel-like red eyes croaked at us in greeting, then hopped off its perch by the spring and landed in the water with a soft *plip*.

Itsuki drew a lidded reed basket from beneath one of the trees, and opened it to reveal clean, carefully rolled – if fraying – cloths of various sizes, bars of his gritty but sweet-smelling home-made soap, and a comb of bone, among other things.

"Use what you wish. There is no hurry – I will stand guard outside and finish whittling this whistle," he said, meaning the small wood flute he had been working on since yesterday evening.

I nodded wordlessly, rendered completely speechless by my overwhelming desire to plunge into the water and get truly *clean*. It was only when he had gone that it occurred to me to wonder what exactly he would be standing guard against.

There are beasts that roam the thorns…

I swallowed a little nervously at the thought. My dreams of the nameless shining *thing* still troubled me, no matter how I reminded myself that such horror could not, could never exist – not even in this magical place. Better not to dwell on such dark fears. Besides, I knew as long as Itsuki was with me, I would be safe.

Movement might have returned to my injured arm, but it was still clumsy and stiff, and much weaker than I would have liked it to be. Luckily there were plenty of flat ledges set into the edges of the pool to sit on, and it was no hardship to obey Itsuki and take my time in the water. The heat, almost scalding at first, relaxed parts of me that I had not even realized were tense. Washing and combing my hair was such a pleasure that I felt almost guilty.

I worried at that thought, trying to make sense of it.

My mind and my emotions were full of dark places, which ached like bruises when I tried to press into them. Every day I felt the compelling sense of urgency – *no time, no time, hurry, hurry* – that nagging awareness of an important task left undone, tugging at me more strongly. Every day I searched my own mind to try to make sense of what I was meant to do. But the more time I spent here with Itsuki the more I had to admit to myself that I half-dreaded the moment when I would finally fit the shattered pieces of my memory back into place.

I loved my home, and I loved my family. I knew that without question. Yet I feared there was something lurking there, something dark, looming, awaiting my return ... and I could not make myself eager to set that shadow free, even as I worked diligently to make it happen.

Blissfully clean at last, I hitched myself up onto the edge of the hot springs and wrapped one large cloth around myself to ward off a faint chill, rubbing at the wet mass of my hair with the other. I rather envied Itsuki his short hair in that moment. It must dry in five minutes or less.

"Are you well?" Itsuki called out, his tone making it clear that the query was habit, not real concern.

"Entirely!" I called back. "Finish your whistle."

I plaited my damp hair with only a little difficulty, and draped the cloth over the branch of a tree to dry. Then I looked around for the robe I had discarded, and began to pull it back on with some reluctance, since it wanted washing just as badly as I had. As I hesitated, I caught sight of the horrible ruin of my scarred, twisted arm and side and hurriedly looked away.

Something stopped me then. Regardless of Itsuki's re-assurances, I was sure that scars like those would never completely disappear. That meant I was going to have to live with them for a long time.

Would I spend the rest of my life flinching from a part of myself – turning in revulsion from the evidence of my own survival?

Taking one or two deep breaths to steady me, I tugged the grubby robe down off my shoulder and arm, and looked at my naked right side.

The bright midday sun was a great deal less forgiving than the dappled firelight in Itsuki's dim stone tower, and what I saw was not pretty. But perhaps I really was healing as prodigiously as Itsuki had said: the long, deep marks were a dark pink – the colour of half-healed flesh – rather than angry red. They were no longer wounds, but were indeed becoming scars, scars that would fade, at least a little, with time. And the skin between was taut and pale. I curled my arm up and down. The pain was still there, but bearable. I truly was getting better – and more quickly than any normal person had a right to. Itsuki was no ordinary healer, and his medicines were as extraordinary as he was.

I had been lucky indeed.

Behind me, a sweet musical note rose up, and a faint smile creased my lips. Itsuki had finished his wood flute. As I listened, I ran the fingers of my good hand over my injuries, testing for tender spots. I had big hands for a woman, and long fingers, but the span of my palm did not cover the breadth of the wounds across my shoulder. What under the Moon's light could have caused me such injuries? What implement of man or creation of nature would leave marks like these?

I tried to imagine myself falling beneath a plough, or being scoured by splintering branches from a great tree as it fell, but none of my imaginings made sense. My wounds were like … almost like claw marks. Yet that was impossible. To create such wounds the beast would have to be immense, with paws the size of—

A glowing white paw strikes out – the bristling pale claws rake my arm, tear my flesh apart – I scream—

The image burned through my mind like a falling star. For a moment, it was more real to me than anything my eyes could see. Lost to all sense of where or when I was, I desperately tried to lurch away.

The small white pebbles shifted underfoot. My ankle gave way beneath me.

With a strangled yell, I fell back into the hot springs.

Eleven

The shock of the hot water closing over my head broke the trance of fear or panic or – or whatever it had been. Unthinkingly I tried to suck in a breath, and choked on water that burned my throat.

My clumsy thrashing made my arm and side scream with pain, while the sodden, heavy robe dragged at me, but I kicked with everything I had. Up. *Up.* My head broke the surface – and a strong hand caught hold of the back of my robe and lifted me bodily from the pool.

Itsuki laid me on my good side and patted with measured firmness between my shoulder blades as I flopped and squirmed like a landed fish, clutching my open robe together with my shaking good hand. Water gushed from my mouth. It felt like half the spring had ended up in my stomach.

"Are you all right? Can you breathe?" he demanded, out of breath himself for perhaps the first time since I'd met him. "Hana?"

I nodded mutely, still coughing. He patted my back a few more times, then helped ease me up into a sitting position. I rested my face on my knees. My head was swimming, my stomach churning as if it was still full of hot sulphurous spring water. Maybe it was. I groaned.

"What happened?" Itsuki asked, bewildered.

I remembered … a nightmare. My waking mind had tried to fit the terrible images from my dreams into the place of my real, missing memories. That was all it was. The creature that stalked in my dreams could not be real. It could not be. Could it?

If it was…

If it was then Itsuki must know of it. Such a beast could only be a product of magic – the magic of this terrible, beautiful place. And Itsuki had said that he did not know what had happened to me.

He was the one who had saved me. He had tended to me with as much care as a member of my own family, and shown me nothing but kindness. He'd just saved me again.

What reason would he have to lie?

And yet.

I wished I could hold myself aloof from him until I had time to think this through, but I was too tired. My choice was to either let myself lean into Itsuki's side, or slump to the ground again. And he was … rather nice to lean on – like resting your weight against a warm, cloth-covered tree.

Belatedly I realized that he was still asking me what had happened, with increasing levels of anxiety. I managed to gasp out, "Ankle turned. Pebbles. Will be well. In a moment."

"I should never have let you go in alone," he said unhappily.

Without thinking I patted him. "Just an accident. Not your fault."

Both of us fell silent – but it was another of those uncomfortable silences, simmering with unspoken thoughts on both our parts. He was probably still castigating himself. To distract him as much as myself, I plucked fretfully at the dripping skirts of the robe. "Stupid of me. Now what am I to wear?"

Itsuki stirred. He sounded almost sheepish when he spoke. "I … had another surprise for you."

"Oh?" I wearily lifted my head, gazing into the darkness under his hood as if I could gauge his expression that way: a habit I could not seem to break. "I shall get spoiled at this rate."

"That doesn't seem likely to me, Hana-san," he said with a small huff of laughter, as he set me carefully aside and stood up.

He reached for a basket from under the roots of a nearby tree.

"You know I had to get rid of your old clothes. They were ripped to shreds and ... the blood ... they were too ruined to save. I hoped you would get better one day, and have need of something else to wear, so I began work on these. And now you are better. I hope you like them."

This was one of the longest speeches he had ever made spontaneously, and he shuffled his feet as I blinked up at him. *Began work—?*

"I'll leave you to... Call if you need help and – I'll be waiting. Outside." He fled, vanishing from my sight nearly instantly in a flash of that incongruous speed of his.

"What in the Moon's name?" I muttered to myself.

But the prospect of – apparently – clean clothes was too enticing for me to puzzle over his shyness, or brood on my misgivings for long. Impatiently, I shucked the oversized and grimy wet robe, towelled myself dry so that I least I wouldn't drip on anything, and reached for the basket containing Itsuki's "surprise".

Within, lying on a bed of dried rose petals, was a neatly folded kimono. I touched it, drawing it out, unfolding it, and rumpling my fingers in the heavy fabric to marvel at its fineness. The material was unembroidered, completely plain, without any pattern or decoration at all. But that only added to its loveliness – for it had been dyed a deep, coppery russet, so vibrant that it was almost iridescent, like the first, most beautiful new-fallen leaves of autumn. Nothing could have improved on such an astonishing shade, or on the quality of the weaving and stitching.

The sleeves were short, wrist length, like the sleeves of a married woman's gown, rather than the heavy and often impractical long sleeves of a girl's furisode. Beneath it in the basket was a nagajuban – an under-robe of pale un-dyed cloth – and last of all, a pair of wide-legged trousers in the same material, gathered at the waist with a draw-string and with lacing that ran from ankles to calves so that, at need, the extra material could be drawn in tightly to the lower leg to prevent it from dragging in the dirt.

Though these garments were simple and unadorned, they were undoubtedly the finest and most beautiful clothes I had ever seen.

Itsuki had *made* these? Made them for *me*? He must have begun work on them weeks ago – when he had no guarantee that I would even survive! The weaving alone would have taken hours upon hours upon hours.

It made no sense that it was this gesture, out of all Itsuki's many kindnesses, that made tears spring to my eyes. But that he knew, or guessed, how an injured girl would feel trailing around in a borrowed, baggy robe that gaped and sagged and caught on things, not even able to wash it, and that he had cared enough to labour in secret, for days, on an entirely new gown for her to wear, mod-elled on her own lost things... And that he made his gift to her as beautiful as he could, as well, so that she would have true pleasure in wearing it... Such great compas-sion would be enough to comfort the whole world if only Itsuki were allowed out in it.

He was good, Itsuki. Truly *good*. The way my mother was – the way Kyo had been. How could I believe such a man capable of deceiving me? I could not. I would not. The beast, the animal I had seen, must be a figment of my confused mind and hazy memories. That was all.

Itsuki would never hurt me.

I felt a smile dawn on my face like the sun breaking through storm clouds after days of endless rain.

Quickly but reverently I donned the trousers and under-robe, and then the kimono itself, tying it closed at the waist with a simple jade green sash found at the bottom of the basket. Then, almost stumbling in my eagerness, I went out of the hot spring garden to find Itsuki.

He was waiting by the opening in the hedge, his whole posture radiating uncertainty. He jumped when I appeared.

"*Thank you,*" I said emphatically. "Thank you. They are the most wonderful things I've ever worn. I – I love them. Thank you."

He slumped a little in what seemed to be relief. "I am glad. I wanted them to be nice for you, but I have never had to make garments for anyone else before. I was afraid I would get them wrong."

I realized with some surprise that I wanted to hug him. He *needed* to be hugged. But although Itsuki had unhesitatingly wrapped me in his arms to warm me, and offered me the support of his hand or shoulder when my strength or balance failed, still he shied from my touch.

Physical affection, anything more than a quick pat on his hand, turned him still and immobile, as if he were becoming the tree I had named him. I did not want to upset him now, of all times, after receiving such a gift.

So I just smiled up at him, hoping my smile conveyed the depths of my happiness and gratitude.

A few days later, something changed.

Itsuki suffered a terrible attack that morning, while chopping wood for our fire. The axe had fallen from his fingers and missed burying itself in his foot by less than an inch. Dropping to his knees by the stump, he clung to it for support, and I watched in horror as his fingers snapped and reformed, curving into bent, claw-like shapes. Through it all I was forced to stand still instead of running to him, because I knew what he would say: "Stay back. Stay away. It will pass."

I was growing less and less able to accept those words.

In only the short time I had known him, Itsuki's suffering had seemed to double. His attacks came more frequently, and lasted longer, and seemed to leave more lasting damage each time. Itsuki limped constantly now. Sometimes he could not pick up or hold things, like the pestle for his mortar, or the small carved wooden jars that held his salves and powders and ointments. He would never let me help him, even when he was forced to slurp his noodles straight from the bowl because he had dropped the chopsticks too many times.

That day, I realized his shoulders had taken on a permanent, crooked shape and that he could no longer fully straighten his back. I was moments from breaking the unspoken promise, and demanding he tell me what was wrong with him, if it was the Yuki-Onna that tormented him this way and if so – for the love of the Moon – *why*?

But as I watched him wearily pick himself up, as I approached him and snatched the axe away – with my bad hand, too, careless in my anger and worry for him – and sunk it deeply into the stump before he could fumble it again and lose a toe this time, a great, rushing gust travelled through the tall distant trees that guarded the maze on all sides. As if caught in an earthquake, the canopy of branches seemed to bend inwards, all at once, leaves rustling and shivering, bowing down towards us. Towards Itsuki.

"The forest. Something has happened. Something's wrong." He took off at a run, his uneven, limping gait hardly seeming to slow him down at all.

I remembered that Itsuki had told me the trees brought him things. Creatures that were dying as I had been dying, which needed help as I had needed help. And if that was what was going on now, then he would need my help – and for once he might even accept it. I gathered up the heavy skirts of my kimono in both fists despite the twinge from the right one, and went after him.

He had said that the forest left me at his door, so I expected him to head for the ruined tower in the tree, the centre of his home. But instead he flew straight past it, and out of the garden altogether. He moved so fast that although he was heading down an almost straight corridor of thorns ahead of me, I could barely keep him in sight.

I was not really fit enough for this yet. My side and arm still caused me pain, I was not perfectly steady on my feet, and I still needed a foolish amount of rest after undertaking quite ordinary activities. So I was surprised and pleased that although my lungs were working like bellows to keep me moving, and my heart battered violently at my breast, and I had an awful stitch, I arrived behind Itsuki only a few blinks after he himself had skidded to a halt.

Here was an entrance in the maze I had never seen before. It was not like the straight openings, cut through the thorns, that Itsuki and I navigated every day; it was a true gateway, a Moon gate woven of twisted branches of bleached pale wood and other long, smooth fragments of white that might have been ivory. Or bone.

This twisted gateway was grown into the hedge, so that the thorns wreathed and bristled through it. As I watched now, they were unravelling from within the circular opening, snaking back out of the way to leave the space clear. Beyond the circular opening, I glimpsed a dense forest of tall, dark pines, swaying and whispering in a wind that I could not feel.

The Dark Wood...

I felt a chill – a sort of instinctive recoil – that I didn't entirely understand. But I had no more time to look, or to think of that, for there on the other side of the gate stood an animal.

I recognized it at once as a wild cat of some kind – like the tiny, shy Iriomote cat, which I had only glimpsed on the mountain once or twice in my life, but at least five times the size – with a golden, black-spotted pelt, and smooth white fur on its belly, and black-and-white tufts on its long pointed ears. It had a tail like a hare's, just a fluffy black nub. Its eyes were round in shape, and amber as topazes.

It looked at us and snarled.

A glowing white paw strikes out – the bristling white claws rake my arm, tear my flesh apart – I scream—

No. No. This animal and its claws were no doubt deadly – but it was not the creature from my dreams. Its paws were not big enough to have caused the wounds on my body. Its front feet were not as broad as my own hands. And besides, hadn't I decided for myself that it could not have been an animal that inflicted my injuries? No matter what my nightmares insisted. It had to have been something else.

I was safe here with Itsuki.

Still, every instinct screamed at me to back away. But Itsuki was bending over the animal, unafraid, making rumbling, purring noises in the back of his throat. What was more, the wildcat was clearly distressed. Its whole body shuddered; a moment later it fell down onto its side, ribs heaving, the snarl transforming into a yowl. I realized then what was the matter. The cat's stomach was massively swollen, with ripples moving over its taut surface.

The beast was pregnant, and the labour was going badly. The forest had brought the wildcat to Itsuki for help, so that it and its kittens would survive the birth.

Itsuki laid one of his hands – the fingers bent and twisted but still gentle – on the wildcat's abdomen, and she snarled again, but made no move to bite him, or to get away.

"I know, I know," he murmured to her. "I will do what I can for you, and the babies."

Then, just as if this deadly animal had been a domestic feline warming itself by the kitchen hearth, Itsuki scooped the labouring wildcat up in his arms. He turned to me, his head tilted questioningly.

"Of course," I said, before he could ask. "Go on, hurry. I will catch up as fast as I can."

He nodded briefly, then broke into a run again and disappeared, a dark blur. I didn't have another run in me, but I could manage a cautious trot, and I used the extra time to think of the labours I had been at – cows and oxen and pigs, and once acting as a helper for my mother when she sat with her friend during a long, though trouble-free birth, because Kaede-sensei had been on the other side of the village dealing with a man badly injured in a fall. Our cats tended to hide away in the roof or other small dark places when they had their litters, so I had never seen one of them in labour.

Regardless, Itsuki would need hot water to clean his hands, and the cat would need somewhere soft and warm to lie, and the babies would probably need to be rubbed dry, although perhaps their mother would lick them, as cows did their calves...

I hurried into the garden of knots, went to the clear, fast-moving little stream, and filled a pail of water. Carrying it with some difficulty in just my left arm, I gathered up as much of the firewood Itsuki had just chopped as I could in the other arm, and went into the tower.

Itsuki had laid the cat down on a pile of furs on his side of the fire, so that it was sheltered from draughts by the curve of the wall. He knelt over it, his hands feeling its belly as if the bulging fur might tell him something. Maybe it did. When he looked up at me and saw that I carried water and wood, his tense body expressed relief so clearly that my heart squeezed.

"You've assisted at births before?"

I nodded as I built the fire up and poured the water into the iron cauldron to heat. "A few. I'm not a midwife. What do you think the trouble is?"

"I believe cats of this kind usually only have one or two kittens at a time. From what I can feel, she has triplets. One of them is lying in the wrong position and blocking the birth canal. It might be dead; it isn't moving."

I nodded again, undoing my obi and pulling off my

heavy outer kimono. "How can I help you?"

He hesitated, and I heard him take a deeper than usual breath. "The kitten must be moved. Turned and pulled out, so that the others can be born. If we don't do it soon, the mother will be too exhausted, and both her and the babies will die. But … my hands…"

"Are too big," I said as he trailed off, knowing that to acknowledge it was his bent fingers which had crippled his ability to help the wildcat would be impossible. I held my own hands out for him to inspect. "Will these do?"

He let out that deep breath, nodding. "Thank the Moon for you, Hana-san."

"The water should be hot enough by now. I'll go and wash," I said, hugging the glow of his appreciation to myself.

Twelve

After I had tied the sleeves of my under-robe up with strips of rag and scrubbed my hands until the skin was pink, I knotted a clean blanket around my waist as an apron and went back to Itsuki and the wildcat.

"Tell me what to do," I ordered.

Itsuki did.

The process of reaching into the animal's birth canal, turning and manipulating the body of the kitten inside it, and drawing it out, was by turns fascinating, disgusting and frightening. Itsuki guided my actions patiently, step by step, holding the wildcat's head in his lap as it panted, and yowled, and occasionally thrashed. I didn't blame it at all. In fact, if I had been in its place, I'm sure I would have torn someone's hand off with my teeth by now, and I didn't even have fangs.

After what seemed like hours, I was finally able to get my fingers around the kitten's head, bring it into the correct position, and, with the contractions of the cat's muscles crushing my bunched-up hand and sending sharp sizzles of pain into my scars, pull the baby free. The mother cat let out a long, low sound, almost a meow.

"She'll be all right now – the others should come out naturally, in their own time," Itsuki said. He let the mother cat go, and sure enough she calmly rearranged herself and within moments brought a second kitten into the world.

In my hands, the first kitten was surprisingly small. Hardly larger than the offspring of a regular house-cat, and half the size of its brother or sister, which the mother cat was now licking vigorously. It lay limp and unmoving. "Is it…?"

Itsuki took the kitten from me and wrapped it in the bottom half of the blanket I was wearing as an apron. He rubbed quite roughly at its back, and then, when it didn't respond, grasped its rear legs and gave it a sort of swing in the air.

The runt let out a plaintive squeak and suddenly began to wriggle. Itsuki laughed – not that quiet huff of amusement which I had grown used to but a real, joyful burst of laughter – and stroked the wet, spiky fur once before tucking the baby in at the mother cat's belly, next to its larger sibling.

Within half an hour the third kitten, which was the biggest yet, emerged, and soon the stone room was rattling with the wildcat's proud purring and the determined, birdlike cheeps of the kittens. I was so happy for Itsuki that I could have burst. Nearly, I wished I might see his face, because it was plain that if I had, a big, foolish grin would have been splitting it in two.

But it was not to last.

As Itsuki bustled around, cleaning up, I noticed that though the mother cat had cleaned the two youngest kittens, and each of them had latched onto one of her milk-filled teats, the oldest and smallest was still damp with birth fluids, and lay a little apart. Its legs worked feebly, and its head moved as if it was trying to sniff out the milk it needed. But when it worked its way closer to the mother, she nudged it away from her.

Biting my lip, I crouched down and, with hands that I had not yet had the chance to wash, and which I hoped would smell strongly enough of the mother cat not to make things worse, lifted the smallest kitten until it nestled back against its siblings.

The wildcat didn't protest, though she watched me narrowly with her fierce yellow eyes as the runt found a teat and began to suckle. I let myself breathe a small sigh of satisfaction. But as I returned from thoroughly scrubbing my hands and arms, and tying my obi into place around my kimono, I heard Itsuki make a low, sorrowful noise. He was standing over the wildcat now – and once more, the runt had been pushed away to the edge of the bedding. It cheeped plaintively, struggling to return to its mother's warmth. She paid it no attention.

"She rejected it," Itsuki said quietly when I came to stand beside him. "Either three babies is too many to care for, or it's too small compared to the other two. Or both."

"There might be something wrong with it," I said as kindly as I could. "Something we can't see. My grandmother said that cats can smell if one of their kittens is damaged, and they let it die rather than waste milk on it."

"Damaged?" he repeated. There was an unaccustomed note of bitterness in his voice.

"You know what I mean. Itsuki-san, she's not a person. She's a beast. They don't feel the same way humans do."

He winced away from me, his shoulders hunching painfully. The kitten made another pathetic cheep by his foot. It was unbearable.

"We could try hand-feeding," I offered rather desperately. "I've seen it done, with calves. If we keep the kitten warm enough, and feed it the milk from the goats, it might survive. We can take turns looking after it at night."

I didn't tell him that usually no one bothered to hand-feed calves unless it was clear that the calf in question was sturdy, and there were younger children in the family or among the neighbours, to take on the responsibility of feeding it every few hours through the night. And that even then such rejected calves often died – and if they didn't, they eventually ended up slaughtered for meat anyway.

It might work, I told myself. *There's no reason why it shouldn't.*

The way Itsuki's stiff, unhappy posture melted was enough reward. As if I had somehow given him permission, he scooped up the abandoned kitten in one hand and cradled it protectively to his chest.

"I'll go and find something we can use for a bottle," he said.

For the next three days, Itsuki and I acted like new parents with a sickly child, carrying the kitten with us everywhere we went in a sling that Itsuki had converted from my old one and padded with a scrap of fur taken from the mother cat's bed. We fussed over it, listening with quivering readiness for its tiniest protesting cry. Though its eyes had not yet opened, and wouldn't for at least another week, I was sure the kitten knew the sound of my voice and Itsuki's, and responded to them. And despite my anxiety, the kitten seemed to thrive. I began to hope, and then to truly believe, that our little runt had a fighting chance.

What was more, in those three days, Itsuki did not have a single one of his painful attacks.

On the first night, I laid on my side of the hearth and Itsuki on his, the kitten curled up in the crook of my good arm, since I had volunteered to night-feed it. Further away, behind a carefully heaped-up pile of blankets, wooden pails and other debris that we had arranged to block her off from the rest of the room – she was getting increasingly territorial – the mother cat growled softly. The fading orange light of the fire painted flickering patterns on the vine-festooned ceiling and I watched them with heavy eyes.

"We should call him—" I began sleepily. Itsuki laughed, and I broke off, then demanded, "What?"

"Haven't you taken the time to check? Our little one is a girl."

"Oh!" It hadn't occurred to me. "No wonder she's such a stubborn creature, then."

"What did you want to call her? Will it still work for a girl?"

"I was going to say Jun – but obviously Kimi would work better for a female."

"Aren't those dogs' names?" He sounded baffled.

"Yes, but… Well, they're names for companions. You know that hand-rearing it – her – this way means she'll think of you as her family. She might go off and hunt for herself or find a mate when she's older, but she will probably stay with you for a long time."

Long after I'm gone.

"I like the sound of Kimi." Fabric rustled as he turned onto his side. "I'll think about it."

On the third night, a groan of distress woke me, and I blinked my eyes open with the confused thought that Itsuki must be having another attack.

But then I felt it. The small, warm shape of Kimi was gone from her place on my breast. My stomach churned with dismay, and when I bolted up into a sitting position,

I saw what I had feared.

Itsuki sat next to me, a dim shadow, outlined only in moonlight, with a fluffy body cupped in the frame of his twisted pale fingers. She was still, just as still as she had been when I pulled her from her mother. The tiny wheezing sounds of her breathing that I had become so accustomed to were gone.

"Oh, Itsuki," I whispered.

"You were right," he said. The words were rough, almost a growl. "You were right in the first place. She was too weak – too damaged – her mother knew it. She – she was probably suffering all this time. It was cruel to drag it out—"

"Don't say that!" I interrupted. "Don't you say that! We gave her warmth and comfort. We did everything we could for her. She knew that she was loved. There's nothing cruel in that."

He bowed his head. "We – we need to – bury her."

"We should bury her here. In amongst the roots of the tree." I sniffed, hiccupped, rubbed my forearm carelessly over my eyes, and got up. "I'll get a spade."

Silently, in the light of the waning moon and a galaxy of glittering stars, we chose a spot – a place where the sun often rested in the daytime – and I dug the hole for Kimi's grave. A small hole. Terribly small. But deep. She deserved to rest undisturbed.

Itsuki wrapped the soft little body in the piece of fur and the cloth sling that we had used to carry her, and then tenderly, so tenderly, placed her in the earth. He used his hands to push the dirt back in on top, and to smooth the soil flat over her.

As he knelt there with me standing at his shoulder, his back gave a single, convulsive shudder, and he curled forwards, leaning his forehead against the tree trunk. "She was dead when I woke up. There was nothing— She was already dead."

"I know," I said, turning the spade over and over between my hands.

"I didn't get to say goodbye. I know she was just a little kitten, just an animal, but ... I never got to say goodbye. Just like before. My mother, my father, my little sisters. All gone. Gone. And I can't—" His voice broke, and he slammed his hand into the tree next to his face. Once. Twice. Then again. Even the vast, mighty tree seemed to tremble under the force of those blows.

I couldn't stand it. I dropped the spade and crumpled down to the grass behind him, wrapping my arms around his wide, crooked shoulders, and my hands around his forearms to hold his hands still. I pressed my face into his back, and for once he did not flinch away from me. Silent tears shook him.

"Do you remember their names?" I demanded, fiercely. "Do you remember?"

"Yes. I do."

"Say them now. Say goodbye now, and Kimi will carry your farewells with her into the Moon's embrace.

She'll be your messenger. Go on."

Soft and slow, he choked the names out. "Kaori. Osamu. Natsumi. Miyuki." A pause. "Goodbye. Goodbye, Kimi. Rest well." He drew in a ragged breath. "Now you, Hana."

I was not like Itsuki. I … did not deserve to have my messages carried into the beyond. Kyo was gone because of me. If it weren't for me, I knew, I knew – even if I did not know how – that he would still be on this earth. *It should have been me instead.*

"Hana. Your lost deserve to hear it. Go on."

I shuddered. Then, almost soundlessly, I murmured: "Grandmother. K-Kyo. Goodbye. Goodbye."

After a moment, I began to sing, my voice cracked and wavering:

"Sakura, sakura,
Covering the sky,
A fragrance blown like mist and clouds,
Now, now, let us go now to see them…"

It took a while longer for Itsuki's voice – rich and deep, yet still a little wobbly – to join mine in the song for the first time. But it did. He did.

We stayed there like that, together, until the sun rose above the dark crown of the trees.

When dawn came, Itsuki insisted that I return to my makeshift bed and try to catch up on the hours of sleep I had lost.

"You are still recovering. Rest is the most important

part of that," he said, weary but kind, himself again.

"And what about you?" I asked. "You were awake longer than I was. Don't you deserve rest too?"

There was a rueful smile in his voice when he replied. "I don't need much sleep – and I want to visit the goats again, and look at that billy goat's front hoof. I'll feel better for occupying myself today. You know what I mean."

I did. Who could blame him for wishing to be away from the sad reminder of the mother cat and her two healthy kittens for a while? The friendly goats would most likely be a comfort to him. I knew that he wasn't trying to coddle me unnecessarily – I honestly was in need of sleep, worn thin by both Itsuki's grief and my own, and dangerously likely to burst into tears again at any moment.

"Don't work too hard," I told him.

"There is no such thing, for me," he said, and left me with a quick, gentle squeeze to my hand before I could ask what he meant.

I sighed, and tucked myself into my blankets, and tried to doze off.

"My mother, my father, my little sisters. I never got to say goodbye."

I didn't get to say goodbye...

My grandmother.

My brother.

I ... didn't get to say goodbye...

My father.

"We might be able to keep him alive until the Moon is next dark…"

Don't go out at the dark of the Moon.

"When a person doesn't move, can't eat or drink much, their body starts to fail very quickly…"

No one ever comes back from the Dark Wood.

"He is already dead, Hana-san."

"It was cruel to drag it out…"

Cats play with their prey.

There is a monster in the forest.

A monster.

A monster.

MONSTER!

The monster's immense jaws unhinged. A colossal, raging snarl clapped at the air like thunder, shook the ground. Behind ivory teeth longer than my fingers, its mouth glowed, dark red, as if some impossible fire raged within its belly. A white-hot cloud of breath rolled out between its fangs like steam, and I watched the arrow that had sunk deep into the cat's flesh quiver and then – somehow – eject itself from the beast's chest. The beast stepped upon the fallen arrow and crushed it to dust with one massive paw and then roared again, its eyes seeking out mine with a gleam of terrifying, feral intelligence.

I saw that no droplet of dark blood marred the monster's white hide. It was unmarked. Unwounded. My arrows could not touch it. And now the beast knew that.

It leapt forwards.

I ran.

My eyes snapped open.

"Never go out at the dark of the moon," I whispered. "No one comes back from the Dark Wood. *There is a monster in the forest.*"

Thirteen

I remembered. I remembered everything. What happened to Kyo. And my grandmother. Father. The impossible thing I had come to the Dark Wood to do.

Dear Moon, how much time had passed since then? Weeks! Last night the Moon had been a thin, sharp crescent among the stars. It would be dark again in a matter of one or two days. That was all the time I had left to save my father's life. And that was if Kaede had managed to keep him breathing this long. If he wasn't already... If he was still there in the healer's house on the other side of the Dark Wood. If it wasn't too late for him, as I had believed, lying alone and bleeding in the earth, that it was too late for me.

It wasn't too late. I would not give up hope of saving my father.

As I floundered out of bed, I felt the heaviness of responsibility settle into place on my back, and the familiar empty ache of Kyo's loss, of my own personal despair and grief, unfolded within and around me as it had not fully done for … for days now, here with Itsuki. Not even last night, after Kimi. It was endlessly cold, like a deep, black shadow, and for just one weak moment, I faltered in its shade, sagging beneath the weight of unhappiness I had carried for so long.

How could I forget so much of what made me who I was? I ought to have been a completely different person – and yet somehow I had still been Hana. Still been me. Just…

Happy.

But that was all over now. I forced my shoulders to straighten, forced my chin up.

I had to go home.

First, though, I must find Itsuki. I must find him, and explain to him why I was here, what I had come to do and what was at stake. He would help me. I knew he would help me however he could.

After pulling my clothes back on and swiftly re-braiding my hair, I left the garden of knots to seek my friend out. I knew where he would be, in the garden of rocks. He and I had walked that way together a dozen times. Before I would have hesitated to travel the thorn corridors alone, but there was no time to worry about myself any more.

No time, no time, hurry hurry hurry, urged the voice in

the back of my mind, triumphant that I was heeding it at last.

When I heard the wavering, plaintive notes of the wood flute drifting through the thorn hedges to meet me, I felt a rush of relief – not only that I had managed to find the right garden in the right part of the maze but also at the knowledge that I would be with Itsuki again soon and could tell him everything and … and…

I stepped into the garden of rocks, my mouth already opening to call out to Itsuki – and felt myself go as still as one of the glittering chunks of stone.

He sat cross-legged in a gently waving bed of reddish ferns, with his small wood flute still at his lips, though the music had fallen silent the moment he had caught sight of me. The morning light fell full on his face.

Of course he had taken off his hood and the bindings around his face in order to play. He hadn't expected me to rush in here like this. Not when he had left me resting, not when he knew I was afraid to walk the maze by myself. And even if he had been given some warning, why would he hurry unduly to conceal himself from me? This was the second time I had seen him unhooded. I had not run screaming before.

But I had not *remembered* before.

I had not admitted to myself, before, that my terrifying, confused nightmares were real, that I had truly walked into the Dark Wood at the dark of the Moon and been savaged by a glowing white beast with green eyes.

And neither, before, had Itsuki's white skin been marked with black stripes that zigzagged over the fine bones of his face, outlining his eyes and radiating out to his hairline and jaw in a distinctive and unmistakable pattern.

My gaze travelled agonizingly slowly over his massive frame as he rose to his feet. Over the twisted, deformed legs that, I now saw, had finally come to bend backwards at the knee like a beast's. Over the curving line of his back, and the shoulders which had gradually inched upwards over the past days, shortening his neck and creating a hulking, cat-like silhouette. Over the long, slender hands that had thickened and curved in upon themselves until they resembled great white paws, with great white talons. No wonder he limped when he walked upright. He was meant to be on all fours.

I had been looking at him for weeks, but until now, I had never realized what I was looking at.

There is a monster in the forest.

"You…" I breathed. "You."

"Hana—"

"My family must be particularly delicious," I croaked. "You just can't get your fill, can you?"

Confusion, sadness, and hurt crossed his black-and-white striped face, so quickly I barely made them out, like ripples of heat rising from a fire. And then … guilt. That was the final, most awful blow of all. I had not even realized that I still held out some hope he would have an explanation that would save me from this heartbreak, until that hope was gone.

It was true.

The flute fell from his fingers, and he took a single step towards me. I fled from the garden of rocks like a hare with a fox at its tail.

There is a monster in the forest. There is a monster in the maze. Savage beasts that roam the thorns… He said it himself. *He* meant *himself*.

Itsuki is the monster. Itsuki is a beast.

I ran into the maze of thorns and kept on running.

I never looked back. Not even when I heard his anguished cries of my name, or his pleas to return.

A fine play-actor indeed, I thought bitterly, dashing the tears from my cheeks. But he had already proved that, had he not?

"*I don't know,*" he had said, when I asked him what happened to me.

"*I promise that no harm will come to you at my hands,*" he had sworn.

He had even told me he did not hunt – did not eat the flesh of animals.

No. Only human flesh will do.

Monster. Beast.

Betrayer.

Stronger than fear, stronger than anger, stronger than any pain I had ever felt – even my physical agony after the beast had raked me with its claws – the sense of betrayal was overwhelming. All my memories of Itsuki – everything

I thought I knew of him – kindness, and trust, and friend-ship… How could it all be lies? I had held him as he cried over the tiny grave of a dead kitten. I had sung to him as he writhed in pain. I had leaned into his side and taken comfort from his strength, believing utterly that it would never, could never be turned upon me.

And yet he was the same creature who had tried to kill me and eat me. Who had nearly clawed my father to death. Who had devoured Grandmother. Who had taken Kyo.

Why – why – why – had he saved me? Fished me out of my grave in the Dark Wood where he had knocked me himself with his great paw, and carried me back here, and tended me with every appearance of true concern? Why lie, why take on that human, or human-like form, why pretend to be my friend? All those details. The way he had tended the animals. The very clothes on my back, made with such tender care and attention. His voice as he whispered the names of his lost family.

Had all of our friendship truly been nothing but some sick *game* to him?

No. No. Don't think of it.

It made no sense. But nothing in this place made sense. The curse on the mountain, my people's suffering, had never made any sense. Magic, enchantment, beasts and mazes… How could an ordinary village girl hope to understand any of it? It was a nightmare, had always been a nightmare, even when it seemed it was a dream.

"Hana-san!" shouted the beast.

No, I thought grimly, forcing myself to crush the first rush of desperate panic down, squeezing my sobs into pants and then slow, deep breaths. *Your game is over, beast. We will play a new game now, and I will make the rules.*

It was already too late to try to employ any kind of tactics. I had lost track of where in the maze I was almost at once, and even if I had managed to run for my life logically and coolly, it would not have done me much good. I did not know the way out, and the only safety was *away.* Away from him.

So his voice became my guide. Whenever I heard him, all I had to do was keep going in the opposite direction.

"Hana-san! Come back!" he cried. "You are too near the centre of the maze! This is dangerous!"

Not as dangerous as you.

Yet soon, it seemed, every other turn led me into the biting cold, or to a dead end. The long curving corridors that I had walked with Itsuki – no, the beast – by my side seemed to have closed up, giving me no choice but to travel around in ever decreasing circles as the sound of his voice grew closer and closer.

Why was I surprised that this accursed place had turned on me too? What else had I expected it to do? It was his home, after all. The whole maze was a wicked trap. But if he caught me now that he knew I had seen through his deception, seen him for what he truly was … the Moon alone knew what he would do to me.

At last I found myself cornered. Ahead was another

dead end, to my left an impassable ice-encrusted corridor. I turned at bay to see Itsuki – the beast, the beast, call him, call it what it is – bearing down on me.

"Please…" he pleaded as he slowly approached, his hands, the same great paws that had nearly ripped my arm from my body, held out in a pose of supplication.

He had taken the time to hide himself – his hood was pulled fully forwards and the wrappings were back in place so that the telltale white and black and glittering green lay concealed. He looked like the man I had known and cared for – once more my dear friend that I could trust above all others. For an eye blink I felt my resolve, my knowledge, waver.

But there! On my right, an opening, a narrow gap in the hedge that I had somehow missed. I dived into it.

It was a garden I had never seen before. A silvery flat pool of water that stretched from one wall of thorns to another, uninterrupted save for a bridge woven of twisted white branches. On the other side of the bridge was a second opening in the dark hedge. Beyond that, an ice-free thorn corridor.

Escape.

"Hana, don't! It is a trap!"

I scurried away from him onto the uneven surface of the bridge. The branches flexed and gave strangely underfoot, and a sense of alarm caused me to glance down to check my balance even as I darted forwards. I saw the sky reflected in the still water, and the bridge's arch of pale branches, and my own face too, staring back at me, white as death with eyes like gaping black holes...

It was not my face in the water. It was a skull. The skull of some large animal that lay at the bottom of the pool. And those white sticks I saw were not reflections of the bridge, but the bones of many other animals, at least a dozen, lying beneath the water, bound in place by chains of bleached wood.

The bridge stirred sinuously beneath my feet, like a creature stretching after a long nap in the sun. I flung myself forwards – and hit a wall of spiny branches that spun up around me. They moved before my astonished eyes, forming a jagged cage. Even as I seized the nearest branch and wrenched at it with all my strength, I realized the bridge was sinking, dragging me down, down, towards the silent still pool and its graveyard of drowned animals.

A thunderous roar shook the air behind me – the beast's roar. It was the most terrifying sound I had ever heard. I was trapped. My knees gave way.

In the next moment some immense force hit me from behind. With a jarring crash, the wall of dry branches fell away, as if they were no more than the thin skin of frost on the surface of a puddle. I was propelled through the hole in the cage, and tumbled down the other side of the bridge, rolling head over heels in a landslide of rattling broken branches. I landed on my front and skidded a good two feet – clear of the water, clear of the deadly garden and its trap – into the corridor of the maze beyond.

Shaken and gasping, I rolled to my knees and looked back into the garden I had just escaped.

Itsuki – the beast – was on the bridge now. He … he must have jumped onto it behind me, ripped a hole in the branches with his bare hands, and knocked me off … but he had been caught in the wreck of the cage. White branches wrapped around his ankles like manacles, and wove around his wrists.

The bridge was dragging him into the pool in my place.

Unlike me, he made no effort to struggle. I was sure he had the strength to break free whenever he wished. But he only crouched, motionless, head bowed, as the bridge spun ever more branches around him, and slowly, slowly sank downwards. I remembered my fall into the hot spring just a week or so ago, the shock of the water surging into my nose and mouth, how it had burned – and the strong hand that had hauled me out and hit my back until I coughed the water out. His hand.

The beast's hand.

What is he doing? *He could easily get loose. Why doesn't he* fight?

Why do you care? asked another part of me – the dry, sneering inner voice that sounded like Kyo. *Isn't this your chance to escape him?*

But he'll drown!

Why do you care? repeated that insinuating inner voice. *He is a beast. A killer.*

But—

But what?

"Beast!" I shouted. "What is the matter with you? Do you want to drown?"

He didn't answer. Didn't look up. Didn't even flinch. He simply stared down into the water as it rose inexorably, past his waist, and lapped at his ribs. As if he'd given up. As if he wanted…

Why do you care, Hana?

Swearing under my breath, I grabbed one of the long, sturdy branches that had broken off the bridge when I burst through its cage of limbs, and surged to my feet.

"Beast!" I called. "Beast, you must take hold of this branch, and I will pull you to safety. Quickly now."

The darkly hooded head lifted, and I felt his gaze on my face like the heat of a blazing fire. Yet he made no attempt to free himself, or to reach for the branch that hovered a few inches before his nose. The water was at his shoulders now, an unnatural silvery stillness, like mercury, undisturbed by a single ripple.

"Beast," I said again, and then stopped. I could not find it in myself to plead with him. Neither could I find it in myself to walk away and let him drown.

With sudden, shocking vividness, that moment when I had lain in what I thought was my grave, in the quiet earth, with the sun touching my face, returned to me – and with it the memory of that glorious feeling of peace and acceptance – and I wondered with a pang of doubt if what I did now was truly kindness on my part at all.

He was a beast. He was alone. He lived in a cursed wood, in a maze of thorns, wracked with mysterious crippling pains, feeding on the corpses of humans. And he had done so for at least a hundred years.

It was a horrible life. Even for a monster.

Perhaps he felt the same peace as I had. If so, he must want this, want it to be over, desperately.

But he had not left me to die.

I could not leave him now.

"Itsuki," I whispered, as the pool washed at his chin. "*Itsuki*. Please."

He did not move. The water closed over him. A single bubble popped on the surface. All was still.

I drew in a long, shallow breath. It whistled hollowly in my chest, shaking me like a death rattle. A strange coldness, colder even than Kyo's icy absence, bloomed at the centre of me, and I felt something crack there, something vital that I didn't even have a name for. It – I – was breaking, shattering to pieces, flying apart—

A bent white hand broke through the water, fragments of pale wood twined about the wrist, and grasped hold of the other end of the branch that I still clutched in both fists. That terrible rattling breath escaped my lips in a desperate high-pitched sound. I braced my legs, leaned back, and pulled for all I was worth.

Fourteen

"Why did you" – *cough* – "turn back?" *Cough.* "Why didn't you leave me?" *Cough, cough.*

Water sloughed off him in long silvery runnels. I dropped my end of the branch and backed away, making room for him on the grass. "I don't know." My voice wobbled. "I don't… I couldn't just let you die."

Shouldn't you be running, Hana? Shouldn't you be hiding? sneered my unkind internal voice.

Too late for that. The furious strength of rage and panic that had fuelled my flight was all used up. I'd made my choice now. I needed answers. But first I had to work out exactly what questions to ask.

I lowered myself stiffly down onto the grass and drew my legs up, ignoring the way the movement pulled at my side, my hip. Perhaps I deserved the pain. I heard the rustle of grass and the wet squelch of his clothes as he flopped over onto his back a few feet away.

Then he began to laugh.

Not the soft, amused huff which I had come to know so well. Not the real, joyous laughter I had heard from him only once. It was a broken, mad laugh that came out gurgling and wet. As I recoiled, somehow shocked despite everything by the savagery of that sound, he dragged himself into a sitting position, and flung away the cloak and the face-coverings, exposing his face with violent, angry movements. My eyes winced from his inhuman beauty – though his expression was so twisted just then that the beauty was almost hidden, like clouds hide the sun.

There was foam on his lips, and it was pink with blood. He swiped at it with the back of his hand. "I wasn't going to die. Don't you think I've tried drowning before?"

It took me a moment to absorb the meaning of his words. *"What?"*

The laughter died away. His shoulders jerked inward, hunching. "I assure you, I have attempted to end my life by every possible method this prison has to offer. It's no good. Nothing works. *'You wear the shape of a man, but to me you have been a beast. Very well then – a beast you shall truly be. Suffer as I have suffered, beast, until you have learned to love, as truly I once loved. And when you have learned that, suffer still more, until you have proved yourself worthy of being loved in return, as once my beloved loved me.'* That was what she said when she brought me here. That was her curse."

Her. The Yuki-Onna. Did that mean what Itsuki had told me was true – that he was indeed a prisoner here, and not the architect of this place? If the maze was truly not of Itsuki's making…

What else was *she* responsible for?

I shook my head, scolding myself for leaping to defend him in my thoughts so quickly, so easily. He could still be lying. "What does it mean, all that?"

"It means never, Hana-san. There is no end to this wretched half-life. Not even death. Not until she judges that I have suffered enough. And it will never, ever be enough."

This wretched half-life. "You are the beast, aren't you? You are that monstrous thing."

His head tilted in acknowledgement, the white mane of hair still dripping. "I … change. With the Moon. When the Moon is new, I am a man. As it ages, I begin to twist and reform. When the Moon is dark, I become the beast. The beast is … a beast. I cannot control what it does. I don't know what it does. I don't want to. But … I know enough to recognize the signs. The claw marks. I knew that it must have been me who hurt you." He put one hand over his face. "I didn't know how to explain. You were already so afraid, and I just wanted to help you get better."

"You don't remember?" I whispered.

It was the answer I had sought, little though he re- alized it. He didn't know. He couldn't know. Itsuki had eaten people, devoured them so completely that even their bones had never been found, and I ... oh, merciful Moon ... *I couldn't tell him.* I could not say the words aloud to him.

To know what he had done would drive him mad. Perhaps that was even the point of it.

It wasn't his fault. It wasn't his will. Itsuki might have killed and consumed humans when he was a beast – but the magic that transformed him, stole away his rational mind and left him a ravening monster that was everything he would hate and fear, was the same vile enchantment which called my people into the wood at the dark of the Moon like rabbits to be slaughtered. And that magic was not his. He didn't have control of its power. He didn't even know it was happening.

It was the Yuki-Onna's doing.

She must be mad. To do this to him. To us. She must be completely insane.

And I was trapped here within her maze. She had seen me through her peacock spy. She had chosen to leave me be so far for reasons that were almost certainly malign. I was filled with fear at the thought of such a vengeful creature and the inimical forces she must command.

Yet at the same time I felt a surge of relief, a lightness in my spirit that approached joy. For Itsuki was the monster in the forest, a terrible, unnatural beast ... but he was still my friend.

There had been no game, and his lies had not been to

torment me but to protect himself. I could forgive that. I could forgive anything, so long as he *was* Itsuki, that gentle kind giant who sang lullabies to his patients to calm them, and let fox cubs play hide-and-seek in the folds of his cloak.

But that in turn raised another question, one that had gone unanswered for too long.

"Itsuki, *why*? Why – by the Moon's sacred face – what happened between you and the Yuki-Onna? What did you do? What could anyone possibly do to deserve all this?"

He shook his head, the movement one of mute misery.

"You must tell me. You owe me the truth."

He flinched, then so quickly that the words ran together, he said: "I killed her."

The bald statement sat between us like a stone. I swallowed hard.

He could not mean as the beast. She had made the beast.

Then the words of her curse that he had repeated came back to me. I remembered that Yuki-Onna were not true nature spirits but the souls of the dead which had arisen again. Usually women who had died of exposure. I got unsteadily to my feet, took two wobbly steps forwards, and knelt again by his side on the smooth short grass. My voice, when it emerged, was like iron. "Explain."

He hunched inward even further, still hiding his face. "I ... I don't want..."

"I know you don't. It's time you did anyway," I said firmly. "I'm caught up in all this, my people are caught up in all this, and at the root of it is you. You, and her."

"Your people?" he asked, letting his hand slide down enough that one poisonous green eye blinked out at me between his fingers.

I met his look steadily. "For one hundred years, we have been unable to leave this mountain. The Dark Wood that rings our village – the wood that hides this maze, that hides you – is cursed. We're trapped. Just as you are trapped. And ... people disappear. They leave their beds at the dark of the Moon and they vanish into the wood and no one ever sees them again. My grandmother. My brother, Kyo. They were both taken. My father was one of those people, too – but he came back. I found him. Somehow he escaped. Only he didn't escape intact. He wouldn't wake up. There was – is – some dark spell on him, the same spell that called him into the Dark Wood, and it will kill him if we can't break it. I came into the Dark Wood to hunt the monster that was responsible, to free my village from the curse, to take vengeance for all I'd lost. I came to hunt you. To kill you if I could."

He shuddered. "And afterwards the wood brought you to my door."

"So you could save the girl that the beast nearly killed. My memories were all ... locked away. I suppose my mind sheltered me until I was recovered enough to remember what I had seen without going mad. But I remember now.

Everything we have suffered. This isn't idle curiosity. I am as bound up in this magic as you are. You must tell me how it happened, Itsuki. You must. *Tell me.*"

The one eye of Itsuki's that I could see slid shut. He seemed to brace himself – and then he nodded.

"First of all … you must know that I am not from your forests. I grew up in the City of the Moon. The great Tsuki no Machi that lies at the foot of this mountain. My house was very wealthy and powerful. Too wealthy and powerful. My father lived in the belief that anything he wanted was his by right. He was not pleased when his first two offspring – sons – died one after the other of childhood illnesses. When I was born, he took me from my mother. He said her coddling was what had made my brothers weak, and that he would make me strong enough to survive. He was content to leave my little sisters to her care, when they came along. I strove to be perfect, to be his exact mirror image. I don't think I ever allowed any idea in my head which he hadn't put there. To waver would have been betrayal in his eyes – and in mine."

"He sounds like a … difficult man," I said, with as much neutrality as I could muster.

"And yet he was everything that they said a man should be. Strong. Proud. Fierce. He allowed no weakness – no womanly weakness, he would have said – to prevent him from doing what he pleased. I don't mean to say that he was some kind of demon. He was just a man, a certain kind of man, the kind who believes he is … entitled. And he raised me to be the same kind."

"But you were an ordinary human then? You were not…"

"A beast?" He drew in a shaky breath. "I will let you be the judge of that. I want to say … I want to say that I fell in love. That is how I thought of it then, although I would never have uttered the words aloud. I want to say that I fell in love – but it is a lie. I knew nothing of love. So the truth is that I *wanted*. I met a girl and she was lovely, and calm, and sweet, and serene and graceful. Everything that I believed a woman should be."

I shifted a little uncomfortably beside him at this recitation of virtues I did not possess, and he took it for impatience and hurried on.

"Her name was Minamoto Oyuki. I decided that she would be mine. I deserved her, didn't I? The perfect son, the perfect reflection of my father, deserved the perfect woman. Of course, she already had a betrothed and she and I had met only once, and I knew exactly nothing about her. Nothing that meant anything. Not what she wanted, or what would make her happy. I didn't care. It didn't occur to me that I should care, do you – do you understand? To consider the thoughts or feelings or wants of anyone else would be a weakness. I don't think I even realized that other people had feelings. Certainly not women. She might as well have been a painted paper doll to me, for all that I knew, or wanted to know, of who she was inside."

I began to get a very uneasy feeling in the pit of my stomach. Though I had been raised in a small, close-knit village, I was still a girl – and all girls knew, or quickly learned, that when a man felt he was entitled to a woman, bad, bad things were very likely to happen to the woman.

"What did you do?" I whispered, and the words came out small and fearful.

"I had my father get her for me. Simple as that. Her old fiancé was cast aside, and plans for our wedding were put in progress."

"Just like that?"

"Yes! Just like that!" he burst out. "I … I was a vile, self-centred toad of a boy, as narrow-minded and small-hearted as … as … Dear Moon … I can hardly bear to think now of the way I spoke and acted. She came to me. She came to me, Hana-san, and tried to explain to me what I had done. She had been engaged to Ren-san since they were children. They had played together, grown up together. They loved one another. She told me he was the only one who saw her – saw *her*, not just the beautiful face she was cursed with. If she was made to marry me, she would be miserable, and our marriage would never be a happy one. Surely I did not want that?"

He moved restlessly, hanging his head low. "I listened to her and heard nothing. All that happened was that my pride was stung. What was Ren-san compared to me? The middle son of a modest family was to be chosen over me, the great son of the great house? No, never. I sent her away, more determined than ever to … to own her, because she had challenged me and no one, no one could be allowed to do that to my father's son."

"Itsuki, you didn't go through with it? You didn't force her to—?"

"No. It didn't come to that."

I let out a breath I hadn't even been aware I was holding. It was bad, bad enough as it was, but that would have been worse. "Then you changed your mind?"

"Oyuki changed it for me. She made a break for freedom, her and Ren-san. They ran away into the forest on this mountain and hid in a tiny village, intending to make a new life. A life where they would be free, and together."

A little village on the mountain? *Our village?*

It had to be. That must be how we had been drawn into this. But… "So they escaped, and made a new life. Isn't that good?"

He dragged his hands through his damp white hair, and did not answer.

"Itsuki?"

"The wealth and connections that my father had offered Oyuki's family were too tempting for them to simply whistle away. And the prospect of incurring my house's wrath was terrible, for my father – and I – were known far and wide for our unforgiving tempers. Oyuki's father and brothers hoped that if they acted very quickly and decisively, they could bring Oyuki home, cover up everything that had happened, and go on with the wedding without any scandal. They told my father and me that Oyuki was ill with a fever, and would be weeks recovering. Then they hired hunters, mercenaries with tracking dogs, and set them on Oyuki's trail. And they found them. They found them."

He shivered. "I ... I was told, shown, later... She showed me, through her eyes, what had happened. They broke into the little house where Oyuki and Ren-san slept, in the night, and they tried to take her. But Oyuki and Ren-san fought like wolves. The commotion brought the whole village out. Oyuki and Ren-san called on their new people, the villagers, to help them. The mercenaries panicked. There was only a handful of them to several hundred villagers, and somehow they had to subdue Oyuki, but they had their orders. They weren't to harm Oyuki – not so much as a bruise on her pretty, valuable skin. So how to make her stop fighting? How to frighten the villagers into letting them take her away?"

I closed my eyes. "Ren-san."

"In that Moon-forsaken place, in the snow, they slit his throat, and told the villagers that anyone who tried to help him or Oyuki would be next. Oyuki ... she screamed at the villagers to staunch his bleeding, or free her from the hunters so that she could go to him ... but the mercenaries' plan had worked, and the village folk were too afraid. Ren-san bled to death while Oyuki watched, and then the hunters dragged her away, and no one did a thing to stop it. Afterwards, the villagers buried Ren-san's body in the forest. Without even a stone to mark the place."

I was trembling, shaken with horror by the images that his story evoked, and the thought of what Oyuki must have felt. For a moment I was so filled with disgust that I could have hated Itsuki again, hated him on behalf of that valiant loving girl I had never met, whom his arrogance had broken.

But he had not been there in that snowy village square that night. He had not watched the knife fall, or heard Oyuki's anguished screams and ignored them. No. That had been my people, hadn't it? Mine.

We were not the innocent victims I had been led to believe. My lost great-grandfather – whom we were taught to revere, and mourn, and pray for – must have been there, watching, that very night. Standing by while the tragedy unfolded and refusing to act out of fear. I knew what would have run through his head, through all of their heads – yes, I knew it well.

Why should we risk our lives for them?

They brought this ill-fortune, this trouble with them.

I am not willing to die for their sakes.

None of us are.

Cowardice disguised as common sense. And when Oyuki had been dragged away and they had had time to look around them, to realize what they had allowed to happen – what had they done then? Thrown Ren's body among the trees to rot as if he were trash, not a person they had known, a person they had betrayed. As if denying his existence would allow them to deny what they had done.

"After all that, when they finally brought Oyuki back to the city, it was too late," Itsuki said. "Word had got out, gossip had spread, and my father's rage had broken over her family's house. I was far too busy nursing my own wounded feelings to consider what would happen to Oyuki. If I thought about it at all, I suppose I imagined that her father and brothers would beat her or starve her as punishment, and that it would serve her right. I told her brother that his family would have been better off if she was never born. We – I – didn't know, then, what had happened to Ren-san. I didn't stop to think how far they would go to appease us … what they might do to her."

He held his head in his hands again, apparently lost in thought. I wanted to prod at him, but I did not. I was beginning to see. He called her Yuki-Onna. Yuki-Onna, angry spirit of snow and ice, that froze unwary travellers to death…

At last I murmured, "It was winter. You said in the village there was snow."

"The whole city was white with ice. There was a storm that night that turned the rivers into stone, that tore out shutters and collapsed houses under the weight of the fallen snow. And in the morning the message came from Oyuki's family. I think they expected me to be pleased. They had thrown her out at the dead of night with nothing but the clothes on her back. But it wouldn't have mattered if they had given her a purse of gold and a horse by then, not to her. She had given up. They found her still on the front steps of the house, as if she had just lain down there to sleep in the frost."

Silence hummed between us for a few uncomfortable minutes. Then I stirred, for this next part was what most concerned us now.

"She rose again. Became Yuki-Onna," I said.

"The next night, when the Moon was dark, she came for me. She showed me, made me live through, all that my actions had caused. I saw her and Ren-san, and what they had been to each other, and how it had ended. And then, as I wept for mercy, she cursed me." He spread his hands out. "Since then, all has been as you see now."

"You tried to get out of the maze? Tried to get away?"

"In those first years, I tried everything. In the beginning I was still filled with resentment and pride, and I fanned those emotions because otherwise ... what was left for me? But they burned out soon enough, despite my efforts. After despair had taken their place, and burned away in its turn, all that remained was the truth: that I deserved to be punished. Unthinkingly – no – uncaringly, I destroyed Oyuki's life, Ren-san's life. I killed them both."

Fifteen

I bit my lip, and after a hesitation that felt longer than it was, I reached out and placed the flat of my hand on his back. His muscles clenched up, and he quivered under the touch, but otherwise stayed still as a stone, as if waiting for a blow to fall.

"Itsuki. That … you…" I clicked my tongue in exasperation at myself and began again. "Itsuki. That isn't true. You didn't kill anyone."

He turned on me instantly – fiercely. "How can you of all people say that? Everything – *every evil thing* – that you have endured, that your people endured, is because of me. The curse on the forest – you lost your grandmother and brother to it! The beast nearly killed you! At the root of everything is me. Just as you said. It is all because of what I did."

I blinked at him and then looked away from his awful face – what a fine irony that was, and how Oyuki must have enjoyed burdening him with his own fatal beauty. I focused on his big, bent hands as they curled and uncurled with tension, just as mine were wont to do.

"You did behave terribly to Oyuki. You treated her like a thing, an object with no worth but what could be bought and sold. You were cruel, and arrogant, and blind. I cannot forgive you for that. No one can but her. She is the one who suffered for it. There is no blessing or … or absolution that I can offer. The responsibility for what you did is yours, and you must bear it."

"I know. I know," he whispered, head bowed again, wretched.

"But by the same principle, you can only take responsibility for your own actions, Itsuki. What *you* did. You did not send the hunters after Oyuki, you did not wield the knife that murdered her beloved. Nor did you cast her onto the street to die, or ask that it be done. You did not put the curse upon yourself or upon this forest. Other people did those things, and the blame for them does not lie with you."

He shook his head wearily. "You don't understand—"

I silenced him with a sharp gesture. "You're the one who doesn't understand. I'm not being kind. I'm not trying to make you feel better. Don't you see? You *lessen* your own responsibility if you try to shoulder the burden of other people's actions too. Then it becomes about – oh, about self-indulgence, lashing yourself with guilt and wallowing in it – and that doesn't help anyone, most certainly not the people you have hurt. The way to atone is to truly admit and face up to what *you* did, and seek to make up for your actions however much and in whatever way you can." I paused, and saw that he was staring at me, apparently so struck by what I had said that he had forgotten, for once, to shield his face. Encouraged, I went on. "If there is any hope of forgiveness or redemption for any of us, we must repent for the evil we have done. And that is *enough*, Itsuki. Dear Moon, it is more than enough."

As the last words left my mouth, I stilled. That was right, wasn't it? It was. I had spoken the truth. I knew the truth of it, felt it down to the bones of me.

But if that was right…

A strangled noise – part sob, part laugh, part something else entirely – broke out of my chest. It was the truth, and that meant… *What happened to Kyo was not my fault.*

My brother's voice that I heard in my head, that taunted me and sneered … it had never been him, not truly. *Of course not.* Of *course* not. Kyo would never have said those things – he had loved me, my brother, and if he had been here still, he would only have sought to protect me. Not to punish me for the fate that had befallen him.

I had tormented *myself*. All these years, shouldering that burden of too heavy responsibility, of guilt and self-hate. Trying to make up to my parents for what I felt I had stolen from them. Trying to be both a daughter and a son, and the perfect child, so that they did not look at me and long for an empty void that followed me at my shoulder. Trying to repay a debt that never, never could be repaid.

I had spent so many years trying to gain forgiveness from my father for a crime I did not commit. Surely, I had known, surely I must have always known ... he was wrong to treat me as he did. But how could I accept that the father I worshipped could be so unfair? I loved him, and needed so much to be loved by him, to cling to *something* as I grieved the staggering loss of my beloved best friend and brother. I had got it all so tangled up. I thought if Father blamed me, then I must be to blame. If everyone else rushed to absolve me, then it was only pity and kindness.

In a twisted kind of way, I could almost understand why he had done it. If I had disappeared from the river by magical means, vanished into the forest on the wings of the curse, it would have been a familiar and inescapable tragedy. It would have been the monster's doing, as so many other losses we had faced. But Kyo's disappearance was different. He was only out there among the trees because my father had sent him away in his fear or his temper, or both. Because my father had ignored one of the most inviolable rules of our home: *never go out at the dark of the Moon.*

No good man could live with having sent his son

straight into a monster's jaws. No decent father could live with the responsibility for his child's death. My father was a good man, and he had been a decent father to us both, loved us and protected us. He would have given his life in exchange for either of ours, I knew that. But he had made a mistake.

It had been wrong of him to send Kyo into danger that night.

I could only take responsibility for my own actions. And what had I done? I had tried to tell Kyo that I was moving up river away from him. In fact, I had shouted it at him in pique as I splashed away! I had not heard him later when he called to me. If I had, I would have answered. I could not have known what would happen. I hadn't done anything wrong. It wasn't my fault.

What happened to Kyo was not my fault.

With that realization, the acceptance of it, I felt my despair, my grief and guilt, the aching, empty hollow which had been rooted in my own heart, growing day by day for four years, begin to shrink, and contract, and close up. I would always love my brother, and I would always miss him. There would always be a scar in his shape on my soul. But the wound he had left within me was healed. At last.

I was free.

I did not hear Itsuki move, but the next thing I was aware of was his gentle, twisted fingers wrapping around my wrists, coaxing my face out of my hands.

"Don't … Hana, please, please, don't…" he begged, just as when he had begged me not to struggle and hurt myself in my delirium.

I steeled myself to look up into his striped, alien face – and stared, astonished. His expression had transformed again, changed from that ugly rictus of anger into … something else. He had altered in some fundamental way, strange, and yet so familiar, though I was unable to name it. He was crying. The repellent beauty of his features was still there, still terrible to gaze upon, but I could look into those cat's eyes now without flinching. I could see the sadness and compassion and caring in them, and somehow it made them human.

"Don't cry," he murmured again, and he sounded broken, faltering and hurt.

Itsuki was no longer that calmly remote, endlessly patient voice, so unmoveable that it had seemed perfectly fitting for me to name him "tree". He was no longer the man who kept his back to me and wept so silently that I could only feel, never hear or see, his tears.

"It's all right," I reassured softly. "I won't cry any more, Itsuki. It's all right now."

He wrapped his arms around me and clung so tightly that it hurt. He was shuddering. While I had been falling apart in my own little world, so had he, in his. I had got through to him.

We needed to break, I thought. *We needed to break so we could both finally begin to heal anew.*

*** *** ***

It took a while for the strange, self-contained storm of our emotions to exhaust itself and blow out. When it did, we both drew back, and shook ourselves, and squinted and sighed, a little self-conscious and awkward in our own skins and with each other.

Itsuki wrung out his cloak and drew it back on with the hood pulled far forwards, although he left the rest of his disguise discarded in a soggy pile on the grass. I wiped my eyes and face on my under-robe and re-braided my hair, although it didn't really need it.

I felt drained. Hollow and empty once more, but in an entirely different way. It was oddly pleasant, as if this new emptiness offered some kind of clarity or space, which I had never known before. An empty bowl will ring with a clear, bright musical note, as long as there are no cracks in it. I had turned out my bowlful of old sorrow and misplaced guilt, and found that I still rang true.

But I was tired as well. Last night we had buried poor doomed little Kimi, and this morning I had thought Itsuki a betrayer and a monster and fled from him. Now all the truth was out, and our tears had been shed, and we were friends again. And still my work was not over.

For all that events seemed to be flowing together with impossible, chaotic speed, there was more to be done before this day was through. The task I had come to the Dark Wood to accomplish still lay before me: I needed to save my father.

He was my father, and I loved him. No more than I could have let Itsuki sink beneath the surface of that pool, even when I believed him to be my enemy, could I leave my own father to die of thirst and starvation under the power of the Dark Wood.

The way seemed clear, though the thought of it sent a chill through my veins. Kaede had been wrong. Even if Itsuki could be killed, and even if I was willing to kill him – which I was most emphatically not – the power which held my father in that poisoned sleep was not his. It was the Yuki-Onna's. Oyuki's. To save Father, I must confront her.

To be sure, I had always known that to get out of the maze, she and I must meet. But now I understood what she had been through, what she had become, and what she was capable of – and I understood that what I planned to do was horribly dangerous. For I would not approach her simply to ask for my release. I had to get her to spare my father's life, too. She, who had been cast out to die by her own father...

"I don't know, for sure, if my father still lives," I told Itsuki, my voice croaky and rough. "Or if the Yuki-Onna can be reasoned with, or persuaded ... I only know that I must try. Will you take me to her?"

"Now?" he asked.

"There isn't much time."

He hesitated. "You will need warmer clothes."

He climbed – almost lumbered – to his feet, and

helped me to mine, and shortly we were back where our friendship had begun, in the tower-tree, in the garden of knots. I looked around me with an odd sort of homesickness, for I could not face quite yet the knowledge that one way or another my peaceful idyll here was over, and that this might be my last chance to see Itsuki's garden for a long time to come.

Itsuki layered thick furs over my shoulders, and gave me knitted mittens and a fur cap that covered my ears. Waddling somewhat, and feeling rather like a barrel, I went across to peek in on the mother wildcat in her nest in the corner – and was shocked to see her and the two little ones gone.

Itsuki joined me, and sighed. "They'll be all right. The creatures I try to help – when they're better again, they always eventually leave and go back to their old lives. It's the way of things."

I caught the edge of his cloak as he went to turn away. "Itsuki, if I survive this—"

"You will return to your home and family." The words were utterly neutral. There was no hint of bitterness or regret or even sorrow in his tone, and I hesitated, unsure what to make of it. Was he so eager to be alone again? That didn't seem like Itsuki.

"Yes," I told him. "I must go home. But that doesn't mean I can't come back."

"You're a kind person, Hana-san." He grasped my mittened fingers, and carefully detached them from his cloak. "One task at a time. Your father is the most important thing now."

He headed for the doorway, and I stared after him for a split second, feeling … rebuffed. I shook myself and hurried forwards before he could notice my hesitation. We were about to seek out a vengeful snow maiden, who might smite me where I stood for my impudence in even approaching her, and attempt to bargain for my father's very life. Perhaps Itsuki was right.

One thing at a time.

Sixteen

As we left the garden of knots, Itsuki turned right, then right again, and right twice more – and although the rapid turns bewildered me and should, I thought, have only led us in a circle, it was clear almost at once that I was now in a new part of the maze. The hedges were taller, and denser, and their wicked thorns were as long as Itsuki's fingers.

All too soon, a thick coat of frost silvered the sharp black thorns. Frost turned to ice, and the ice formed giant, bristling spikes, some of which were big enough to pierce a man right through. I was grateful that Itsuki had insisted I wrap my feet up in layers of fur and leather before we reached this icy place, for the ground was thick with snow and hard as iron.

I tucked my mouth and the tip of my nose into the

ruff of grey fur around my neck and hid my hands in my armpits. Tiny specks of ice formed on my lashes and eyebrows, and though we were walking at a brisk pace, I couldn't control the occasional shiver. Without a word, Itsuki wrapped his arm around my shoulder, sharing his own blazing warmth.

The dark maze that I had grown accustomed to – even if only partly – had become a landscape of sheer white by the time we came to the end of the thorns, to the very centre of the maze. It didn't seem to take very long at all. In his hundred years trapped here, Itsuki had learned its ways well.

I blinked, sending a miniature flurry of snowflakes dancing in my vision.

It was a wide, kidney-shaped lake, surrounded by the white-frosted cones of dark pine trees. The water was an unbroken sheet of ice, and at one end a great waterfall, which must once have been the lake's source, had frozen in mid-flow, ice forming into fantastic curls and bulges that seemed to glow from within with a ghostly blue light.

The frozen lake held an island. It was a long way from us, where we stood at the water's edge, but I could see that it was white too, and glinted and gleamed in the sun.

"That is the heart of this place. I call it the Moon maze," Itsuki told me, pointing to the island, his voice carefully devoid of emotion. "The Yuki-Onna's home."

"Oyuki's home," I murmured.

Itsuki grasped me firmly by my arm and turned me

to face him. Only his chin and his mouth were visible under the hood, but they were set sternly, and his voice was almost harsh when he said, "You must never call her that. She doesn't like it."

Fighting a shiver that was nothing to do with the temperature this time, I nodded firmly. "Are we to walk on the ice?"

"No. We wait. She knows we're here. She always knows. If she's inclined to meet us, she will send us a way."

"What if she's not? The Moon will be dark again soon!"

"I am well aware of that," he said, and though his voice was not reproachful, I fell silent, chastened. "You cannot force her to do anything she doesn't wish to do, Hana-san. If she doesn't want to see us, we will come back first thing tomorrow and hope for better fortune then. Believe me, we do not want to set foot on that lake without her permission."

I sighed – a curling plume of white dissolved into the air – and nodded again. This was no occasion for impatience and temper. Reaching deep into myself, I tried to find a sense of stillness, my hunter's patience. It came with surprising ease, slowing my breaths and my heartbeat, and I remembered thinking, days and days ago now, that simply being around Itsuki had taught me more patience than I had ever known before.

"Forgive me," I said, nudging him remorsefully with my shoulder.

He put his arm around me again and drew me back to

his side. "There is nothing to forgive."

At length, there was a noise from the lake that drew both our attention – a cracking sound, as if of ice splintering. And indeed, a moment later a great split opened in that sheet of frosted white, practically at our feet. The crack widened and arrowed away from us to create a straight path in the ice. The water beneath it was dull black, like tar.

Far ahead, a tiny piece of the gleaming white island seemed to break away. The fragment glided slowly towards us, traversing the black path of water as smoothly and steadily as if some unseen creature in the lake's depths towed it in our direction. When it arrived at our feet, it was seen to be a boat. A narrow little boat of ice, shaped like a rice seed, with no sail, and room enough for two to sit inside. Both the prow and stern curved upwards into graceful, flowing figureheads of ice, taller than the top of my head. The one that faced us was in the shape of a ferocious white cat, snarling. Its body was poised in mid-leap. The eyes were lumps of green ice, and its fangs were icicles. It was very clear to me whom it was meant to represent.

Itsuki looked away from it as he helped me to climb into the boat. I had little experience of such craft, but it struck me as strange that it didn't rock or shift at all, despite the addition of my weight, and then Itsuki's as he climbed in after me. As I sat down, I examined the other figurehead in silence. It was a peacock, the long white tail swept out behind it, like the dragging train of the heavy

Uchikake robe that brides in my family had passed down for five generations.

Was this the Yuki-Onna's personal symbol? Did it represent her power, her all-seeing eye within the maze? Or her resentment over the striking beauty that had doomed her in life?

Itsuki sat down opposite me. I caught a glimpse of his venom-green eyes, shadowed by the hood, and they seemed wide and anxious. I nodded at him with all the reassurance I was capable of. In the next moment, the boat lurched a little, and a thump echoed through the hull. Then it began to move. Away from the shore of the lake. Towards the island.

I stared down worriedly between my feet, at the bottom of the boat, hoping that the delicate-looking ice was thick enough not to dissolve. I didn't like the look of that lake water. But under the smooth ice that seemed to be the boat's main material I saw the fine swirling grain of some pale wood. And there was no tell-tale sloshing of water. It seemed the Yuki-Onna didn't intend to try to drown us twice in one day.

Not yet, at any rate.

"Do you have any advice before we … arrive?" I asked softly, not sure if she could already hear us.

He only shook his head. In his lap, his hands curled and uncurled, curled and uncurled. I wanted to reach out and put mine over them, but he had brushed my touch away last time – and he seemed so far away from me, even though our toes were bumping together in the bottom of the boat.

I shouldn't have brought him. I should have found my own way here, I thought. *This was too much to ask. I'm sorry, Itsuki.*

It was too late for apologies now. With a shrill scrape, the boat arrived at its destination. The island was bordered by a narrow crescent of pale fine sand – perhaps the same sand that edged the turf in the thorn maze and the garden of knots. Still attached to its invisible tether, the boat drew itself up onto that sand and clear out of the water. As it halted, it tipped gently, as if to invite us to step over its shallow side onto dry land.

Itsuki seemed frozen in place. Even his hands had stilled their restless motions. Pity and guilt stabbed at me again. Though I did not want to do it – though I doubted whether I could so much as climb out of the boat without help in all these bulky layers, let alone face the architect of this place and emerge in one piece – I leaned in until I knew I had his attention and said: "This is as far as you need come. I can do the rest alone. Please wait here for me."

I thought at first that his silence was agreement. Then he made a little low huff of laughter. "I am not afraid of facing her, Hana-san. I may be a coward, but not such a coward as that."

"I don't doubt your courage. It hurts you to see her," I said gently. "There is no need."

Annoyed with my own hesitancy, I tugged off one of my mittens and laid my hand over the back of his, where it rested on his wide, distorted knee-joint. But as soon as my hand made contact with his skin – blazing warm still, in this cold place – the thought flashed through my mind: *he used this hand to tear Kyo apart and eat him*. I went still.

Itsuki shook his head and shook off my touch in the same moment, standing abruptly. And I was glad, for I was not sure if I had been about to recoil from him.

It isn't his fault. But it is still true.

Hurriedly, I shoved my fingers back into the knitted glove.

"I am selfish," he said lowly. "No matter how much time has passed, no matter how I have tried to be better, I am still as selfish as I ever was."

"What do you mean?" I asked, distressed for him even in the middle of my own distress.

He had already clambered over the side of the boat and was reaching back to lift me out. The tormented, beastly shape of Itsuki's body might pain him, but it didn't seem to have impaired his strength one bit. "We should move on. She'll be impatient otherwise, and we don't want her to feel slighted."

Unable to argue the sense of this, I found my balance and turned away from him to look at the Yuki-Onna's home closely for the first time.

The Moon maze, Itsuki had called it. The towering construction was a cross between a forbidding fortress and the glittering diamond crown from a children's fairy tale. It shone. It glowed. And yet, the closer we came to it, the more I felt wrongness radiating from its walls, as tangible to my senses as the waves of cold that caused the air around it to ripple and waver.

My eyes traced the shapes in the diamond-bright walls with a mixture of revulsion and fascination. They were woven of twisted fragments of every cold white thing imaginable, from bleached white branches to shining ivory, to brittle bones, to translucent horn and jagged quartz. And ice. Everywhere, coating everything, the ice. The same intricate curling patterns that had been worked into the grass in Itsuki's garden home made up the very fabric of the Moon maze – carved into its quartz, braided into its branches, cut into its bone. These markings had never bothered me when I walked over them, had never seemed more than a pretty repeating pattern designed to please the eye. But now that I saw them writ large upon such a canvas, I felt as if every knot and tendril were looking back at me, and more, that they were moving, shifting in the corners of my vision, snaking and changing where I could not watch.

Itsuki caught me as I stumbled, and steadied me. "Better to keep your eyes on your feet if you can," he advised. "I've grown used to it, over the years – I forgot."

I stared down and found, thankfully, that my head stopped swimming almost at once when it was no longer required to make sense of such an unnatural thing. "Are we close to the way in yet?" I asked, trying not to sound too plaintive.

"The way in is wherever—" He hushed and went tense.

I wrenched my eyes up off the ground to see what was coming.

Directly before us, the white wall of the maze was changing. The twisting rigid fibres were indeed moving now, silently and inexorably, curling back on themselves as if they were alive, and not solid dead wood and ivory and stone. As the fabric of the wall dilated, a white circle of bone, many feet higher than our heads – a Moon gate – pushed forwards into the gap, and the same fibres which had shifted to make way for it now twisted around it to hold it in place.

Beyond the gate of bone, in the newly revealed blue-white shadows of the maze, something moved.

Itsuki seemed to become even stiffer, like a tree in truth – save for his hand that suddenly latched onto the back of my fur cloak. "She has sent an escort for us."

It was a – a thing. I wanted to label it "creature", but how could I? It was no animal, not even a monster – not a living thing at all – just a collection of rattling bones and branches held together with sinews of frost. The stiffly moving bone and branch limbs supported a torso that was nothing more than an irregular, twisted block of ice lit from within by a cold glow and wreathed in ropes of dead white matter. A dark, spreading shape, like a spill of blood, huddled at the centre of the body, misted by the ice so that its true form could not be discerned – and the sight of it filled me with visceral quaking revulsion, though I could not have guessed what it was, nor why it made me feel that way. The thing's head was a dense tangle of dry pale sticks, resting directly on the body with no neck to support it. All told, it was at least seven feet tall, towering over even Itsuki.

It stepped out of the gate and walked towards us with mechanical clumsiness, and it was not until it had come near enough for me to reach out and touch one of its spindly limbs if I wished that I saw the most dreadful part of all.

Among the dry dead branches of the head, there was a face.

A human face.

The skin was pallid blue-grey, like clay dug up from the riverbed, and the mouth gaped vacantly, and – oh no, no, dear Moon—

I twisted sideways violently, stumbling and going down on one knee in my desire to hide from those blank frost-dulled eyes.

"Hana-san?" Itsuki's hands encompassed my shoulders, and I realized he was crouching beside me, as if to shelter me from the sight of the … the *thing*. I was trembling so badly, fighting so hard not to simply crumple up and cry that he was actually having to hold me upright.

"What. Is. *That*?" I demanded, my voice thick and slurring with unshed tears.

"It is one of the Yuki-Onna's servants," he said tentatively. "I know it's … horrible to look at, but it is only one of her creations, a magic thing. It doesn't suffer. She has many of them. Dozens. Some of them are part of the walls of the maze, to guard it, others patrol the island, others— *Hana*, what is wrong?" he asked urgently as my gut heaved, and I slapped a hand over my mouth.

"It is not a creation. It is a person. Or was. There is a woman inside that thing. I knew her. I knew her when she was alive. She was called Hyouta-san. She was taken from my village seven summers ago."

She had been a friend of my mother's, and a kind of honorary aunt to Kyo and me. Plump and cheerful, filled with matter-of-fact kindness and good sense, she had once given me a little red silk fan that had belonged to her as a girl, since she had no daughter to pass it onto. I thought the fan was still tucked into a dusty box of my childhood treasures somewhere – long forgotten. But I had not forgotten how her youngest boy had cried in his father's arms the morning they had discovered her gone.

Never, never had I forgotten that.

I felt, though I could not hear, the low rumble of the groan that vibrated in Itsuki's chest. "You mean that her servants were humans once? Alive once?"

I nodded. "There are … dozens?"

"There may be even more than that." He looked around helplessly.

Dozens of ice and bone servants, with human faces.

This was what had become of them all, the lost ones, our loved ones – and it was worse than we had ever known. They had not even been granted the respect of true death. Being eaten would have been better than this obscenity, twisted and ruined and forced to serve the one who had stolen them from their families and homes.

And if Hyouta was here ... so must be my grandmother, who was taken barely six months later.

So must be Kyo.

Then, in a blinding flash that seared away, for an instant, all sickness and grief, I knew something else: *Itsuki had not eaten anyone.*

There had never actually been any evidence that he had, after all. Only the assumption that if a monster lived in the forest, as the trees said, and took humans, it must be to consume them. But Itsuki did not call the humans from the village. The Yuki-Onna did. The Yuki-Onna had stolen our people and changed them, stolen their bones and faces and condemned them to this unspeakable living death in her service, and it was vile, vile, vile, but—

But she had not made the beast eat them. At least she had not engineered that. The beast had nearly killed my father and me – but we had both survived – and the Yuki-Onna had the rest of our people, and so *Itsuki was not a murderer.* He was not a maneater. The relief was almost enough to do what the sight of poor Hyouta's face had not been, and make me sick then and there.

With a dry rattling, the thing that had once been my

mother's friend shifted from one foot to the other, and made a swooping gesture towards the Moon gate with its long bent arms. Itsuki was still gazing up at her – it – in spellbound horror, but I recognized the movement as impatience, and remembered what Itsuki had said about the dangers of keeping the snow maiden waiting.

"Come on," I said, climbing up Itsuki's broad shoulders until I could stand on my own feet again. I looped my arm through his as he rose too, rather shakily. "We must do what we came here for."

"But that woman…"

"She is dead. If the Yuki-Onna has done this to them, then everyone who was taken is dead. There is nothing to be done." I avoided the dull gaze of the Yuki-Onna's servant as it bowed jerkily. It turned away and walked into the maze, clearly intending us to follow. "But I pray my father is still alive. It is not too late to hope for him yet."

The words were pure bravado. This new evidence of the Yuki-Onna's power and evil made me fear for my chances of success more than ever. No matter what had happened to Oyuki, no matter how much she had been wronged, *nothing* could justify this. What hope had I of reaching someone who could do such a thing to poor Hyouta?

My argument seemed to reach Itsuki, though. He moved forwards determinedly. And perhaps we leaned into each other more than was strictly necessary as we went – but if so, no one but us two knew it.

Seventeen

I saw the truth of Itsuki's words as soon as we stepped through the Moon gate: two more vaguely human shapes, cocooned in cobweb layers of frost and bone, were fused into the fabric of the maze on either side of the entrance. A permanent guard.

Try as I might to stop myself, it was impossible to resist. Fearfully, I gazed into each face, searching for the long-remembered features of a loved one. The one on the left was familiar, I thought, but neither were well known to me. I was ashamed of my gladness. Each of them had been a person, with thoughts and hopes and fears and dreams. Each of them had loved someone, or been beloved by someone. Each of them was precious. And now, each of them was dead and imprisoned in this Moon-forsaken place, and there was nothing I could do to help.

What would I have done if one of them was Kyo? Or Grandmother? Dear Moon, what was I to do if I saw a face I loved staring dully out at me from one of these "servants"?

You will think of your still living father, and not fall apart, I told myself grimly. *And in the meantime, follow your friend's excellent advice and keep your eyes on your feet.*

Side by side with Itsuki, I walked the twisting corridors of the Moon maze, following the remnant of the woman who had once been dear to my family. The sustained horror and fear were having a strange effect on me. Or perhaps all this dark magic was too much for my merely human brain to withstand. I felt numb, remote, as if my true, vulnerable self had curled up small, somewhere deep inside, where no one could reach or hurt it. I watched what my body did from far away, through a sort of blurry veil, and could almost pretend that none of it was real at all.

It was a relief of sorts, to finally leave those haunted pathways behind and emerge into the centre of the Yuki-Onna's web – but the kind of release that brings new pain, as when a knife is drawn from a wound and the blood gushes forth.

The heart of the maze, its hub, was surprisingly small. Not much larger than our village meeting hall. It was almost empty. A mere bleak field of snow, edged by some stunted, leafless black trees and, here and there, clustered groups of the snow maiden's "servants", standing to attention. This time I successfully wrestled the temptation to check their faces, and kept my eyes firmly averted.

At the far end of the barren clearing was a throne – it could only be called that – hacked roughly from what seemed to be another, smaller, frozen waterfall. The seat of the chair was backed by cruel spikes and spears of ice. On top of the waterfall, where once perhaps the rocks had been home to shrubs and plants, a single dead white tree remained. The trunk curved forwards over the cascade of frozen water, its bony branches heavy not with leaves or blossoms but with razor-sharp frost crystals. The trunk bowed so low that these strange frost flowers very nearly brushed the head of the thing that sat on the throne.

She had been a woman once. It was clear that she was no longer anything of the kind. She was nothing like any mortal human being.

If Itsuki's beauty was repellent, the Yuki-Onna's was monstrous. Her flawless face was lovelier even than I had imagined, and I could see that she had been no older than me when she died. Her skin was the same absolute white as her ice, and it glittered fiercely, iridescent, so that other colours were seen within it: green and blue and purple. Her eyes were as dark as a Moonless night, burning cold. Her hair was a sweep of onyx that reached her waist, clad in a glimmering veil of frost, and her gown was white peacock feathers, trailing around her tiny feet in luxuriant layers, with the black eye pattern standing out stiffly behind her neck, like a ruff.

One glance was enough to etch her image into my mind forever, and I wrenched my gaze away from her face, blinking fiercely. I was surprised that my eyeballs didn't smoke even from that brief contact.

"My dear, how kind of you to bring me a visitor," she whispered – and though her voice was low, and gentle, and sweet, it wailed around the walls of the Moon maze like the shrill, hopeless pleas of the dying. "Is she a new pet of yours?"

I felt the great shuddering breath that Itsuki drew in and the momentary tremble of his arm where I clutched at it. But when he spoke, he managed to sound his steady, calm self.

"No. This is Hana-san. She is not of the maze. She came here by accident and seeks only to return to her village and her people."

What? No! Swiftly I released his arm and straightened up. "I seek more than that. I have come to beg for my father's life." In my fear, my own voice emerged with a kind of stiff defiance, and I felt Itsuki's warning look on my face.

A deep, rolling chuckle – sick children screaming for their mothers, condemned men crying for mercy – and Yuki-Onna seemed to shift forwards, eager. "Interesting. She has fire. Not to your usual taste. Perhaps that is why you seek to be rid of her?"

Something, some brittle note, some falsity in her delivery of the line struck me as … wrong. It *seemed* like a line, a piece of dialogue written down and memorized, then delivered by some puppeteer in a play – and not a particularly good one.

Involuntarily my gaze flickered up to hers, and for less than an eye blink, I could have sworn I saw something else – something that was still human – looking back at me from within or maybe around the edges of that immense and malevolent power. Then it was gone. Gone so completely that I was no longer truly sure I had seen anything at all, and had to look away once more.

Itsuki did not rise to her taunt, but merely inclined his head towards me, encouraging me to speak up for myself since I had forcibly disrupted his plan to play intermediary. I swallowed, and my throat clicked dryly. But I lifted my chin and fixed my eyes on the flowers of frost behind the snow maiden's head.

"My lady, at the last dark of the Moon, you … you called a man here into the wood. But he escaped. I found him the next morning at the edge of the trees. Though he was – wounded – the wound was not fatal, and he should have recovered. Only he was – is – still held in the same magic that had called him to the wood. He rests in a sleep that no one can wake him from, and if he sleeps for much longer he will die. That man is my father."

Her head tilted slightly sideways, as if in confusion. The birdlike gesture somehow made her seem a little more human, and, encouraged, I went on. "In fairness, my family begs that you break your spell upon him, and let him go free."

"Fairness?" she repeated sibilantly, and at the hissing sound all her dead servants stirred with a dry, uneasy rattle.

"Yes." I pressed my lips together tightly. But the Yuki-Onna did not continue. She seemed to be waiting. I forced myself to speak again. "You – you had your chance to capture him, my lady, and you failed. He returned to us. It is not fair to make us slowly watch him waste away out of ... of spite."

Itsuki made a jerky, aborted movement beside me, and the Yuki-Onna seemed to go still.

"Your people were not fair to me," she said, and the softness of her voice now was like the rattle of death in an old man's chest. "They had the power to save me once, and they refused to help. Why should I care for fairness now? Now that I have the power, and they do not?"

"What you say is true," I admitted. "But the people you speak of, who did not save you – they are all long dead, and you have punished many, many others since then who were and are innocent of any crime." Strangely, it was Hyouta's face that flashed before my eyes, and urged me to speak my thoughts aloud. "How much more suffering must you inflict before you are satisfied? Is your vengeance not complete yet?"

There was a beat of quiet. Itsuki shifted slightly in place but stayed where he was, as if to move would incite the snow maiden, the way a mouse fleeing for freedom captures the attention of a cat.

Then the Yuki-Onna rose to her feet in a jerky, furious movement. "None of you are innocent!"

She made a furious sweeping motion with one hand. Faster than I would have believed their clumsy bodies could move, two of the dead servants lunged forwards. Their spindly twisted limbs came up like spears, bone shards and icicles bristling, to pierce me or rend me in two.

Roaring like thunder, Itsuki threw himself into their path.

He sent the closest one flying with a swipe of his arm that reminded me irresistibly of the great white cat that lurked within him. The servant tumbled head over heel, crashed against the wall of the maze, and was still. The other one was still reaching for me. Itsuki turned on it. He ripped its arms from its body in a single brutal movement. It toppled to the ground, legs thrashing.

Spinning in place, Itsuki threw the disintegrating bundles of sticks that had been the thing's limbs at the foot of the Yuki-Onna's throne, and roared again.

"You shall not harm her!" The gentle rumble of his voice was almost unrecognizable, transformed into a growl of pure ferocity – and I realized with a shock that I had never heard him angry before, not ever. "Torment me as you will, I have earned it, but Hana-san has done nothing wrong. You will have to kill me before I let you touch her, do you understand me?"

The Yuki-Onna and the beast stared one another

down, each of them breathing hard, two raging creatures of dark magic – with me, the soft, unprepared human caught between them. Then the snow maiden put back her head and laughed.

It was a wicked, gloating laugh of mean delight, and the sound made me shudder.

"Oh, yes! Yes! This is perfect. I have waited for this day, and now at last it has come. Take him!"

As one, the army of servants rushed forwards from every corner of the maze, converging on Itsuki where he stood before the Yuki-Onna's throne. They brushed by me as if I was not there, sending me stumbling back with no more effort than I would use to wave away a fly.

The things spun and bent and twisted, surrounding Itsuki with a forest of white branches and bones, spiked with shards of ice. In less than a moment they were no longer free-standing individuals but a single structure. A woven cage, pockmarked everywhere with dead human faces. The cage enclosed Itsuki completely, and then contracted, forcing him down onto his hands and knees.

I cried out – but at my first step in his direction, the Yuki-Onna closed her fist, and Itsuki collapsed, curling up in an all-too-familiar spasm of pain.

She wagged a finger at me gently, smiling a terrible smile. "You asked me, child, if my vengeance was yet complete. The answer is no. Never has this brute loved anyone or anything as much as himself – and so himself was all that I could take from him, little as it was.

But you, you have made something wonderful possible. In such a short time, you did what I could not achieve in one hundred years. You have placed him in the position to watch helplessly as what he cherishes is wrenched away from him."

Itsuki uncoiled and slammed against the inside of his cage, sending chunks of bone and ice and one of the human heads flying as he snarled at the snow maiden through the bars.

"Hush now. Don't worry, my darling," the Yuki-Onna crooned. "I shall not hurt a single hair upon her fair head, never fear. I don't need to." She fixed her burning black gaze on me, the smile dying from her face. "You can go. My maze is not for such as you – you should never have come here."

Frozen in place, yearning desperately to run to Itsuki's side yet fearing to make his agony worse, I stared at her in dismay.

She clicked her tongue. "Are you paying attention, child? I grant your request. Your father will live. You may walk free of this place, unmolested, and the moment you are gone from here, your father will open his eyes again and be just as good as new. Isn't that what you wanted?"

"I – I – yes – but – I…" My gaze returned to the cage. Itsuki's claw-like fingers had curled out of his prison, nails digging deep into carved horn and bone. His hood had fallen down, and his poison-green eyes stared out at me from between the bars.

"There is just one more thing," the Yuki-Onna said. "A price that must be paid for my fairness. The moment that you leave this place, the maze will close to you, and the Dark Wood will hide it. You will never, ever return here. You will never see this beast again. Your father's life and your own, in return for the beast's happiness. Doesn't that seem fair?"

She was offering me everything I wanted, everything for which I had been willing to risk or even sacrifice my life. Yet I met Itsuki's eyes, and I could not move. I could not turn, I could not take a step, no more than I could have grown wings and flown. I couldn't.

Itsuki spoke, his voice the same soft rumble I had grown to trust, though it was hoarse now with deep, panting breaths. "Hana-san. You must go."

"No." I shook my head furiously. "No, I won't leave you like this. I can't!"

"Your father." Itsuki's great pale head came up to the bars, pressing against them as if he could not help but try to get closer. "It's his life. It is your life."

"He's right," the Yuki-Onna said, and my stomach turned. "If you don't go now, I may change my mind. With a snap of my fingers, your father could die, and it would be all your fault for being so ungrateful."

"Itsuki—"

"Go. I'll be all right. I promise. Go."

Heartsick and torn, I stared into his eyes. He nodded, and despite everything, despite the cage around him and the Yuki-Onna towering over him on her throne, there was a kind of … happiness on his face, a kind of peace. He wanted me to go. He truly wanted to help save my father, and for me to be free. Slowly, hating myself, hating the Yuki-Onna most of all, I turned away.

The walls of the Moon maze peeled back silently before me, clearing the path straight down to the shore of the island where the white boat waited in the black water. The snow maiden's triumphant laughter rang in my ears, following my every step.

From Itsuki there was no sound at all.

Eighteen

By the time I reached the shore of the island and allowed myself to look back, the maze had reformed itself behind me, and the snow maiden, and the dead remains of the villagers, and Itsuki, were all hidden from view behind its shining walls. I struggled with myself for another moment, my hands aching for the grip of my bow, hearing Itsuki's last words to me in my head – urging me to go, reminding me that this was about my father's life. And then, with my heart like a lump of rock inside my chest, I climbed gracelessly back into the boat and sat down.

With nearly indecent speed – as if the Yuki-Onna or whatever force served her was desperate to have me gone – the boat slithered smoothly from the narrow sandy shore. The hull sank into the water. The boat moved forwards.

Staring blankly at the figurehead, I didn't notice at first when my vision began to cloud. I blinked rapidly. My eyes felt dry but – could I be crying? I tugged off one of the mittens Itsuki had given me and raised my hand to my cheek. No. It was not tears that blurred my sight.

Snow. It was snow.

The sky was a vivid cloudless blue, and yet flakes of snow as tiny as flecks of dust drifted down from it, falling perfectly straight, like beads running into place on the silk thread of a lady's necklace. Faster and faster the snow fell, thicker and thicker, and I could not help but stare in astonishment. The bottom of the boat was full already. The snow had covered my feet and lap and arms, and I could no longer see the lake, the path of dark water, or even the boat's icy figurehead.

The world was still, and silent, and cold, cold, cold.

My hands clutched at each other as my eyes searched the blankness around me. Was I still on the lake? Still in the maze? Had the Yuki-Onna broken her word and banished me to some new prison?

Gradually my ears began to perceive a sort of distant roaring. I thought perhaps my mind sought to fill the unnatural silence with sounds that I knew, to save me from going mad, for the noise that I heard was that of wind moving restlessly through trees. Of a forest bending and moving in the gale's embrace, like a dance. The music of leaves, whispering and singing.

Hana.

Hana.

Hana.

Welcome home…

The boat lurched beneath me, as if it had hit a rock. Then it jumped, tipping forwards, capsizing into the flurrying snow. I closed my eyes tight and flung my hands out before me, bracing for the fall into icy water.

I landed on my knees, on solid ground, as softly as if I had simply sunk down into that position of my own accord.

At once I felt a change in the light and the air. The warmth of the sun on my face, and also the absence of that biting chill which I had felt everywhere in the Moon maze. I found myself peering blearily at late afternoon sunlight, dappling red and yellow and orange through fiery autumn leaves, and green and brown moss, and brown tree bark, and splotchy yellow lichen, and soggy lumps of leaf mould, and mottled grey stones.

Nothing like a garden.

Nothing like a maze.

The very disorder, the natural chaos of it, was like a balm to eyes that had grown too used to staring at artificial, fearsome beauty. Sitting very still on a branch not far above my head was an ordinary, common robin – not even obliging enough to sing – and I could have kissed it for being little and brown and every day, with its drab orange head, instead of bright or extraordinary or magical.

The trees shifted and sighed around me again, with

relief or sadness, I could not tell.

Hana.

Home, Hana.

Welcome. Welcome. Home.

Feeling as wobbly as a newborn foal, I got to my feet, and took a couple of testing steps forwards, and then a couple more, patting trees as I passed them, hanging onto branches where I needed to. It was enough to bring me to the edge of the trees, to the ridge. I looked down.

Spread out before me was the valley. The rice terraces, edged in vivid green, reflecting a cloudy afternoon sky, and beyond that the river, like a strip of liquid amber in the last brilliance of the sun's rays. And there, as if cradled gently in our valley's cupped hands, was the irregular wood and thatched-roof jumble of the village.

Smoke trailed upwards in lazy white ribbons. A cow lowed. A door closed somewhere, and someone shouted a greeting or a goodbye. Pigs stirred in the mud, and a grey goose flapped its wings on the peak of Hideki's house. In the river, a trio of children laughed and splashed in the shallows, long brown legs drawn up to their chins like the frogs that they hunted.

"*Home.*" This time the voice that spoke the word was my own.

I let out a long, shuddering sigh.

It was all just as it had ever been. It was as if I had never left. Yet somehow everything seemed strange and new, and my eyes traced the lines of these well-known things with the curiosity and incomprehension of a stranger. I had returned, and everything was the same. Except me.

"Your father will live..." the Yuki-Onna had said.

I drew my shaken breath back to me – it tasted of crisp autumn leaves, and musky mushroom spores, and wood fires – and began my descent from the ridge.

No one noticed my return. There was no shout of recognition or disbelief, no rush to greet me. It was like any other day, sturdy Hana-san trudging home from the wood, weighed down by her day's work. By the time I reached my house, nestled in the curve of the hill on the edge of the settlement, I felt I was drifting, borne up on a cloud of dreamlike normality that seemed too real to be real. My geta were waiting for me under the step of the porch, as always. The smooth wood was cold against my weathered soles as I slipped them on.

I stepped up onto the porch and drew back the screen, looking in without stepping over the threshold. The kitchen was empty. The table was scrubbed clean, the floors swept, the fires out and the ovens cold. A thin layer of dust, sparkling gold in the rays of sunlight that spilled in through the gaps in the shutters, lay over everything. I did not have to call out, or search the house, to know that my mother was not here.

Reluctantly – part of me wished to keep the last things Itsuki had given me close – I stripped off my cap and the furs. I spread them out under the porch roof, just as I had always done with whatever prize I dragged home from the forest for my parents.

For the first time I really noticed the deep, misty blue and glossy black of the furs, finer by far than any pelt I had ever seen before. A prince's ransom in furs, though we had no prince to buy them. Itsuki would not have killed any animal for these, I knew. He must have taken the pelts from creatures he knew in the maze that had died of old age, or he had been unable to heal. That made them all the more precious. Yet he had given them to me so carelessly – no, not carelessly, not that, but – *gladly*, as if their value had meant nothing to him.

Or as if their value, no matter how great, was not equal to yours.

My fingers clenched tightly in the soft fur they had been stroking. I felt my face crumple, and my shoulders heaved with the desire to fling myself down and weep. I had left him. I had left him there in that cage, alone, while the Yuki-Onna laughed.

He told me to go, I reminded myself, clinging to the thought as I clung to the furs. *He wanted me to go. He promised it would be all right.*

I forced my fingers to unknot. Straightening up, I mechanically brushed down the wrinkles in my clothes, and drew the kitchen screen and door carefully shut. Then I left my parents' home and stepped down onto the stone path that would lead me to the centre of the village. To Kaede's house. To my mother.

And my father.

The first person I saw on the walk to the healer's house was the village tanner and leatherworker. He was heading in the opposite direction with a barrel under one burly arm and a satchel of tools over the other. He looked at me in passing, blinked as he took in the glowing finery of the kimono that Itsuki had made for me, returned his gaze to my face – and walked straight into the wall of a house.

I did not pause as the tools clattered to the ground and the barrel rolled away, although on a normal afternoon I would have rushed to help. There was more important work for me to do today. Head held high, I strode past him.

A garbled shout went up behind me. Near by, a shutter slammed back as someone came out to see what the commotion was. On the smaller path that branched off to the left, one of the pig-keepers, driving a couple of his charges down towards the river, turned to look at me and went stock-still. The fat, speckled pair of sows escaped and ran past me, squealing. A housewife who had been beating a rug on her porch peered around its frayed edge, dropped the beater with a muffled yelp, and then screeched for her husband. I moved on.

More doors and shutters opened. More voices rang out, questioning, fearful, and then disbelieving. Like a tide sweeping away from my footsteps, the news spread.

"Hana-san! It is Hana-san!"

"The girl's come back! Ichiro-san's girl!"

"What? Returned? Alive? From the Dark Wood?"

"She's alive? By the Moon, she's alive!"

So, I thought, with a hint of bitter humour, *they told themselves I was dead, did they? A fair enough assumption, I suppose. But will my unexpected resurrection be seen as a blessing – or a curse?*

I saw Hideki and his wife, and Goro, and Shouta amongst the faces of those who lined the path to gawp and point, but I did not slow, even to nod in acknowledgement. In my quick, determined march and refusal to lower my eyes, some message must have been clear, for no one tried to stay me. No one put out a hand, and no one stepped in my way. In fact, any preoccupied souls so unobservant as to stumble onto the path ahead of me were seized by the others and hauled off so that they did not impede my progress.

By the time I reached the sensei's house, practically the entire village must have been following me, muttering and exclaiming and sounding like nothing so much as a gaggle of geese. It was annoying, but I had no time to turn and remonstrate with them. The few persons that I really wished to see were in that low, quiet house ahead of me – and trails of blue, pine-scented smoke were spiralling up from the incense holders on either side of the door. *I am in time, then. I must be. Surely I must have made it in time.*

Before I could even reach out to knock, the door flew open and Kaede herself was there. Her face was more deeply lined than ever, and her stance showed a great weariness. Yet her eyes, meeting mine, brimmed with warm brilliance that I recognized with a sharp pang of hope. It was the look of a healer whose patient has turned a corner.

"Hana-san," she breathed, and her hand reached out to clasp my arm and shake it a little, as if she was a doting grandmother and I the long-lost child for whom she had prayed each day. Perhaps she had.

"My father?"

"He is well, he is well, Hana-san. You are returned to us by the glory of the Moon, and whatever you did, however you did it, it worked. He woke this morning as the sun rose, and he is himself. He will recover."

The last anxiety as to the truth of the Yuki-Onna's words fell away from my shoulders like a robe whose pockets had been filled with stones. The fact that she had somehow freed him before I ever spoke to her I did not allow to trouble me, for Itsuki had said that time passed strangely, or differently, within the maze. All that mattered was that it had worked. I lifted my face up to stare at the sky for a long quiet heartbeat, and then looked back at Kaede and smiled. "Thank you."

"I didn't do much." She jerked her head uncomfortably. "I didn't do anything, really."

I put my hand over hers on my arm and squeezed it. "You kept him alive long after almost anyone else would have given up, and you gave me the time I needed to do … what I must. Thank you, Sensei. I will not forget. Not ever."

She stared into my face, her expression arrested. "Well. My goodness. If ever there was a story that was begging to be told, my girl ... but for now, come inside, come in. There are some people who will be even more impatient than I to hear you tell it, once they know you are here."

Staying only to take off my wooden sandals, I stepped up and into the house, and Kaede shut the door in the faces of the gawping onlookers with an air of some satisfaction. There was no sign of the healer's apprentice. The inner door to the great room was closed. Unable to restrain my impatience any longer, I rudely reached out to open it for myself. The healer waved off my look of apology and gestured me through, then wordlessly pulled the door shut between us.

And then it was just me. Just me, and the two who laid there in the quiet light-filled room beyond.

My mother was sleeping, curled on her side with her pale, sad face pillowed on both her hands and a light blanket pulled up over her. Beside her, propped up in a half-reclining position by stacks of pillows, was my father. He did not move at the click of the door, but continued to stare down at my mother. There was a strange expression on his face. As sad as hers, but not at all as peaceful.

The sight of him, eyes open, mostly upright, and with colour in his face, was enough to strike me dumb with wonder and relief. I had not realized until then how deeply the memory of his waxy stillness had haunted me. All I had done, everything I had endured, each hour of suffering and each moment of doubt and fear, was worth it to me. I knew then that no matter what had happened, I still loved him, and always would.

Smiling a little nervously, I stepped forwards. Father's head lifted, without much interest, I thought, to look at who had come in. His gaze fixed upon me without recognition at first, and almost I allowed it to wound me, to cut that still vulnerable place in my heart. Then his eyes seemed to focus. They widened, and every bit of colour in his face fled – then rushed back all at once.

The cup that he had held absently in his left hand dropped to the tatami mat with a soft thud and he jerked forwards off the pillows, both his hands lifting up towards me. His fingers grasped at the air without dignity, like a child's, until I rushed to his side, and knelt there to take them in my own. His hands were icy cold. They closed around mine painfully tightly.

"Hana, Hana, *Hana*," he whispered. "Please tell me it wasn't true, what they said. Where have you been? How could you – how *dared* you – do such a crazy thing?"

I ignored the second part. "You know where I've been."

"I prayed against reason that you had more sense, you reckless unthinking child!"

"Sense?" I repeated. "What would you have had me do then, Father? Fling the chance aside like trash, simply because it was small and fragile? Someone had to do something. Someone had to save you."

He shook his head. Opened his mouth. Closed it again. Then he buried his face in the back of my hands. His shoulders shook, and I felt warm droplets running over my fingers. I stared down at him, speechless and disbelieving. I had never seen him cry.

His tears were not as silent as Itsuki's had been. Beside him, my mother murmured, and stirred, and opened her eyes. For a moment she stared, wide-eyed, as she slowly pushed the blanket away and sat up. Then her arms were around both of us, her slim strong hands clutching like bands of iron.

"If I am dreaming, do not let me wake. Do not let me wake," she murmured.

"In a dream, dearest, I would be shaved," my father said, rubbing his face self-consciously – pretending that it was his patchy beard and not the evidence of his tears that discomfited him.

My mother and I both laughed much more heartily than such a feeble joke deserved. After a blink of surprise, Father's laughter, dry and rusty with disuse, joined ours. We embraced one another as we had not done in years, not since Kyo had vanished into the Dark Wood, and if none of the three of us were really sure by now if we were laughing, or crying, or both, well, what did it matter?

Nineteen

Kaede, despite her occasional irascibility, really was a patient woman. Perhaps all healers must have, or learn, such vast and stolid patience in the course of their profession. In any case, she left us alone there long after anyone else would have been battering down the door in curiosity, and gave us enough time to talk through many things that needed to be talked of, though not quite everything that we might have wished.

Both my parents took me to task for recklessness and disobedience, and for scaring them half to death by running off into the Dark Wood alone on such an impossible quest. Given the happy outcome, the scolding was not as harsh as it might have been, but it was stern enough. I apologized for scaring them, but I did not make any promise to refrain from such behaviour in future. I couldn't have promised that, not even at that moment, not even for them – and I thought my father at least guessed this.

Father then horrified us by revealing that he had heard all, or nearly all, that was said near him while he had lain paralysed in what had only seemed to be sleep. Although he had not been able to twitch so much as an eyelash, he had been aware the entire time, vainly straining every fibre he had. So he had known when I ran away that night all those weeks before, because Kaede had broken the news to my mother at his bedside.

"I wished I had died," he confessed lowly. "Died there in the forest like the rest, rather than send you out to face the beast for my sake. You can have no idea how I railed and cursed and wept, all without ever making a sound."

He sounded devastated by the experience. I understood that very well. And yet ... yet for all that, for all that he had lost too much weight from his already rangy frame, and was rumpled and unshaved, there was an odd lightness about him, I thought. His hair might be straggling and in need of a wash and his eyes sunken into grey bruises, but he seemed ... younger. Somehow. Or at least, not as weighed down by age.

The thing I could not get used to was how he looked at me. He met my eyes straight-on, without turning his face away in that gesture I had come to know and hate, and not once did I suspect him of gazing wistfully over my shoulder for a boy who was not there.

I wanted my father's love, but I did not need his forgiveness any more. Or rather, I had come to accept that I had never needed it. But I had an odd sense that he had somehow shed a similar burden of his own during the course of his "sleep". I longed to know just what it had been, and how this had come to pass.

Hoping a little wistfully that the change was not some effect of his recent healing that would wear off with time, I told them, "The beast was not the one I had to face in the end. The beast … was not truly a beast at all."

Father gave me a look that searched for answers at the same time as it offered understanding. He reached out to me as he had not reached out since I was a child, and touched my face. "I know, I think. For I dreamed … such strange dreams, while I lay here under that dark magic, Hana. And now that I see you again, I think at least some of them must have been true."

I stared at him, open-mouthed, while my whole body went hot and cold with the implications of this. Mother exclaimed with surprise, and demanded to be told what he had dreamed, what he knew, exactly where I had been and what I had done. "Oh, everything, tell me everything! What in the world can all this mean?"

Before any more of the mystery could be unravelled between us, there was a knock at the door. Kaede's head poked in. She looked at us warmly for the length of a smile, and then, as one who briskly ties up her sleeves before undertaking an unpleasant but necessary task, she pulled on her familiar grumpy expression.

"No more time to gossip, I'm afraid," she said. "The elders are outside – the whole village is outside – demanding to be told if Hana-san is really back, if Ichiro-san is really awake, if the curse is finally broken. And most likely if the sky is blue as well."

I sagged in place, holding in a groan.

Of course. Hana-san had marched off into the forest to kill the beast, break the curse, and save her father, had she not? And now, against all expectations, Hana-san was back, and alive, and her father was indeed saved.

They thought I had done it. They thought the curse was broken and that Itsuki – the beast – was dead. They thought they were free at last.

Nothing could have been further from the truth.

I looked down at my neatly folded knees, clad in the shimmering cloth that Itsuki had woven, and felt the last of my strength drain away. I was tired. So very tired. I had not eaten a morsel all day, and I now noticed that my mouth was parched with thirst, too. Every part of my body that did not ache with exhaustion throbbed with still healing scars, or previously ignored bruises, or hunger, or sheer cussedness.

The last thing in the world that I wanted was to have to face the villagers, and the elders, and explain to them that, despite my miraculous return, the mountain still lay as deeply under its enchantment as ever. They would not want to hear such news. But they would expect to hear my story, just as my mother did. How ... *how* could I tell even a fraction of what I had seen, and learned, and done? Of what lay beyond the bounds of the Dark Wood? The terrible things and the beautiful, the truth of the beast, and the maze, the Yuki-Onna – and the poor dead remnants that served her?

The thought of even trying made me feel ill.

All I really wanted right now was ... to eat a bowl of Itsuki's delicious vegetable noodles, and drink some of his mock-tea. To listen to the calm, deep rumble of his voice. To lay myself down on the other side of the fire with the solid bulk of his body comfortingly close by. I wanted to sleep for a hundred years like that, safe and watched over and ... and cherished.

But none of that, not the least part of it, was within my grasp.

My breath hitched, and I bore down on my emotions, squeezing my eyes shut.

"Hana..." my father said softly.

"Can Mako-san not turn them away?" my mother asked with an abruptness that was not at all characteristic of her. "We're all so tired – Hana most of all – and she has only just returned to us. Surely they could wait until tomorrow!"

"Mako-san left me a week ago," the healer said with a *humph*, and I heard her footsteps as she came fully into the room and approached us. "Finally decided to marry that charcoal-maker on the other side of the river. Waste of all my training, and a fine pair of steady hands. No, no, I didn't expect you to notice, not as things were at the time. But if she were still here, even she couldn't put these fools off. One or two are threatening to take my door from its hinges and come in to speak to you themselves, and the rest of the elders aren't saying much to dissuade them. It'll probably avoid a lot of fuss if you just come out your-self and answer a few questions before they riot, my girl."

I raised a hand to my forehead and rubbed, as if I could wipe away the hard band of tension that encircled my temples. "I... Very well. Can we roll the screens back, in here? I don't want to have to—"

"Go out and stand among the whole lot of them? Of course. It's a good idea. They're used to me shouting at them from the porch anyway."

"Listen to me," my father said, claiming my attention. "You don't owe anyone apologies or explanations. Say only what you wish to say, and dismiss them. They have no more right to command you than – than—"

"Than a dog has to command the Moon Prince," my mother finished. Then she pulled a face. "But do try to be polite, Hana."

"When we've got rid of them, you can eat something, and then rest here for the night," Kaede said encouraging-ly. "I've just finished making my famous soup dumplings. You'll like those, I promise."

This was offered rather in the tone of someone calm-ing a toddler's tantrums with treats, I thought wanly.

I nodded in agreement and tried to compose myself.

Together, my mother and Kaede rolled back the paper screens and then one side of the wooden door that blocked the great room of the healer's house from the covered front porch. The noise of the crowd gathered outside swiftly filled the quiet space, and surged up still more when they realized that this door and not the front one was inching open. I heard everyone rushing around to try to get the best place, and had the impression of feral creatures baying for scraps.

You're only tired, I admonished myself. *Get this over with and you can rest, as Kaede said.*

With a quiet groan I got up – my father awkwardly patted my ankle – and went to stand at the healer's side by the open door. My mother backed up a step but stayed behind me, as if to offer support. My father's place on the other side of the room was still hidden, and I was sure he was grateful. I wished I could hide there with him. Dusk was deepening, and a few torches flared orange here and there among the gathered villagers, but that only seemed to intensify the dimness everywhere else. Most of the light was coming from the lit lamps of the healer's house itself, which meant that I was bathed in it. I must be shining in their gaze, while they seemed like a restlessly shifting, anonymous mass, the half-hidden shadows of people I knew in the daylight.

"Hana-san is worn out," Kaede said severely to the crowd. "So you'll take it as a favour that she's come out to answer your questions, and not keep her standing here too long."

"Where have you been?" someone unfamiliar shouted.

"Did you see my little girl?" a woman asked in a high, quavering voice. It was Misaki – the beautiful, laughing weaver's daughter, upon whom Kyo had had such a crush – whose five-year-old daughter had vanished just this past winter. The child was the youngest the village had ever lost.

No one had heard Misaki laugh since.

As I cringed at the thought of the fate which must have befallen the little girl, the first voice bellowed again: "How did you find your way back?"

"Now, now, that's enough!" One of the torches shifted forwards to the edge of Kaede's porch, and I could make out the faces of the elders, Yuu, Hirohito and Hayate clustered around it, with Yuu's gawky grandson holding it up.

"Don't bark questions at the girl, don't overwhelm her, you heard what Kaede-sensei said," Hayate went on, but even as he spoke, he directed an anxious look at me.

As soon as he was finished, Yuu blurted out: "Is it really … her? Not some demon or yokai, come back to taunt us?"

The sensei let out a long and dramatic sigh. "She is as real as she ever was, and as human as you or me. And you should be ashamed of yourself for asking, Yuu-san. Do you think I would let a demon into my house?"

This could go on all night, I realized, as Kaede continued

to bicker with the other elders. Gathering up what fortitude I still had – and the idea of enduring this for a single
breath longer than I must was enough to remind me that
one always had a little fortitude left, if there was the right
incentive to dig it out – I edged forwards and raised my
hand. The elders broke off their fight abruptly, and the
mumbling, shuffling crowd grew quieter and more still.

"I am the same girl who left here nearly four weeks
ago," I said. My voice sounded as thin and done-in as I
felt. "I have been into the Dark Wood, and there I saw …
many awful and astonishing things. My return came about
through a combination of luck, and stubbornness, and the
– the contrary nature of the creature who holds the Dark
Wood in her thrall."

"What of the beast, then? What of the monster?"

"Yes – did you kill it, Hana-san? Is it dead?"

"No," I shot back. "It was not in my power to kill it – nor
anyone else's power, either. The beast cannot be killed."

"But your father is awake. The curse must be broken!"

"No," I repeated, more gently this time. "I could not
do that, either. The enchantment on the mountain is as
strong and dark as it ever was."

A low moan of denial, despair and disbelief, and a
sharp faint edge of anger, ran through the crowd. Someone
– Misaki, probably – burst into tears, and was hushed.

"Then what good did you do by running away?" a
new voice demanded, and I looked down almost directly
into the face of Shouta. His brows were drawn together

and his mouth was a tight, resentful line. "If all you accomplished was to disappear for a month and leave us to mourn you for dead, and then come back dressed like a painted—" One of Shouta's brothers, who stood just behind him, gave him a powerful shove, and Shouta broke off, looking chastened for a moment. But then he shook his head angrily and finished, "Why go at all if you were to come back having changed nothing? What good did you do us, Hana-san?"

In the course of my life I have felt many strong emotions, some so deeply that I feared they would rip me apart. But never in all my years had I experienced such an incandescent, all-consuming rage as boiled up inside me then.

My heart thundered against my ribs until I thought it should crack them, my nails curled into my palms with enough force that they cut the skin, and when I opened my mouth, the words rolled out like a female version of Itsuki's ferocious roar.

"What good did I do? What *good*? The only good I sought! I did not walk into the Dark Wood at the dark of the Moon, alone, with a bow in one hand and a wood hatchet in the other, for any of your sakes – I did it because it was my father's only hope *and none of you had spine enough for the job.*"

Shouta leaned backwards as if the force of my response was a strong wind blowing in his face, and the ranks of others behind him shuffled uneasily.

"Don't take offence," Shouta's brother said, stepping in front of Shouta as if to shield him from my wrath. "He didn't mean it that way."

"I know exactly what Shouta-san meant," I snarled.

"Come, young lady, this is pettiness," Hirohito quickly interrupted. "There's no need to point fingers or rake up the past—"

"You are the ones who threatened to break the healer's door down if I did not come out here and let you rake up the past. You! And now you stand here before me with whining and complaints, and imply that I have *failed* you? That I would have done better to have stayed home instead – as Shouta-san did – as all the strong men of this village did when we needed your help? Because I didn't do *you* any good?"

With a rough jerk I dragged Itsuki's shining kimono down my arms, letting the top part sag over the sash, and shrugged the pale nagajuban off over my right shoulder, pulling it as low as I could without exposing my breast. An audible gasp of shock ran through the crowd as they saw the deep livid pink scars carving the flesh of my shoulder and arm.

"Yes, I walked into the forest, yes, I fought the beast – *and, yes, I survived*. You who would judge me may do the same. Take up your spears! Take up your scythes and bows! Do as I did. The Dark Wood awaits you. If you return in one piece, then you will have earned the right to question and criticize me. But until that day comes, I will tell you now that I do not answer to you, or to anyone here. *Do you understand?*"

There was a long, hushed silence, and not a living thing within the valley seemed to dare even to breathe. And then, one by one, the people of my village – even the elders, and Kaede herself – bowed down to me, the deep, wordless bow of respect.

My mother sighed. "Perhaps asking for politeness was too much…"

Twenty

I half feared, half hoped to dream that night, as I curled up on the spare futon Kaede had rolled out for me beside my parents. My time in the maze had been characterized by vivid, barely understood nightmares: memories fighting to break free of the strange barrier that my mind had imposed to protect my sanity. The barrier was gone now, and all my memories were free to roam through my dreaming mind at will. I had seen much that was worthy of dreams, and even more that was the stuff of nightmares. Nor had I forgotten that peculiar – almost prescient – dream which I had the night before I went into the Dark Wood, even if I could not now truly convince myself that I had seen my father looking at me with Itsuki's eyes, and talking to me with his voice. I was no seer.

Both hope and fear were wasted. I was too exhausted

for dreams, and slept so deeply that I believe I barely stirred the whole night through. When I woke it was not on account of my own bad dreams but my father's.

The muffled gasp – an unmistakable sound of panic – jerked me from slumber into a sitting position, with my hands raised before me in defence. I was disoriented and dizzy with the speed of waking, and my blurry gaze shot into every corner of the shadow-shrouded room, seeking danger. There was no one there but me, and the long, thin shape in the futon that was rolled out next to mine. The shadows lay quietly, like soft shreds of grey silk edged with the warm gold of mid-morning light that crept in around the edges of the shutters and door. Outside I heard the usual noises of a small busy village at work. Dawn had come and gone. There was nothing to fear here.

At last I turned to look again at where my parents had lain. Only Father was there now. My mother's space beside him was empty, blankets smoothed carefully down. My father's eyes were open, and when they caught mine, he made a calming gesture.

"Your mother is well. She woke a little after sunrise and could not sleep again, so she went back to the house to throw open the shutters and stoke up the fires and do all the other things she worries about. The sensei said I should let you sleep and try to sleep myself. I seem to have failed on both those counts."

"Oh." I sighed, allowing myself to fall backwards onto the pillow again. It felt very soft and giving under my head. Too soft, after the pillow of moss I had grown used to. Just as the futon was different to a fur spread over packed dirt, and the crisp autumn chill that stole into the room with the light seemed to get in under my blankets in a way no chill had ever defeated my sleeping furs beside Itsuki's fire.

"I'm sorry that I woke you," my father said.

I turned my head sideways to find him watching my face intently. I wondered what my expression told him. "That's all right. I was most likely ready to wake anyway – I'm not used to sleeping so late."

"I know."

The stilted exchange trailed off, but the awkwardness lingered in the air like pungent smoke. Perhaps I should pretend to sleep again. Then he might fall asleep in truth, and so rescue us both. *Our happiness and ease with each other did not last very long, did it?*

"Hana," my father said, and I worried for a second that he had somehow read my mind. But he went on, "I was dreaming. I dreamed of a maze of black thorns, and a maze of ice and ivory. I dreamed of a beast who fought and snarled within a cage made of the bones and faces of people I knew. And there was a white creature there that once might have been a woman, who laughed at the monster's roars, and made it writhe with a twitch of her finger."

My eyes snapped open and I sat up hastily. "You still dream about what lies within the Dark Wood?"

He nodded. "Some vestige of the enchantment must cling to me, even now. But I am grateful for that, because it means I know … something of what you have done, and where you have been. I think, although you may not be able to speak of those things yet, you do need someone who can understand. At least a little."

I swallowed thickly, and blinked fast, my shoulders easing as the sense of sitting beside a distant stranger faded away. Perhaps we did not know one another as well as a father and daughter should, but strangers … no.

"You saw him. He was in the form of a beast?" I asked, voice small.

"Half a beast. Parts of him changed as the white woman laughed, and parts of him were still human. There were words in his cries."

I closed my eyes again. On my lap, my fingers curled, squeezing tight on nothing, and then uncurled to lie straight. *I will be all right. I promise…*

"Hana—"

"Father—"

We both broke off. I nodded at him to continue first.

"You have left the job half done," he said, a faint smile quirking his lips. "Never could you bear that. Even as a child, you always had to see things through, complete what you had started. You are returning there, are you not? To finish the job."

I drew in a long breath. "The job I must finish is not to slay the monster, Father."

"No. You are going to save him."

My breath whistled out, and left me light-headed with relief. "You do understand."

"A little," he repeated. "When will you go?"

"Soon. Today, if I can." I said it firmly. "You've seen what she is doing to him. It's…" I shook my head. "Her vengeance brings her no peace. I believe it has driven her mad, warped her into something cruel and wicked. He has suffered enough for a hundred lifetimes, more than anyone but he could have endured, yet still she is not able to let go. They are like … like a lightning storm caught in a bottle, trapped in that place, with only their memories and their hurt, and each other. Someone has to stop it. Or it will go on forever. And we will all suffer with them."

He made no reply at first but gave me a glowing, watery eyed look, with a small smile tugging at his lips. It took me a moment to recognize the expression, for I had never seen it on his face before: pride, and the respect of one equal for another. It was a look that said, *Daughter, you have honoured our house.* It silenced me, and as he realized this the smile died away and he bowed his head.

"Don't you think it might be wiser to wait? Not long, perhaps, only to rest and recover before returning? Tonight is—"

"The first night of the dark of the Moon." I twitched my shoulder and, perhaps in response to that new look I had seen upon his face, felt my own face reorder itself in some unfamiliar way. "I survived the last time, and I was less prepared then. At least this time, if what you have seen is true, she has not set him loose to wander the Dark Wood and play cat and mouse with me."

"I distrust that smile," he said, eyeing me with brows wrinkled. "You look exactly as my mother once used to, when she had some labyrinthine scheme in mind."

I let the smile, now that I realized what it was, stretch my lips wider. "That I will take as a compliment."

Rising, I began to roll up my bedding and the futon. There was no sign of the clothes Itsuki had made, which I had left neatly folded near the bed last night, and so I assumed my mother had taken them with her to hang up or wash, or simply to marvel over. Kaede had loaned me a worn pink yukata to sleep in, and though it was a little wrinkled, it would do to walk home. I needed to look out some supplies, and … I needed to talk to my mother.

"Follow the sensei's instructions, and rest," I told my father as I went to the door. "You still have much healing to do. I am glad you are well, Father."

"Wait." The urgency of the word turned me back. "Come here for a minute."

I moved swiftly to his side, worried by his tone, and knelt there as I had the day before. And, just as he had the day before, he took both my hands in his – but today he kissed the back of each one, and then cradled them gently between his.

"I wish you all the good fortune of your ancestors and all the strength of our house," he said formally. "Where you go, you will carry the Moon's grace, for your errand is good, your heart is virtuous, and your intentions are pure." His lofty tone deserted him as he finished. "Come back to us, Hana. I ... cannot lose another child to the Dark Wood."

Gravely, I said, "I will."

But although I spoke the words like a vow, they were not a promise. Any promise would have been empty. It was obvious by his face that he knew it.

He drew in a long breath, and I heard it catch in his throat. "I must ask this. Will you – can you forgive me? I am sorry. So very sorry."

The apology carried a nearly unbearable weight: years of words left unsaid, and silent, festering unhappiness. A burden of anger and guilt that he, perhaps, had not known how to shed any more than I had, until Itsuki had shown me the way.

"That is all forgotten now," I whispered. "It is behind us. We need never speak or think of it again. There is nothing to forgive, Father."

I leaned in and kissed him on one whiskery cheek, and smiled, and kept smiling as I left him. But as I closed the door to the great room behind me, my smile faded. I slipped on my sandals and stepped out of the healer's house, determination straightening my shoulders.

My father had been rescued from the Yuki-Onna's grip – but it had never been more than petty cruelty that had made her toy with him, and her grasp had been careless.

Itsuki was the true focus of all her madness and anger and grief, and like my father for all those years, she did not know how to set that burden down. And I did not know how to make her. I had no idea how to free Itsuki. All I knew was that I could not leave him there at her mercy. I had to try.

Even if trying was the death of me.

I had fully intended to take the central path through the village and head directly home. But once there I must face my mother, and explain to her what I planned to do – and I did not expect her to take it with anything like the calm acceptance my father had displayed.

And so, exactly as the last time that I had walked out of the healer's house, I found myself lured away by the peaceful murmuring call of the river.

Unlike last time, all those I met on my short walk went out of their way to catch my eye, to exchange short nods or more formal bows, or even to stop me and pass a few polite words. Some of them stared uneasily at my right side, where the beast's dramatic scars were now safely hidden again, and some just as conspicuously kept their eyes away. The general attitude was a mixture of admiration and apology, and, perhaps, a trace of fear. There was no pity. I had not known, until then, how used I was to seeing and accepting pity from everyone. Without it, it was as if they hardly knew me. Or I them.

Hideki stayed me briefly to ask after my father – did I

think Kaede would permit visitors soon? – and to let me know that he had butchered and hung the serow I had caught so many weeks ago, at my mother's request, and nothing had been wasted.

"A fine pelt," he said, a slightly nervous edge to his heartiness. "I have hardly ever seen the like. You did well."

I thanked him, and puzzled as I walked away on how I would have treasured these words of praise once – not so very long ago – and yet now, although they brought me pleasure, they altered nothing within me at all. Always, I had felt as if I must prove that I was worthy, as if my very right to exist hung over me like an unanswered question. But no matter how hard I worked to gain the respect of others, true confidence had remained just out of my reach, for I had believed that whatever place I had won for myself within the village hierarchy could be snatched away at any moment. Perhaps I had been right.

I was different now. The difference was not that I no longer cared, but that I no longer cared enough to let it affect my own decisions or actions. It felt like a kind of victory.

With all this stopping and bowing and smiling, it took me twice as long to reach the river as I had expected – and once I arrived, there was no stillness to be found, for a group of women whose family houses clustered over the river shallows on wooden stilts had brought their children out to play together while they worked on their mending. The little ones' screams of laughter and shrieks as they chased up and down the low bank and splashed each other nearly drowned out the water's music entirely. I moved upstream, climbing over a green hump of land and then down onto a tumble of large stones. It might even have been the very same bend of the river where I had hidden from Kyo to hunt frogs all those years ago; it looked too different now to know.

The footing was not good, and the inflexible wooden soles of my geta made it hard to navigate the smooth, rounded boulders. Since I was not wearing socks I tugged my footwear off, letting them dangle from one finger by the cloth thongs as I scrambled down to the water's edge. There must have been a hard rain in the past few days. The river's mood today was tumultuous, and it was a pale cloudy green, like jade, topped with creamy foam crests.

The autumn colours of the sloping hillside and the peaks above were even more glorious now than they had been the last time I came to the river. Soon, within only a few days maybe, the leaves would turn crisp, and begin to fall in earnest, and then there would be a windy night, and in the morning all the branches would be startlingly bare. The delicate autumn frosts would turn to thick ice, and winter would stalk into the valley again.

I wondered if trees ever felt wistful about their changing nature. Did they mourn for the bright spring greens when they deepened into gold, or sigh over the loss of their golden beauty when the snow coated their black empty branches? Humans would. But human changes were not so swift, or so easy to perceive.

After kneeling to drink, I turned to look at the village again. It was a very different vantage point than my usual one up on the ridge, among the trees. Here I stood at the heart of the settlement, close enough to pick out not only individual homes but individual people.

In the distance I could hear the lady whose rug-beating I had interrupted the day before getting back to work: *whack, thwap, thud*. There was Goro's father, stumping determinedly at the ground with his polished ash stick and limping on the bad knee that always told him when the weather was about to change. His married daughter, Goro's sister, walked beside him, smiling wryly down at the wisps of white hair on his shining head. And there was poor sad Misaki, carrying her new baby – clutching him really, as if she could somehow preserve him from sharing his sister's fate by holding him close enough.

I could not see her face, for she walked with her head down.

There, on the lowest rice terrace, Shouta and two of his brothers were arguing instead of working. One of them shoved him. He shoved back. Sturdy old Yuu, on the terrace above, shouted something at them and shook her fist, and they shuffled apart, sheepish.

Nothing had changed here for a very long time. We had grown less, and more fearful, and we had dug more terraces and built different homes, but in all important parts the village was just as it had been one hundred years ago when Oyuki and Ren had sought sanctuary here, and when our villagers had first allowed themselves to be made monsters by fear. They had turned from Oyuki when she needed help – as they had turned from my mother and me – disguising their cowardice as common sense, and in the process, they had created a worse fate for themselves than any they could have known was possible.

But my people were not truly monstrous. They were only ordinary families, ordinary men and women, who loved and hated and cried and laughed, and had the capacity to be kind – so very kind – or terribly, unbearably cruel, given the right circumstances.

Fear is contagious.

But perhaps bravery can be too.

The villagers had found the courage to face me this morning when less than one month ago they had diligently avoided me instead. Like the trees and their seasons, like me – and like Itsuki himself – people could change, given the chance. They could become better.

One hundred years was long enough for any place to be held in stagnation and in fear.

The time had come for us to be free.

When I went into the woods again, into the maze, into the toils of the Yuki-Onna, I would fight to save Itsuki if I could, but I would fight to free this village too. And I would carry their clumsy, well-meaning greetings this morning in my heart like a blessing.

That same heart lifted at the thought. Even if I did not succeed, perhaps I would not be the last to try. Perhaps somehow, inadvertent as it might have been, I had begun the process of teaching my people how to be brave again.

When at last I arrived at the house, I found my mother caught up in a cleaning frenzy, scouring every inch of our little home of dust, raking out the fireplaces, polishing the wood, turning out and relining the drawers, reorganizing the pantry. I had much that I needed to say to her, things to explain, even if I was unsure of my ability to do so adequately. But Mother did not seem to be in a talking mood.

She swept me into her whirlwind of activity, relentlessly setting me to work at all the small fiddling tasks which could be accomplished sitting down, and disappeared whenever I tried to engage her in conversation. When the time came for the midday meal, I was firmly pushed into the kitchen to kneel at the low table, and became involuntarily speechless at the feast she produced. Half the contents of her store cupboards seemed to have been emptied for this one meal.

"Mother, how can we eat all this?" I asked, after staring for at least two minutes at the tray.

"I will not. You will," she said, arranging a large bowl of stewed pheasant udon with dried mushrooms and steamed pork dumplings at one of my elbows, a bowl of rice fried with egg at the other, and a plate of crispy gyoza and preserved plum onigiri before me, along with a small bowl of wilted river greens. "And it will get cold if you sit there gaping, so close your mouth, please."

In the event, she had judged my appetite better than I did. I had eaten only one meal yesterday and none so far today, and the moment I began to chew my stomach played the same trick on me that it had in Itsuki's tree-home and began growling as if a wild creature were trapped inside.

My mother let out a faint grunt of satisfaction, but when I swallowed and opened my mouth to try to broach the subject that I most needed to discuss, she only pushed seared cutlets of the serow at me and left the room. I eyed the path of the sun's shifting light, which was now a little past its zenith, and devoured the cutlets. Perhaps once every plate was clean, she would let me speak.

Yet when Mother finally returned, my voice died in my throat. In her arms were a bow, and a quiver of arrows, and a small hatchet with a gleaming quartz blade.

My bow and arrows. Our wood axe. The ones I had borne into the Dark Wood and sacrificed to the battle with the beast. I had given them up for lost. Never had I imagined I would see them again.

"How – *where*—?"

"Shouta-kun found them in the woods – on the ridge, where you found your father – the morning after you went. He brought them back here to me. He thought I would like to have them."

Her work-roughened fingers ran gently over the leather

of the quiver, and tilted it towards me so that I could see the dark splatters and streaks of dried blood that stained much of the surface. "Shouta-kun tried to scrub these away before he returned them, but they wouldn't come out. He really did think you were dead. I think he blamed himself for driving you into the woods. Don't judge him too harshly, Daughter."

I reached out to take the precious things from her, and laid them across my lap. "I won't. But, Mother … why do you give me these things now?" *Now, when I need them more than ever, although you cannot know it.*

She smiled down at me, and though the lines around her eyes were tight and worried, and her lips thin with tension, her eyes were as warm and as understanding as they had always been. She touched my hair fleetingly with one hand.

"Because you still have work to do. You never needed to tell me that. Your father may have seen you in his dreams, my little flower, but I have always seen you in my heart."

Twenty-one

The Yuki-Onna had said: *"If you leave, you shall never be able to return. You will never see your beast again."* She had said: *"The moment that you leave this place, the maze will close to you, and the Dark Wood will hide it."* She had also said: *"You should never have come here. My maze is not for such as you."*

That meant something. It meant that the forest had brought me to Itsuki the first time without her permission or her knowledge. The Dark Wood had chosen to save me that night. It must, in fact, have been the Dark Wood that had brought my father home and left him at the edge of the treeline to be rescued, just as somehow it had saved the bow and quiver and the quartz axe which I had lost, and deposited them where Shouta could find them.

I had been used to thinking of the woods as two

distinct entities – believing that the friendly forest of non-magical trees was my forest, because I knew its voices as well as I knew the voices of my mother and father, and that the Dark Wood was foreign, wicked, even evil. But when I had first wandered into the Dark Wood, the voices of the trees had been so similar to the ones I knew that I had not been able to tell the difference. The Dark Wood was as alive as my forest was, and it had a mind of its own and magic of its own, too – even if it had been brought into being by the Yuki-Onna.

Perhaps the Yuki-Onna did not know that.

The Dark Wood had been willing to defy the Yuki-Onna all those times. I hoped it would be willing to do so once more, to help me again. To help me find my beast – and to save him, this time.

It was mid-afternoon, and the light was clear and golden when I walked into the trees at last. This time I had made no hurried, fugitive escape from my house. In fact, my mother had insisted on helping me to prepare – and it showed.

I wore my shabby down-stuffed jacket over the thickest winter kimono I owned, and my winter leather leggings. We had folded the gown up around my waist and tucked it into my obi, but I would let it down when I needed to, for extra warmth. A pair of my father's rough old boots, made snug to my smaller feet with the addition of two pairs of socks, were laced up to my knees. Rolled small together in a pack on my back were the mittens and cap, and one of the furs that I had carried home with me from the maze, ready to be donned when the time came. I had not forgotten the biting, near-fatal chill of the Moon maze.

Also in the pack were flints and tinder, a full leather waterskin, and a quantity of dried meat and fruit. My quiver hung next to these, the strap crossing my breast, with the bow inside it. The wood axe I carried in my hand. The weight and heft of it was reassuring. The weight and heft of everything else I carried would likely make my back ache before very long. But mother had been firm, and I wanted her to have the comfort of knowing, this time, that she had done the best she could to arm me for what was to come.

I halted at the treeline, turning back to look down at the village one last time before I left, just in case I did not see it again. But my eyes would not focus. In my heart, I had already said my farewell to this place.

My eyes strayed away of their own accord, back to the shifting yellow and red-gold of the wood.

There is a monster in the forest, a spiny sugi tree, one of the few evergreens in this part of the forest, murmured softly.

"I know," I began, as I often did – and then it struck me, for the first time, what the trees were trying to tell me – what they had always been trying to tell me, and all of us.

"You don't mean Itsuki at all, do you?" I breathed. "He isn't a monster. He earned the right to be called a man long ago. You're talking about her. The Yuki-Onna. She's the one who must be defeated to end the curse. And you knew it. You knew it all along – you were always trying to warn us. The monster in the forest is Oyuki."

Monster! the sugi said again, as if in agreement.

"I understand you," I told it. "I finally understand what all of you have been trying to say. But I still need your help, my friends. I must find the Dark Wood, and within the Dark Wood, the maze. Will you guide me as you did before?"

A gentle shudder moved through the trees, scraping the dry leaves together overhead with a soft lonely sound, and it was only then that I noticed how quiet, how unusually still the forest had been since I had stepped onto the ridge.

Hana… the trees breathed. I heard sadness, and worry, and reproach in their voices. But also … acceptance. Maybe even hope.

"You will help me?"

Walk. Walk. Walk.

"Thank you," I said. Turning my face in the direction that the trees called me, I set off.

With the light, and a full belly, and an excellent night's rest behind me, the first part of my journey to the Dark Wood felt easy. At least, easier than the nightmarish trek through the dark and the wailing wind I had made a month ago. Nor did I have anger and despair and the awful weight of guilt sitting on my back.

Yet then I had been at the peak of my strength – a strength I had barely noticed, because it had always been mine. I was not so strong now, despite all Itsuki's care and his remedies. It did not take nearly as long for me to begin to feel the distance I had walked, and I noticed the aches and pains in my body as a recent invalid does, with the fear that something important might choose to give way at any time. The longer I walked, too, the more I felt my anxiety for Itsuki rising, a creeping foreboding about what the Yuki-Onna had done to him while she had him in that cage, and what state I might find him in when I finally arrived. *Hurry. Hurry. There's no time. No time.*

My progress was determined, and as quick as I could make it, but the light had still faded into a silvery grey dusk before I found myself in a part of the wood that was unknown to me. I was forced to stop for a short rest there, taking a seat on a tree stump and washing the sweat from my face in a tiny stream that trickled near by. After the enlivening splash of the water had woken me up, I drank from and refilled my waterskin, and ate around half of the food. My knees creaked as I pulled myself to my feet, making me grimace.

There was no wandering into the Dark Wood unawares tonight. Though it was night by the time I reached the boundary, and everything was draped in deep shadows, the line of dense dark pines was unmistakable – and impassable. Their heavily scented branches seemed to have woven together into a single wall of green-black foliage, and if there were any gaps or holes, the thick thorny vines that grew around the pines' feet – a cousin to the maze thorns perhaps – blocked the way just as thoroughly.

I moved up and down the line of the trees, seeking some opening, any chink in that wall that might reveal itself if I looked hard enough. The trees at my back shuddered and shifted, as if in encouragement. But no opening did I find.

Hurry, hurry, hurry, said that familiar voice in the back of my mind. *No time, no time…*

Reluctantly, for this was the edge of the Yuki-Onna's territory and I did not want to alert her to my presence yet, I stopped where I was and leaned my body into the strong, springy wall of pine boughs. Softly, I whispered:

"Sisters. I know your mistress has commanded that I be kept out. But I also know what she does not – that you have thoughts and feelings of your own. You saved me once before, and I think that you love Itsuki in your way, and would help me to rescue him from his suffering if you could."

The pines rippled and shivered against me. Then they sighed, *Hana.*

I smiled, encouraged. "Yes, it is me. I have come to help, and to try to mend what has needed mending for a hundred years. I am going to slay the monster. Will you aid me? Will you let me pass?"

The dark trees moved again, as if a great silent wind

had buffeted against them. Then, as one, they murmured, *Hana.*

Help. Mend.

Hana.

Friend.

The closely knitted green wall began to part, the branches drawing back. Below them, thorns curled into themselves and slithered out of the way. A narrow opening appeared, just wide enough for me to squeeze through if I turned sideways and was very careful with my pack and quiver.

"Thank you," I told them. "I will do the best I can."

With that, I slipped into the Dark Wood.

I did not see the narrow ravine where Itsuki in his beast form had played cat and mouse with me. For that, I was grateful. My path remained simple and straight, as if the trees were falling back before me to ease my way, and only a few minutes' walk brought me out from under the dense canopy of leaves to open sky. Black as pitch and depthless, the night was filled with great glittering drifts of stars so bright that it was almost possible to not miss the light of the Moon.

Before me stood the tall outermost hedge of the maze, looming and dark as ever it had been. I approached cautiously. The thorns had never spoken to me, nor to Itsuki that I knew of, or given any indication that they were sentient like the trees. But they had rolled back of their own accord to allow me in, I presumed – and I had seen them open for the wildcat.

"Thorns, thorns, you know me," I whispered, softer even than I had spoken to the dark pines. "I am Hana, Itsuki's friend. I have come to help him, and bring an end to the suffering here, if I can. Will you let me pass?"

There was no response – not a dry rattle, not a twitch, not a sigh – from the hedge.

Very well.

I took off my pack and quiver, tested my grip upon the axe, and swung it hard.

The blade was sharp and my aim was true. I felt the stems of the thorns part beneath the hatchet. Yet when I reached the bottom of my swing and made to pull the hatchet back, I had to drag it free with both hands and the whole weight of my body, as if the thorns had already grown into place behind it. Or reached out actively to try to seize it. My blow had left no gap in the hedge. I sighed.

A woodsman's methods would not avail me, then.

Turning back to the trees of the Dark Wood, I appealed to them. "Is there no way in? No way to break through?"

The trees quivered, wordless. Frightened? I frowned. They knew something, then, but did not wish to speak it. Yet they had not been too frightened to help me so far, despite the threat of the Yuki-Onna's wrath. What could frighten trees more than magic?

The answer came as if my own grandmother, tree-whisperer and wood walker, had breathed it into my ear: *Fire.*

Itsuki had said that winter never came to the maze properly, and in the weeks that I had been with him the skies had always been blue. I had not seen so much as a light drizzle, let alone rain. These tangled hedges might have been forced to grow for decades on magic, instead of water. What was more, didn't the stories talk of Moon Priests driving out demons and yokai with flames?

Dry wood was vulnerable to fire. So was magic.

For a heartbeat I quailed at the thought, for I had grown up in a village of wooden houses with thatched roofs, surrounded by forest. If there was one single thing that we had been taught to fear more than the monster in the forest, it was fire. The maze was home to dozens, perhaps hundreds, of harmless animals. I could not allow them to be trapped and burned to death. Nor did I wish to be trapped myself.

But Itsuki was on the other side of those thorns.

Hurry, no time, hurry, hurry...

I must do more than make a path for myself to the Yuki-Onna's island; I must burn the maze down, so that all the denizens of the thorns – and I, if necessary – would be able to get free and escape into the woods.

Bringing out the tinderbox, then my bow and some of the arrows, I offered a silent apology to my mother before I began to rip strips off the bottom of my naga-juban. I wrapped them in little bundles around the tips of the arrows, working as quickly as my fumbling fingers would allow. Itsuki was waiting for me.

A few paces into the trees I found a long, sturdy stick of dry wood, perfect for burning. I rolled its end in the dark sap that oozed from the boles of the pine trees, and made a torch of it by binding layers of the fraying fabric over that, then rolling it in pine resin again. Then I set to work with my flints. The torch smoked sullenly for a few moments, but eventually smouldered and began to burn steadily. Once I was sure that no stray breeze would put it out, I went back to the hedge.

"This is your last chance," I told the thorns, unsure if they could hear or understand. "If you won't open, I will have no other choice."

Nothing. After a few beats just to make sure, I leaned in and held the fire to the thorns.

The dry tangle of the hedge caught light instantly, as if it had been waiting for fire all its life. With a soft *whoomph* and a shower of sparks, a gout of flame streaked away up to the top of the hedge. I jumped back in alarm. The sudden heat made my cheeks feel red and raw, and the yellow-white light caused my eyes to water as much as the smoke.

New tongues of flame crackled out in either direction as I watched anxiously, waiting for the fire to eat a hole in the thorns. Slowly, the place where I had first set the blaze began to fall down into ash, all its fuel consumed. I shrugged my pack and quiver back on, shoved the handle of the axe into my obi, then took the bow and my handful of wrapped arrows firmly in my right hand and the torch in my left.

I backed up to the trees. Braced myself. Ran forwards as fast as I could – and leapt through the gap in the burning thorns.

The smoke hit my eyes and throat, blinding and choking me at the same time. Coughing, I staggered away from the flames as fast as I could, examining my clothes and braided hair for smoking patches. There were none. Well, I had not set fire to myself then, at least.

By the light of the torch, I searched for a gap in the hedge that would let me through to the next ring. When I did not find one, I set fire to the thorns again. Behind me the fire was spreading almost too quickly to be believed, until it seemed that at least half the first wall of the maze must be alight or burned away to ash.

I progressed steadily through the maze, moving in as straight a line as I could navigate, always working towards the centre. Wherever a dead end tried to block my way, I sacrificed an arrow to set it aflame. Stringing and drawing my bow again, after a month of no practice and with the still healing wounds in my arm, shoulder and side was … not pleasant. But it did allow me to make fires in the dangerously flammable hedge from afar, so that the risk to my clothes and hair was minimal.

Soon animals began to flee past me, back the way I had come. The friendly goats nearly trampled me into the grass, and the slim weasel-creatures tripped me by darting between my feet. I even imagined that I saw the distinctive tufted-eared silhouette of the mother wildcat, her shadow edged in gold, as she slunk away.

The creatures' eyes rolled and their nostrils flared with panic at the scent of the fire, but when I looked back, I could see them flying through the gaping holes that the blaze had left in the thorns, and knew they would be able to make it to the wood.

Of the white peacocks, I saw no sign.

When the cold began to cloud my breath and rime the hedges of the maze, I stuck the unlit end of the torch into the stiff embrace of the thorns to keep it alight so that I could untuck my kimono. The patched fabric fell in thick, warm folds around my legs. Then I donned the cap and fur I had carried with me, but reluctantly left off the mittens, for they not only seemed a risk when handling fire arrows, but would also interfere with my ability to hold the bow steady and draw its string precisely. Remembering how my hands had turned almost blue before, I held them as close as I dared to the flaming tip of the torch as I walked on, and flexed them, and shook them, trying to keep them limber. Either it worked, or perhaps the fire had affected the ice magic of the Yuki-Onna, for my hands remained pink and warm enough to move, if a little stiffly. I thought that the frost was less thick and the air less bitter, too.

At last, more weary than I wished to admit, I came to the centre of the maze, and found myself on the shore of the Yuki-Onna's lake once more. The boat of ice awaited me there, at the end of the path of dark water.

The snow maiden was eager for us to meet again.

I hesitated, suddenly struck by the worry that she would decide to get rid of me by sinking the boat halfway across the icy lake.

Hurry! Hurry! No time!

The maze burned behind me. Itsuki was ahead. It was too late to turn back – even if I wished to.

I shrugged off my pack and placed it and my bow in the bottom of the little craft. Then, holding up the thick layers of my clothes with one hand, and clutching the torch in the other, I climbed into the boat.

Twenty-two

The little boat barely gave me the chance to sit down before it was off. I held the torch between my knees and assessed my situation quickly as the island got larger and larger beyond the peacock figurehead. I only had two of the cloth-wrapped arrows left, and no time to make more. But my hatchet was still secure in the thick wrapping of my obi, and I thought the torch would last for a little while longer. It would have to do. I slung my strung bow over my right shoulder and put the two arrows into the same hand that held the torch, so that my right one was free.

The Yuki-Onna did not make me walk her icy maze of horrors again. Each ring of shining white opened and rolled away on either side of me as I approached – and snapped shut behind my heels with the nasty, final sound of a metal bear-trap springing.

She's angry. I shivered with the knowledge of what I was about to attempt. *Very angry.*

I stepped into the heart of the Moon maze with a face as calm and unrevealing as willpower could make it, and a body that vibrated with long, convulsive tremors of panic. The snow maiden stood waiting for me on the steps of her throne. Her hair and gown flowed around her slender form, fluttering faintly in an unfelt breeze and illuminated by the steady, sickly glow of the maze's walls. Her dress was not of feathers, this time, but of moths. Black and white moths as large as my hand, still opening and closing their wings, as if they were alive despite having been pinned or sewed together.

My glance at her was fleeting. As soon as I had fixed her location in my mind, my gaze fell away from her to the cage of bones and dead faces at the bottom of the frozen waterfall.

Itsuki was not moving. I could barely make him out through the layers and layers of white bars. He was only a large, still shape, huddled in one corner of the cage beneath a fraying dark cloak. I was so busy looking at him, praying for something, anything – a twitch, or moan, some proof that he still lived – that I did not notice the first dead servant lunging at me until it was nearly too late.

The thing moved fast. So fast that its bluish face, looming above me, was thankfully a blur. I barely managed to duck the sweep of a scythe-like arm, and warded it back for a precious second with a wild swing of my torch as I fumbled the wood axe from my obi. The servant came at me once more. With a cry of fear and effort, I flung the hatchet.

My throw might have been hasty, but my aim was still good: years as a hunter had seen to that. The gleaming quartz blade made a pale arc in the air and sheered through the place where the tangled head of twigs met its smooth icy torso.

The head tipped one way. Its body went another. The servant fell without a sound, and the ball of twigs that held its face rolled off into the snow. It was awful. I wanted to retch. But I could not stop, for a second dead thing was already running towards me.

I lit one of my arrows and hastily dropped the other and the torch at my feet, where it smoked but did not quite go out. Then I swung my bow up, aimed, and loosed the flaming arrow directly into the second servant's head. The tangle of branches exploded into flame, just as the thorn hedge had done.

The servant made a high, inarticulate scream – almost like a baby's – as it collapsed. I swallowed, tasted bile, and looked away. *They are already dead,* I reminded myself fiercely. *Dead. You cannot truly hurt what is already dead.*

Can you?

The Yuki-Onna let out a scream of her own, of fury and frustration. Quick as a flash, I bent and lit my one remaining arrow from the last guttering flicker of the torch at my feet, and raised my bow to aim it at her.

"Is that your plan?" she demanded, and madness echoed through the words. "To set fire to me, and my entire realm? I am powerful enough to raise everything you have burned again in a single night of the dark Moon, even if there is nothing left but ashes. Even if you burn *me* to ashes, you cannot destroy me."

I sucked in one shaky breath, two … and then I allowed the tension of the bow to slacken, and the point of the flaming arrow to drop until it pointed at the snowy frozen ground. "I have not come to destroy you. I want to save you."

Her smooth, icy brow wrinkled. "To save … me?" she repeated uncertainly.

"Yes." I released the arrow completely, so that it fell into the snow and was extinguished. With an effort, I fixed my eyes on the ruff of her dress, and refused to let my gaze stray back to where Itsuki lay, still unmoving. "From the beast you have become. You don't deserve to suffer this way. I don't think any of this is what you wanted."

Her head tilted in that curious birdlike manner. "I wanted revenge. I wanted … wanted justice. The power to set right what had been ruined."

"I understand," I told her. "That's why I came here, into the Dark Wood, to hunt the beast. I wanted vengeance too. But do you think you have found that here, in this place? Do you think what you have made here is truly righting the wrongs that were done to you?"

"Understand?" She laughed, a shrill, creaking laugh. "How could you possibly understand me? The grief I suffered? You cannot possibly know what it is to *hate* – you're nothing but a girl!"

"You were a girl like me, once. Your grief and anger are still that girl's. We are not so different. I, too, stood before the people of my village – my own people! – and begged, begged them to save my father's life, and they would not. They turned their backs on me, just as they turned their backs on you. They expected me to accept their cowardice because I was a just a girl, and they did not fear me. And when I did not listen to them, when I defied them and did what they could not, they tried to paint me as a demon or a liar, tried to turn on me. I despised them as you must have done, loathed and hated them for it."

"But then you forgave them," she sneered. "And so? Do you now preach forgiveness to me?"

"I don't expect you to forgive anyone. But you have had your revenge, one hundred years of it, and it has brought you no happiness. No peace. Hate is a burden that never gets lighter, and its weight does no one any good. It would harm *me* to cling to it – and so I chose instead to lay it down. Not for their sakes, but for mine. And so may you. You may choose to lay that weight down … *Oyuki*."

The snow maiden became – if possible – even more still. She stared at me, transfixed. I forced myself to meet her eyes, though the sight of that grotesquely perfect face, and the terrible burning eyes, made my stomach churn and the bile taste surge into my mouth again. I could feel my own fate, and Itsuki's fate, and the fate of my village, teetering on the edge of a knife, as she and I looked into one another's faces. Something flickered in her expression, and I saw it: the humanity inside her. The spirit of that passionate brave girl whom Itsuki had known so long ago. She was still in here. If only—

She jerked in place, like a horse that feels the lash of its rider's whip. Her hair and gown flared around her as her eyes began to burn once more, black with ancient power and fury, searing away all trace of Oyuki and who she had once been.

"No! No one shall take my power from me. I will never be powerless again!"

Before I could speak, or even move, I was seized from behind. A dead servant lifted me from my feet as if I weighed nothing, its dry, spindly arms crossing over my chest so that my own arms were trapped, clamped to my sides. A second servant plucked the bow from my grasp, wrenching my fingers painfully when I tried to cling to it.

"Give her to him!" The Yuki-Onna was screaming as the servants dragged me towards her. "Put her in the cage with her precious beast, and let us see how she deals with his true self. My curse will have its due!"

The curse…

Oyuki was not in control here. She was no longer

the mistress of the dark magic that she had unleashed, if she ever had been. It was the curse that ruled the maze, the curse that governed her – and with a terrible sinking of despair I knew that this meant my quest had always been impossible, for a curse could not be reasoned with. It would not give up its victims, whose suffering were the source of its own existence, and willingly dwindle away into nothing. The curse would seek only to perpetuate itself, on and on, forever, extracting its "due" from beastly Oyuki and beautiful Itsuki until there was nothing left of either one of them.

There was never any hope. I had failed before I even began.

With a sickening grinding of dry bones, the top of the cage opened. The servant dropped me inside. I landed ungracefully, letting out a hard grunt as I sprawled on the frozen ground. The top of the cage fell back into place with a crack that rattled the bars and made the dead faces set into them moan softly. I had no attention to spare for that, though – for the noise had also caused the huddled lump of Itsuki to stir beneath the dark, muffling folds of his old cloak.

"He's going to kill you," the Yuki-Onna said, speaking softly now. She had come down from her throne, and the snow-dusted white and black folds of her moth dress swept softly past the bars of the cage as she trailed around it. "He won't be able to help himself, for that is his true nature. He will kill you, just as he killed me – and when he awakens and realizes what he has done? Oh, then, at last, he will taste the suffering I know, the agony that I endured when I watched the man I loved die because of me."

A sort of rumbling moan – nothing at all like the soft rumble of Itsuki's human voice – emanated from under the cloak.

Every nerve in my body turned to a wire of steel, trembling with tension, and I scrambled backwards, drawing my knees up and pressing myself against the bone bars of the cage so hard that they stung the skin of my back, even through all the layers I wore.

I knew what it was that was under Itsuki's cloak.

It was not Itsuki.

It was not my Itsuki.

"This will destroy him," the Yuki-Onna murmured, bending low, as if she spoke a secret. "The grief, the guilt, the horror. Nothing else has, but you will, Hana-san. When he sees what he has done to you, he will go mad. Just like me. But I would not want you to think me … unfair. So here. I've fixed this for you."

Something slipped through a narrow gap in the roof of the cage and landed near my feet with a dull thud. I reached for it automatically. It was the quartz hatchet, its battered wooden handle smooth and familiar under my fingers. But the simple blade was changed. It glittered with a scintillating, dead white frost that I would not have dared to even brush with my bare skin.

"It will cut him now. Perhaps you will even survive – if you are willing to tear him apart the way he tore you apart. Are you merciful enough to end his life before he ends yours? Let's see if you really are willing to break the curse. To save us both. Let's see how much your fine talk is worth."

The Yuki-Onna turned and swept away, and as she did, Itsuki's cloak at last slid off to reveal the creature underneath. A monster with a glowing silver-white pelt, jagged black markings, and a long silky mane. A great cat, with paws as large as gig-wheels, and glassy, poison-green eyes.

Seized by the instincts of an animal which knows it is prey, I froze in place, desperately trying to evade the hunter's attention through stillness. But those eyes found me all the same. They considered me with the chilling, alien intelligence I remembered … and no hint of recognition at all.

The eyes slid down to the weapon I still clutched. The beast's muzzle wrinkled back from its teeth, and the jaw gaped in a snarl. The mouth and tongue burned, red hot, behind the teeth. Steam filled the cage.

It was going to leap at any second. Either I would get in a wild, lucky blow, sever an artery or do some other awful damage that would fell the cat – or I would die horribly under its teeth and claws, screaming and bloody and struggling.

And then Itsuki, brave, kind Itsuki, the most decent,

most human person I had ever met, would have to live with my death for the rest of his life. Powered by his anguish, the curse would make that life last an eternity. Because Itsuki loved me.

How could I not have seen it? Everything that he had done proved it. Bringing me fully into his peculiar life with every bit of warmth and comfort he had. Laying out all the truth of what he had done for my judgement, and holding nothing back, not even his most shamed self-loathing. Bringing me here himself to confront the Yuki-Onna, and facing her down, and then sending me away, back to my family, without ever a word that would reproach me. He had cared for my safety and happiness more than for anything the Yuki-Onna might do to him.

Did I love him in return? The moment I faced myself with that question, it seemed ridiculous even to ask. I loved Itsuki not like a raging fire or a crashing wave, or any of the other things named by besotted young men in their serenades, but like a woman loves the golden sun on her face, the sweet clean air in her lungs, the good earth under her feet. I loved him the way that you love all the things which are both vitally necessary and absolutely reliable. Things that you never even have to stop to be grateful for, because they just are, and without them you would not be.

I had failed to save Oyuki, and I had failed to free my village. At this, I would not, could not, fail. I would not allow myself to be used to destroy Itsuki.

In a frantic movement, I raised the quartz hatchet high above my head. The frosted blade flashed and trembled between my shaking hands. The beast roared, blasting me with another cloud of steam. It uncoiled and stood, every line of the sinuous muscular body exuding menace.

I shoved the hatchet up, as hard as I could, back through the gap in the lid of the cage. Then I let go. The weapon clattered down the outside of the bone bars and landed in the snow, out of reach.

The beast lunged forwards.

I lifted both hands to show they were empty, closed my eyes and sang.

"Copper fish, dance, dance
Leaves falling on silver pool
Autumn rain, fall, fall.
Autumn leaves, dance, dance
Float in pool of copper fish
Silver rain, fall, fall."

Even as the words wobbled and croaked out of my dry throat, I expected the monster's terrible breath to scald me, the crushing pain of its bite, the tearing swipe of claws.

They did not come.

The animal made that strange rumble-groan again. My eyes snapped open to see that it had stopped dead, within arm's reach, shaking its head fretfully from side to side as if its ears hurt.

Can it truly be … working?

I moved into another song, this one about maidens

milking white cows under the full Moon. The beast reared back and roared once more, the force of the noise shaking the cage and ruffling the hair around my face. Steam rolled out in great waves. The huge paws raked at the earth, gouging long black furrows in the snow. But it came no closer.

I sang on.

Songs about sakura, and fishing, about sweet plums in summer, about catching birds of gold and silver to win a princess's heart, about snow falling in the winter, and the right way to cook rice. Nursery rhymes and ballads. Every song that Itsuki and I had ever sung to one another, and every song that Grandmother had ever sung to me. My voice lost its nervous croak and turned smooth and sweet, and then gradually became hoarse with dryness.

The creature snarled, and roared. It paced away and back again. It flung itself at the walls of the cage. It laid on its stomach and clawed at its face with its own paws. But it did not attack.

Finally, as my voice was truly beginning to die, fading to a thin rasp, and I was starting to tremble again with the thought of what would happen if it gave out completely, the beast began to belly towards me through the raked up mess of snow and frozen dirt that it had made.

Inch by inch, the monster crept forwards, nose twitching, mouth gaping slightly to reveal the ivory glint of fangs as it drew in gusts of air, scenting me. I held myself utterly still, fearing even to flinch. My memory failed me and I ended up back at the beginning, singing "Copper Leaves".

With a low, deep sigh, and a little rush that nearly paralysed me with fright, the beast laid his great head down in my lap.

I finished the song. The cage was silent, save for the thunderous beating of my own heart in my ears. The beast sighed again, letting out a small ribbon of steam. The heat of the creature was overwhelming – through kimono and leggings it was still almost cooking the flesh of my legs. I raised one hand and touched the silky mane. The fur was softer than a cloud beneath my fingers.

The great cat whuffled, and I found myself looking down into those venomous eyes.

It was not Itsuki looking back at me. Not my Itsuki. But it was something that … knew me. Something more than just a monster. The beast's long tail curled lazily, and its eyes closed as it nestled safe in my arms.

"Itsuki," I whispered, my head curling down towards the creature's. My hands moved without thought to gently stroke the small, round ears and the heavy cheekbones of the face. The face of the monster that held Itsuki's soul. "I love you."

Somewhere outside the cage, I heard the Yuki-Onna let out a low, wavering moan.

And then … lights. Lights everywhere, suddenly, white and soft. They blossomed around me, silently flickering to life in midair and spreading in delicate swirling patterns like white apple blossom stirred by a gentle wind. They danced around my body and around Itsuki's beast form, filling the bone cage. I peered out, through the bars, and saw the same lights coming to life in the heart of the Moon maze, gathering around the throne in the frozen waterfall and blocking the Yuki-Onna from sight. Blocking everything from sight.

I looked down at the beast and it – he – was looking back at me. The last thing I saw was the deep green of Itsuki's eyes.

Twenty-three

I n that first moment of blindness I felt the beast push closer to me, as if in fear. I clutched at him, held his face tightly, but it didn't matter. The silky warmth of his fur, the heat of him, and the solid weight of his skull leaning against my stomach and legs just … dissolved. The light dissolved everything, replacing reality with soft, starlike whiteness, until it was all I could see, all I could feel – thrumming against my skin – all I could hear – whispering in my ears – all I could smell – the scent of flowers, and frost, and the tingling taste of lightning in the air. I imagined that I was dissolving too, that the light was replacing me fibre by fibre, skin and blood and bone, washing out scars and shadows, painlessly fading me into its whiteness.

Am I dying?

Then I heard a sweet, lovely voice – far lovelier than mine had ever been – softly sing:

"Autumn leaves, dance, dance..."

Gradually the light began to take on colours, like watercolour paints washing across a blank sheet of paper and darkening, deepening, as they dried. In the distance, a smudged line of dusky blue-grey solidified into the craggy, familiar lines of the distant mountain peaks above the village. Below, the dark dense shadows of the forest. Above, streaks of pink and yellow and peachy-orange: ragged clouds flushed with dawn.

And all around me, rustling and stirring in a warm wind, scented with distant lightning and ice, there were flowers. Blowsy, cup-shaped white flowers on long, waving stems, with deep golden centres, unfurling to the sun.

The last thing to take shape was a girl. She was slender, a little shorter than me, dressed in a very fine pink kimono with long, full sleeves. Her hair, neatly coiled and knotted on the top of her head, gleamed lustrous black against a spray of the same white flowers that grew all around me.

She turned to face me as the last words of the lullaby left her lips, and smiled.

The girl had a beautiful face, ageless and unlined in the pink light of the rising run, with pretty, soft skin and delicate features. But her smile was something more – something better – than beautiful. It was wide and crooked, wry and friendly, like the smile of a big sister, and it lit up her eyes with happiness and affection. I had never seen that smile before, but somehow I recognized it – and her.

"Oyuki," I whispered.

"Hana," she said, coming towards me through the flowers. Her arms lifted, and so did mine, just as naturally as breathing, and we embraced like the dearest of friends.

"They called me for the snow, my family," she said softly. "That was how they wanted me to be. Cold, elegant, pure. But I always loved warmth, and flowers, and the sun. I was never meant to be a snow maiden. Only Ren ever understood that about me. Ren – and then you."

"Ren? Your…" My voice trailed off. Ren who had been murdered right before poor Oyuki's eyes.

"Yes." She sighed. "I miss him so much. Even now."

And yet her words held no echo of the fury or madness of earlier. Only sorrow, and love.

How did this girl become the Yuki-Onna? And how did the Yuki-Onna become the girl I am looking at now?

As if she had heard my thought, Oyuki drew back, and looked up into my face.

"You know – I know you do – that anger, hatred and guilt … if we let them, they can become so powerful they have the ability to consume us. We are left only an empty shadow of our own pasts, reliving the same hurt over and over again. Well, that is what happened to me. At the moment of my death my soul had become a scream of torment, of pure rage, and that purity gave me power, or unleashed a power within me I had never known of before. I turned my back on heaven. Transformed myself into the Yuki-Onna, spirit of ice and vengeance, and made your Itsuki relive everything I had been through at his hands – and when that was not enough, I cursed him.

"The curse made all the swirling thoughts and pain within me real, gave my anger and hatred form. That form was the beast, and the maze, the Dark Wood, and the enchantment on this mountain. And then there was no turning back. By the time I realized I had created a prison not only for him, but for everyone on the mountain, including myself … it was too late. The curse had a life of its own, as all magical things do, and it wanted only to endure.

"For one hundred years I was trapped in the maze with Itsuki while the curse fed on our despair and on the poor unfortunate people of your village, and grew stronger. Long after my hatred had shrivelled into weariness and longing to join Ren in heaven, the curse kept on. I made it, but I did not have the power to break it. We, all of us, who had been caught in the coils of the curse, had one hope. The only thing that would break the curse was if its original terms – the words that I had spat at Itsuki in my first explosion of power and rage – were fulfilled."

"'*You wear the shape of a man, but to me you have been a beast. Very well then – a beast you shall truly be. Suffer as I have suffered, beast, until you have learned to love, as* truly I once loved. And when you have learned that, suffer still more, until you have proved yourself worthy of being loved in return, as once my beloved loved me,'" I quoted softly. This had been burned into my brain since Itsuki repeated it to me, but I had never worked out its true significance – that this was the curse itself, laid out plainly.

"Oh, those impulsive, terrible words!" Oyuki said. "I wanted him to suffer so badly, you see… I made it nearly impossible to break the curse. It was impossible. Until you came stalking into the forest, raging and determined to kill him, and taught him to love you instead. He proved that when he persuaded you to leave him behind. And you proved he had become worthy of love when you returned, and were willing to embrace even the beast that almost killed you, to save him. You did what you set out to do, Hana. You slew the monster. You saved him. You saved us all."

The tears that had been welling up in her eyes finally slid down her cheeks. Even after everything that had happened, I felt my face heat at the extravagant praise. I looked around a little desperately, and then frowned.

"But if – if the curse is truly broken then where is Itsuki? Where is this place? And what about you?"

"Do not fear. Itsuki is just where you left him, and he is well. I promise. This is … a tiny pocket of spare time and space that I snatched, so that I could meet you before it is really all over, and I … move on. I had to see you, Hana. I don't know if either of us will remember this once it's finished, but I had to thank you. For doing the impossible. For teaching a beast to love, and for loving him in return. I will do what I can to make sure you are rewarded. I have a little of my magic left... Not much, not enough to undo every ill that the curse is responsible for ... but just enough, I think, to right one last wrong. For you, Hana. My friend. My sister."

She hugged me again. When I allowed the tip of my nose to press into her hair, it smelled of frost and flowers and distant lightning, and the heady scent muddled my thinking, so that all I could say was, "Thank you for giving me the chance to know him. And you. It is – probably very selfish, but – I'm glad."

She squeezed me tightly, and then stepped back. "Time for me to go. Ren is waiting. I can almost hear his voice..." She drew in an awed breath, turning her face away, into the light of the sun. Her eyes went distant, and tears gleamed on her cheeks once more. "I can hear him, Hana. It's been so long... I can hear him!"

And she laughed in joy and relief.

Before I could open my lips to say farewell, the pink light winked out. The field of flowers disappeared. Oyuki was gone.

I knelt on springy grass, on an island at the centre of a dark lake. The water, glinting black and silver under the soft starlight, lapped softly at the shores of the little scrap of land. Around me, the Moon maze and its tortured dead servants were no longer. Not fallen or destroyed, but simply disappeared – the way that Oyuki had disappeared – as if none of it had ever been.

And before me, in the near darkness, knelt a young man.

My eyes travelled over him slowly, thoroughly sketching out his shape as I adjusted to the faint light. He was slim, almost slender, with a build more suited to speed than power: square shoulders and long whipcord limbs. I could not make out all the details of his face no matter how much I squinted or widened my eyes, but I thought that it was long-ish, and square too, with a determined chin.

His hair, which was neatly pulled back, was dark. His skin was dark too, though not as darkly tanned as mine, and so were his eyes. I could see the straight, stubborn line of his brows but not his expression.

Then it occurred to me that all the while I had been staring at him, studying him silently, he had been staring back. What did he see? Now that the curse had been broken and my beast had become a man again, what did he see when he looked at me?

"I…" My voice was a hoarse whisper. "Itsuki?" Then I flinched. "No, that isn't your real name, is it? Forgive me."

There was a pause, and then a heartbreakingly familiar soft huff of laughter, and that beloved deep rumbling voice. "There is nothing to forgive."

Oh, please, please… I drew in a trembling breath. "Do you … remember? Me?"

"I remember a barely human beast with no name, and a girl who gave him one, out of kindness and friendship. I remember the first time you said it, and how it made me feel as if maybe there was still a person worth knowing within the monster. I remember that to hear the name you gave me, from your lips, brought me more happiness than any of the fine empty titles I had in my old life." He stopped, and there was a dry noise, as if he had swallowed, before he went on. "My real name is Itsuki. I was honoured to be your Itsuki, Hana – and I always will be. If … if you will have me?"

The sob that burst from my mouth should have embarrassed me, but I had no time to be embarrassed. The space between us was gone in the next instant, and we were in each other's arms – truly in each other's arms – for the very first time.

"You saved me," he whispered.

"You saved me first," I said, half laughing, half crying.

"Will you take me back to your village?" he asked, endearingly eager. "Shall I meet your family, and learn how to … to plough fields and tend pigs and mend roofs, like a proper villager?"

"You already know how to do all those things, you liar," I told him firmly. "No. You will be Kaede-sensei's apprentice, and she will teach you how to use ordinary non-magical medicines, and you will teach her all that you know in return. The village will be more healthy than it's ever been, and everyone will love you."

"And your family?"

"Of course you'll meet them. You'll probably have to live with them, at least at first. If my father doesn't frighten you away. But I don't think he will."

"Well, I have faced down a Yuki-Onna and lived to speak of it," he said dryly.

"That's why I'm confident you won't run away from Father. Mostly."

He huffed again, pressing his face against my hair. We were both still laughing weakly, giddy and clinging as much for support as for the sheer delight of touching one another this way. For some time – I didn't know how long – we stayed like that, our need to be close, and still, and safe together all the greater for being unspoken. We had won. We had saved each other.

We were free.

Eventually I managed to convince my hands that if they let loose their bruising grip on those neat shoulders Itsuki would not evaporate, and to draw back enough to look up at the sky. The stars had faded to distant glimmerings amongst ragged steel-grey clouds.

"Dawn is almost here. I think I can find the way home now."

"Then we should go," he agreed, and hugged me all the more fiercely.

"Itsuki—"

"A moment." His voice was a faint rumble, more felt than heard. "Just one moment more."

I could not resist the appeal in his words. I wrapped my arms around him and felt the warm press of his lips against my forehead.

And he will kiss me again, I thought, almost dizzy at the wonder of it. *He will kiss me a thousand times more, and in a thousand ways.*

At last we climbed unsteadily to our feet. I found the wood axe, its quartz blade marred with a long crack and deep nick in its cutting edge, lying in the grass. My bow and arrows were there too, unharmed. Itsuki took the axe, and my fur, and I carried the rest.

Everything else might have faded away like nightmares in candlelight, but the boat that had carried me to the Yuki-Onna's island was still there. It even still had my pack in it. The little craft was no longer majestic and white with frost and sculpted ice – just a plain little bleached wooden boat – but it was good enough to carry us over the lake to dry land, when we had unearthed the dusty oars from the bottom of the hull. The trees whispered and rustled as we arrived at the shore, the clatter of the leaves – dry, golden autumn leaves – almost like applause.

Hana Hana Hana...

Itsuki Itsuki Itsuki...

They said nothing else. There was nothing else for them to say – no monster in the forest, no warnings to give. The forest was free, too. The curse was done.

"Thank you," I said, laying my hand on the first trunk that I came to. "Thank you for your help. I could not have done any of it without you."

Hana Hana Hana...

"Do you always talk to the trees?" Itsuki asked.

"Always," I said, a little warily. "Why, does it give you a disgust of me?"

"I think I can learn to live with it," he said, amused, and gave the tree next to him a gentle pat. "They have been my friends these many long years, you know."

Itsuki Itsuki Itsuki...

"They like you too," I told him, smiling.

We walked on. At first the trees had to guide us here and there, but the light was growing, gentle gold settling in the highest leaves like a fiery crown. It was much more lovely than the fire I had created in the maze with my arrows. After a short while, I began to recognize landmarks, and simply to enjoy the peaceful walk, with Itsuki's hand clasped firmly in mine and his footsteps, not quite as silent as my own, keeping me company.

Every time I glanced at him now, I could see more of him. He was only an inch, perhaps two, taller than me. And I had been right: his eyes were dark, a dark ashy brown with little flecks of paler grey-brown within them. His face was long and his cheekbones broad, and his brows heavy and straight. His lips, though well-shaped, were a little thin to be perfectly in proportion. I would have bet a good brace of pheasants that when he grew angry those stubborn brows bunched up and that chin jutted out as if it was just begging to be hit with someone's fist.

He was not beautiful at all, and yet he was the most beautiful man I had ever seen. Every time I looked at him, I found him looking back at me, as if he too could hardly stand to tear his gaze away, and those eyes – those imperfect, ordinary, human eyes – told me that what he saw in my face was just as lovely to him. For he was Itsuki. And he was mine. I let myself smile, and smile, and smile.

A little noise of surprise escaped me as I looked ahead and realized that the woods before us seemed lighter than they should, as if the trees were thinning, and we were reaching the end of them. But we had only just passed the great white standing stone with the curling green ferns at its base, and the ridge was not so close as that.

"What is it?" Itsuki asked.

I smiled again just at the sound of his voice. Nothing could be wrong this morning. So I tugged at his hand. "Something is different and I wish to see what it is. Come on."

I pulled him into a trot, and he laughed a little but let me. Together we burst out of the trees – I had been right, the treeline was different – and both of us made noises of shock and pleasure as we stumbled to a halt.

It was just like my dream, like the little stolen moment of space and time where I had met Oyuki. Ahead, the pink-streaked sky, and the mountains, and not so very far away the familiar ridge above the valley that held my home. But here, where once there had been trees, was a broad, open meadow filled with tall green grass, and blowsy, cup-shaped white flowers with golden centres that swayed gently on long stems.

"Beautiful," Itsuki breathed.

"I … I know this place… How did she do this?" I said, half to myself. "Is this how it looked before the woods were cursed?"

There was a sound behind me: the snap of a twig under an incautious foot. I turned quickly, still holding Itsuki's hand. A man walked out of the bronze shadow of the trees into the warm pink dawn light, a little unsteady on his feet, yawning as if he had just woken from a long slumber.

No, not a man. A boy, really – no older than fourteen – tall and lanky and still growing into his limbs, with wild, too-long, shaggy hair. He squinted, rubbing at the back of his neck as he looked around in confusion, and then his eyes caught upon me.

We stared at each other, both so still that I knew the boy was holding his breath, just as I held mine. Behind me, I heard Itsuki make a tiny noise of shock, his grip on my hand squeezing tight. And in the back of my mind there was a faint whisper of a voice – perhaps only a memory – that said: *I have a little of my magic left … just enough to right one last wrong.*

And then the boy rushed forward. "Hana – it is you! Where have you been? I've been searching for you for *ages.*"

Zoë Marriott is the author of many critically acclaimed and beloved books, including *The Swan Kingdom*, which was longlisted for the Branford Boase award. *Shadows on the Moon*, the companion title to *Barefoot on the Wind*, won the prestigious Sasakawa Prize and was an American Junior Library Guild Selection. Zoë lives in Grimsby, Lincolnshire. Visit Zoë's blog at thezoe-trope.blogspot.co.uk or her website at ZoeMarriott.com. Follow her on Twitter (@ZMarriott).

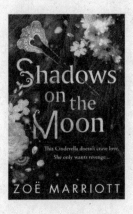

**A magical retelling of "Cinderella"
set in a fairy tale Japan. A companion title
to Zoë Marriott's *Barefoot on the Wind*.**

Suzume is a shadow weaver. Her illusions allow her to
be anyone she wants – a fabulous gift for a girl desperate
to escape her past. But who is she really? A heartbroken
girl of noble birth? A drudge scraping a living in a great
house's kitchens? Or Yue, the most beautiful courtesan
in the Moonlit Lands? Whatever her true identity, she
is determined to capture the heart of a prince – and use
his power to destroy those who murdered her family.
Nothing will stop her. Not even love.